JAMIE GLANCED AT HELENA and raised his eyebrows. "He's a lively one. He'll need to settle down a fair bit before someone rides him."

"He'll be fine," Helena replied, half to herself. In the pale late afternoon light that filtered over the stable door, the stallion looked like a shadow, his mane and tail black with rain. The horse snorted again, but more gently this time, and lifted his head to look straight at Helena.

She held the intelligent dark-eyed gaze, trying to read his thoughts. Where had he come from, this mahogany-dark stallion? Whatever had happened to him in the past to make him so wary of strangers, Helena was determined to prove to him that he had nothing to fear in his new home.

ALSO BY VICTORIA HOLMES:

The Horse from the Sea

VICTORIA HOLMES

Rider in the Dark

AN EPIC
HORSE STORY

AVON BOOKS

AN IMPRINT OF HARPERCOLLINSPUBLISHERS

www.harperchildrens.com

Library of Congress Catalog Card Number: 2003024279
ISBN-10: 0-06-052027-2 — ISBN-13: 978-0-06-052027-4

Typography by Karin Paprocki
❖

First Avon edition, 2006

ACKNOWLEDGMENTS

I WAS HELPED IN my research by the following people, who have been infinitely generous with their time and knowledge. Any historical inaccuracies are entirely my own.

Chris Chapman; Sue Clark, Dorchester County Council, Dorset; Dai Evans, Uppark, Hampshire; Ashley Gething; Terry Hearing, retired magistrate; Nicholas Mander, Owlpen Manor, Gloucestershire; the staff at Poole Local History Centre; Sam Powell, master stonemason; James Wild and family, Puncknowle Manor, Dorset.

Weymouth, West Bay, Chesil Bank, and Beacon Hill are all real places. The village of Roseby and all characters therein are fictitious, and any similarity to any persons alive or dead is entirely coincidental.

Rider in the Dark

DORSET, ENGLAND, 1740

THE CHESTNUT HORSE'S HOOVES thudded on the close-cropped turf as he galloped up the hill. Helena Roseby risked a glance over her shoulder. The gray mare was thundering steadily behind them, her nostrils flared and breath coming in rasps. There was less than half a furlong between the two horses now and the ancient hill fort was still some distance ahead, a flattened green bulk on the horizon.

Helena stood in the stirrups, wincing as the hard leather rubbed unfamiliarly against the inside of her right knee. Her mother would be horrified if she knew Helena was riding astride; ladies were expected to ride decorously on heavy high-pommeled saddles. But with the gray mare gaining on them, there was no time to worry about ladylike behavior. Clutching the reins in her left hand, Helena reached down and tried to tuck her skirt more thickly between her knee and the saddle flap.

Piper threw up his head and snorted, scattering sticky white foam back over his neck.

"Steady, lad," Helena soothed. She looked up between the pricked chestnut ears. A hawthorn hedge loomed in front of them, with a stony track running beside it.

Piper's ears flicked back and forth as he assessed the height in his quick equine mind. Helena closed her legs against him, ignoring the rawness inside her right knee. She felt Piper's stride shorten as his quarters bunched under him, ready to push into the air. There were four, maybe five, strides left before the hedge. It was taller and broader than anything Helena had jumped before, but it was the most direct route to the top of the hill. Her father's voice echoed in her head as she recalled the jumping lessons he had given her that summer in the paddock beside the orchard. "Look to the top of the fence and don't have a moment's doubt about getting to the other side, or the horse will doubt too."

Piper's neck tensed, uncertainty registering in a flicker of his ears. Three strides left, two strides, and suddenly the doubt that she had been warned against flooded Helena's mind. Piper may have been the horse her father was intending to ride in the Bridport gentlemen's race next month, but, like Helena, he had never faced a jump this big before. A horse would need wings to clear it! And a braver jockey than she, Helena admitted wryly to herself. She yanked hard on the left rein, turning Piper away from the hedge. The gelding stumbled and his hooves skidded on the stones.

Helena clapped her heels to his sides. "Come on, Piper!" she cried, throwing the reins forward to give him his head as he fought to get his hindquarters back under him.

As they galloped up the track that ran beside the hedge, the sound of hooves rang in double time, and Helena realized that the gray mare had taken advantage of her hesitation at the hedge to close the distance between them. Not daring to look back, she crouched lower over the straining chestnut neck and leaned into the curve of the track as they followed the contour up and around the hill.

Still at a gallop, Piper swerved through a gap in the earthen ramparts that led to the open grassy summit. Helena sat back in the saddle and dropped the reins, allowing Piper to slow to a trot. They had made it! She pushed back her light brown hair, which had long ago escaped from the pins under her hat, and looked around. In front of her, the ground fell steeply away to Chesil Bank. This mast-straight stretch of pebbles ran for more than ten miles along the south coast of England, all the way from the harbor at West Bay to the Isle of Portland. Helena's father owned several quarries on the tear-shaped island that was joined to the mainland by a narrow strip of stones.

NOW THAT THEY HAD stopped galloping, the wind was light enough for Helena to hear the pull and suck of the sea as it rattled over the stones. Helena reined Piper to a halt beside the beacon that gave the hill its name. On top of the tall wooden pole was a metal cage in which wood was burned at night to keep ships away from the treacherous reefs that lay barely half a mile from the shore. Today the waves were flat and shiny gray like slate, giving away nothing of the reefs beneath the surface. The pale linen-colored sun had been swallowed up by thick clouds that hung low and heavy overhead, bringing a tang of salty rain on the breeze. This autumn had brought as much rain as Helena could remember, and Piper's hooves left deep muddy crescents in the smooth green turf.

Suddenly Piper stiffened and whipped around, his tail streaming behind him like an amber kite. Nearly jolted out of the saddle, Helena muttered a distinctly unladylike oath and scooped up the reins. The gray mare was cantering across the turf toward them. Her rider looked out of breath, his right leg crooked uncomfortably over the pommel of the sidesaddle.

"Was it you or Piper who changed his mind about that hedge?" he panted, grinning as he pulled up the mare beside her.

Helena flushed. "Jamie Polstock, I'll thank you to remember who won that race," she retorted. "I believe that's one farthing you owe me!"

Jamie shook his curly brown hair out of his eyes and laughed. He was two months younger than Helena and they treated each other with the easy familiarity of brother and sister, having known each other since before they could walk. "Fair enough, Nell, you proved your point. An' I have to say, you were right not to jump that hedge—I don't think even Piper could manage that yet." He glanced proudly at the chestnut gelding, whose flanks shone with sweat. "But we've a few more weeks before the race an' I reckon by then he'll be clearing anything your father puts him to." The annual Bridport horse race was a chance for local landowners and farmers to show off their favorite horses, and Helena's father had high hopes for Piper.

Helena nodded. "I still think he could be fitter—he tired on the steepest part of the slope. Perhaps we should take him to Eggardon Hill for a longer gallop next week?" She twisted in the saddle to look across the Bride Valley to the ridge of rounded green hills. Behind them, Helena could just make out the silhouette of Eggardon Hill, a thin brown shadow on the horizon.

Jamie unhooked his leg from the pommel of the saddle and slithered down to the ground. "Good idea," he said. "Come on, Nell. I should think poor old Snowdrop's had enough of my weight, an' we ought to get back before those rain clouds break."

Helena smiled down at the mare, more than a hand

shorter than Piper, her head hanging low after the gallop. Snowdrop had been her mother's hack until Helena's thirteenth birthday, two years ago. Helena loved her dearly, but couldn't resist persuading Jamie to let her try her father's horses when they rode out together. Jamie good-naturedly put up with folding his long leg around the cumbersome pommel of Snowdrop's sidesaddle, and joked to Helena that he'd never hear the end of it if someone from the village spotted him. For this reason, and to keep secret Helena's determination to try out Lord Roseby's more difficult horses, they were always careful to leave and return on their original mounts.

Helena kicked free of the stirrups and swung her right leg over Piper's neck. Jamie stepped forward to help her jump to the ground, Snowdrop's reins looped over his arm. Feeling her boots sink into the chalky soil, Helena shook out her heavy skirt, then let Jamie lift her onto the gray mare. Her right leg felt cramped and useless when she hooked it over the pommel, and she looked back wistfully at Piper's saddle.

The faint outline of a triple-masted sailing ship in the distance caught her attention. Helena tucked an escaping strand of hair behind her ear and narrowed her eyes.

"A revenue cutter, by the looks of it," remarked Jamie, turning to follow her gaze as he lengthened Piper's stirrup leathers, identifying the lightweight ship favored by the customs men who patrolled this stretch of coast. He swung himself into the saddle and grinned at Helena, his brown eyes sparkling with mischief. "You'll need to watch the wall tonight, my lady, if there are smugglers about."

Helena smiled back. As if the peaceful village of Roseby would ever have its own company of smugglers! The most daring crime all summer had been the theft of the sexton's pig. And even if anything suspicious did happen in the middle of the night, the daughter of Lord and Lady Roseby would never be asked awkward questions by customs men, especially as her father was a magistrate at the courthouse in Dorchester, eleven miles away.

Jamie picked up the reins and closed his heels against Piper's flanks. "We'll take it slower down the hill," he warned. "These two need to cool off." The chestnut gelding tossed his head, then began to walk toward the gap in the ramparts. Helena nudged Snowdrop with her left leg and followed, tucking her shawl more securely around her neck as the first cold drops of rain spat at her back.

RAIN WAS FALLING STEADILY as the two horses trotted along the village main street and turned into the gravel drive that led to Roseby Manor. Snowdrop's reins were slippery with foam, and Helena felt wet through to her shift.

A wiry middle-aged man stepped forward to meet them as they clattered into the stable yard, his black hat speckled with raindrops. "Good afternoon, Miss Helena," he said, reaching out to take Snowdrop's reins. "How was the mare today?"

"Fine, thank you, Watkins," Helena replied, gathering up her skirt to dismount. She took the groom's hand as she slid down. "Please see that Snowdrop is rubbed dry before you put her blankets on. She got quite hot after a gallop and I don't want her to catch a chill."

"Of course, my lady," said Watkins. He rubbed affectionately at Snowdrop's damp forelock. "Come on, lass, let's get you inside. An' you too, my lady," he added, frowning at Helena's bedraggled appearance.

Helena nodded absently, looking around for Jamie. He was leading Piper into the stable block, his hair plastered darkly to the back of his neck. Helena was about to call out to him when she noticed two unfamiliar horses tied to a rail in the open-fronted barn at the top of the yard. One was a sturdy dun cob, not much taller than Snowdrop, and the other a rangy iron gray with a walleye.

"Whose horses are those, Watkins?" she asked.

Watkins glanced over his shoulder. "Visitors for Lord Roseby, my lady," he replied. "They're with Lady Roseby now."

Helena frowned. "Isn't my father back from Dorchester?" She knew he had been dining with stone merchants from London the night before, but it was unusual for him to be home this late.

Watkins shook his head. "Perhaps he's stopped to shelter

from this rain?" he suggested.

"Maybe," said Helena. She turned to Jamie as he came out of the stables with Piper's saddle balanced on one arm and the bridle hooked over his shoulder. "Jamie, I think you should give Piper a bran mash to warm him up. And make sure his legs aren't hot after that gallop."

Jamie ducked his head respectfully, but when he looked up again, his eyes were alight with humor. "Very good, my lady. Will you be riding tomorrow?"

Helena met his gaze and smiled. "Yes, I will. Please have Snowdrop ready for me at eleven."

She felt a familiar pang of gratitude toward Jamie for accepting that she had to play the part of a proper young lady when they were back at Roseby Manor. It seemed a long time since they had played together in the orchard, sun-freckled seven-year-olds in identical white smocks swinging from the lowest branches of the apple trees. Her childhood companion had grown up to be a stable boy, a surprise to no one considering the number of hours Jamie had spent scrambling under the bellies of patient carriage horses or pestering Lord Roseby's head groom with a thousand questions as soon as school was finished for the day.

But as the young lady of the manor house, Helena's duties lay in a very different direction. Her lessons came from a governess, not from the vicar's wife who ran the tiny village school.

She studied literature, French, drawing, and accounting; and once a month a rather intense young man—his face so fat and pale that it resembled a peeled potato—traveled from Bridport to teach her how to play the spinet. These were considered to be the necessary steps to turn Helena into an accomplished and charming hostess so that she could marry well and manage her husband's household. And now that she was fifteen, her mother had already started to introduce her to suitable young men from Dorchester and Weymouth—heirs to estates like Roseby or sons of wealthy businessmen. Their eyes gleamed when they saw Helena's beautiful home, but she hated the way they treated their horses with no more emotion than they would their carriages, or even their stable lads. To Helena, nothing was more important than horses, and her needlework lay untouched whenever she had a chance to go down to the stable yard instead.

As Jamie respectfully ducked his head and walked toward the tack room, Helena smoothed down her damp riding coat and, holding up her skirt with one hand, ran up the steep stone steps that led to the back hall of the manor house. The impressive slate-roofed building was built of creamy Portland stone from her father's quarries, with two stories of mullioned windows in carved stone frames and a tiny row of windows set into the roof marking the rooms where the servants slept. The front entrance was at the other end of the house, where a gravel drive swept through carved pillars to a magnificent stone porch with walls thicker than Helena's outstretched arms.

As Helena reached the top step, the door to the back hall flew open and a plump, pink-faced woman appeared with a broad piece of linen in one hand.

"Lady Helena, what on earth are you doing out in this weather?" she scolded, shooing Helena into the oak-paneled back hall. "You need a change of clothes this instant. I don't know what Jamie was thinking of, keeping you out in the rain."

Helena smiled as she took the linen and began to rub the ends of her hair. "It wasn't Jamie's fault, Mary," she said. "We took the horses up to Beacon Hill, and it only started to rain when we were coming back."

Mary Polstock pursed her lips and shook her head. She was Jamie's mother and had been the housekeeper at Roseby Manor since before Helena was born. Because Helena and Jamie were so near in age, Mary had often looked after both babies when Helena's nursemaid had her afternoon off, and she never missed a chance to fuss over her Roseby chick.

"Who are my mother's visitors?" asked Helena, handing Mary the linen and unwrapping her sodden shawl from inside her riding jacket.

Mary took the shawl from Helena, clucking with disapproval when she felt how wet it was. "Customs men, my lady," she said. "They came to speak with your father, but he isn't back from Dorchester so your mother is with them in the front parlor. They'll be here on court business, I expect. Now, I'll go and tell Louise to set out some dry clothes for you."

She folded the shawl and bustled away up the stairs. Helena was about to follow her when one of the doors opened along the stone-flagged passageway that led to the main hall. A footman emerged from the front parlor, dressed in a long jacket—dark green like all the Roseby livery—and carrying a silver tray. "Good afternoon, Lady Helena. I have just taken some tea to your mother," he said. "Will you be joining her?"

"Yes please, Hawk," said Helena. The sound of voices made her stop. The parlor door behind the footman opened to reveal a tall, dark-haired man wearing a navy-blue riding coat and mud-spattered white breeches.

"Thank you for your time, Lady Roseby," he was saying. "I am sorry to have missed your husband. Please tell him we will call again tomorrow." He caught sight of Helena and bowed politely. "Good afternoon, my lady."

"Good afternoon," Helena replied. She wondered who this well-spoken stranger could be. His accent wasn't local, and she felt a little unnerved by the strength of his sharp blue gaze as he studied her.

"Helena, this is Mr. Roger Chapman," said Lady Roseby, coming out of the parlor behind the visitor. "He has just been appointed as supervisor to the Riding Officers at West Bay."

Helena raised her eyebrows with polite interest. Riding Officers were land-based customs men, whose job it was to gather information about smugglers for the revenue cutters and to catch them red-handed as they unloaded their contraband. The last supervisor of West Bay's six Riding Officers had been a good-natured sixty-year-old local man called Mr. Jessop. He had been a regular visitor to Roseby Manor, and Helena had always suspected that Mr. Jessop's ruddy face owed more to his fondness for French brandy than to patrolling the cliffs on horseback in all weathers. Roger Chapman was less than half Mr. Jessop's age, Helena guessed, and his eyes shone with a barely contained energy that made his predecessor seem like a lazy old spaniel in comparison.

"Pleased to meet you, Mr. Chapman," she said, acknowledging the introduction. "What's happened to Mr. Jessop?"

"He has taken up a post in Warwickshire, my lady," replied the officer. "I arrived in West Bay yesterday and came to speak to your father about some urgent news."

"News of smugglers?" Helena couldn't help asking, as her heart quickened. Could Roseby have its own company of smugglers after all?

2

"THERE ARE ALWAYS SMUGGLERS, Lady Helena," Mr. Chapman replied quietly. "This is an even more serious matter."

Behind him, Lady Roseby drew in her breath. Helena frowned, wondering what could have upset her mother so much.

Roger Chapman gave a small bow toward Lady Roseby. "Forgive me for troubling your daughter with such grave concerns, my lady. But I believe everyone should be kept informed, in case they notice anything that might help us catch these villains." Then he turned back to Helena, his face grave. "My men and I have reason to believe that a gang of wreckers is coming to Chesil Bank."

Helena felt a jolt of fear clutch in her chest. Wreckers! These men plied a deadlier trade than smugglers. On stormy nights, they went down to the beach and kept watch for ships in trouble, not with any intention of helping the unlucky sailors but to steal whatever washed up on the shore—cargoes of wine and cloth, even the passengers' luggage and timber from the wrecked ship.

Roger Chapman obviously saw the flash of fear in Helena's eyes, for he stepped forward and laid a hand on her arm. "Please don't worry, Lady Helena. My men and I will catch this gang before they have a chance to set foot on the Bank. The reefs here offer a tempting harvest for these murderers."

Helena nodded, unable to speak. She knew that the most black-hearted wreckers were not content to let bad weather and dangerous tides send a ship into trouble. To add to the wrath of wind and water, they lit false beacons to confuse the sailors who relied on cliff-top fires like the one on Beacon Hill to guide them around the timber-cracking reefs. Worst of all, wreckers had been known to murder any sailors that made it to the shore, to make certain that there was no one else to claim the washed-up cargo.

But Helena had never heard of wreckers coming this close to her home before. She drew her arm away from the Riding Officer's hand, uncomfortably aware of her rain-soaked sleeve. "I wish you luck, Mr. Chapman. I'm sure my father will do everything he can to help."

Another Riding Officer appeared in the parlor doorway. He was shorter and more heavily built than Roger Chapman, with curly sand-colored hair and slate-gray eyes like the sea. "We should leave now," he said, "if we want to get back to West Bay before dark."

Mr. Chapman bowed to Helena's mother. "It has been a

pleasure to meet you, Lady Roseby. And thank you for the wine. Your husband clearly has an excellent cellar."

Lady Roseby acknowledged the compliment with a dip of her head.

The Riding Officer put on his broad-brimmed black hat and walked briskly toward the back door, followed by his companion. The officers disappeared down the steps toward the stable yard and shortly afterward reappeared on the drive, Mr. Chapman riding the dun cob and his colleague the long-legged gray.

Helena stood at the window and watched them trot out of the gate, her stomach churning at the thought of wreckers coming to Roseby. Smugglers would have been bad enough! A ship carrying a cargo of rope from West Bay had run into the reefs last winter, and she had seen the vessel's scattered wooden bones when she rode down to the beach with Jamie a few days later. What sort of man would be able to watch a ship break up and think only of stealing the cargo and killing any survivors? Helena shuddered.

"Helena, you must go and change out of those wet clothes." Lady Roseby's voice broke into her thoughts, reminding Helena that her shift was clinging uncomfortably to her back.

"Yes, Mama." As she turned, a flash of movement on the drive caught Helena's eye. A lightweight carriage pulled by a handsome bay horse had turned through the gate.

"Papa is back!" she exclaimed. Then she frowned. Another horse was tethered behind the carriage, trotting with its neck stretched awkwardly by the rein as if it was too exhausted to keep up. "I didn't know Papa was buying a new horse," Helena remarked to her mother.

Lady Roseby came to join her by the window, narrowing her pale blue eyes. "Nor did I," she said dryly. "I should have thought we had more than enough horses already!"

Helena turned to the footman. "Hawk, bring me a dry shawl, please."

"Oh, Helena," protested Lady Roseby. "You're not going out again, are you?"

Helena smiled as she took the shawl from Hawk and tucked it around her neck. "The rain has stopped, Mama, and I won't be long. I just want to see the new horse."

There was a clatter of small feet on the staircase, and a fair-headed boy dressed in a velvet waistcoat and breeches swung himself around the end of the banisters and jumped into the middle of the hall. "New horse? What new horse? Can I come and see? Please, Nell!"

"Come on then, Will," said Helena, holding out her hand to her little brother. "But you must promise to be very quiet when we get near, in case he is nervous of us."

Will looked up at her, his blue eyes round and serious. "Of course, Nell. Watkins told me that not all horses are as friendly as Bumblebee."

Bumblebee was the elderly Dartmoor pony who had taught Helena to ride ten years ago, and now carried Will patiently around the orchard while he pretended he was competing in the Bridport gentlemen's race.

Will's nursemaid, Charity Buckle, appeared at the top of the stairs, carrying a black velvet jacket. "Master Will, you need to wear your coat if you are going outside. Here it is, now."

Will ran up the stairs and shrugged on the jacket. Then he raced back down and tugged at Helena's hand. "Let's go," he urged.

Hawk held the door open as Helena led Will outside. Even though the rain had stopped, the wind was blowing strongly, cold and sharp like a salt-edged knife as it swept over the cliffs. Helena shivered and broke into a run with Will trotting beside her, down the path and around the corner of the house to the stable yard.

Watkins was unhitching the bay horse from the carriage, its flanks steaming after the drive from Dorchester. Lord Roseby handed his whip to Jamie and turned to greet Helena and Will. He was very tall and slim, and his light brown hair curled as thickly as Will's. Dark shadows beneath his eyes betrayed a late night, but he smiled warmly and held out his arms to hug Helena and ruffle Will's hair.

"Hello there," he said. "Have you come to see my new horse?

He's feeling a bit sorry for himself right now, but I think he's just tired from the journey."

Helena walked over to the horse, who was leaning his chin on the taut rein that tied him to the carriage. His ear flickered uneasily as she held out her hand, but he didn't shy away when she stroked his warm damp neck. He carried his weight on three legs, resting one hind leg so that just the tip of his hoof touched the ground. With a pang of alarm, Helena noticed that he was so thin she could count his ribs. And underneath the slick of rain, his coat felt dirty and unbrushed. "What is he called, Papa?" she asked over her shoulder.

Lord Roseby came and stood behind her, holding Will by the hand. "Oriel, the fellow said. He's a scrawny old thing, isn't he?"

Helena turned to face her father, still resting one hand on the horse's neck. "Then why did you buy him?" she asked curiously. Even though she would have happily given a home to any horse on earth, her father usually had a more critical eye.

Lord Roseby smiled, crinkling the skin at the corners of his eyes. "I didn't exactly buy him, Nell," he told her. "I won him in a card game."

"A card game?" Helena echoed. "How?"

"One of the stone merchants suggested a game of cards after dinner yesterday. He had a friend with him, some fellow from Yeovil, who had bad luck with his hand. He didn't have any cash on him, but he said I could take this horse he'd just bought. It seemed like a good deal to me, and I daresay the horse will be fine after a few days of decent feeding."

"So you don't know anything about him?" Helena persisted.

"Who, the fellow who lost at cards or Oriel?" her father teased, raising his eyebrows.

"Oriel, of course!" Helena said. "How old is he, and what's his breeding? I can hardly tell what color he is underneath all this dust."

Lord Roseby shrugged. "Well, I know he's a stallion, about five years old, and as for his breeding, we'll just have to see what he looks like when he's had a bit of attention. What do you think of him, young man?" he said to Will.

Will screwed up his face as he studied the horse. "He looks a bit sleepy," he said at last.

"We'll soon sort that out," said his father, straightening up and beckoning to Jamie. "Put this fellow into a stable and make sure he gets a good feed. Best to keep him on his own for now, I think, rather than put him in a stall next to the others."

Oriel had lifted his head in alarm when Lord Roseby called across the yard, and Helena instinctively moved closer to his shoulder to soothe him. The stallion turned his head and looked at Helena, his liquid brown eyes filled with wary curiosity. Helena stretched out one hand toward him, and Oriel's delicate nostrils flared briefly as he blew hot breath onto her palm. Then

Jamie walked over and Oriel jerked his head away.

"I'll help Jamie," Helena offered. She didn't want to leave the horse before he was settled into his new home.

Lord Roseby frowned, then nodded. "Very well, but don't be too long out here. You've already had a soaking today, by the look of you. Did you ride out with Piper?"

"Yes, Papa," said Helena, her eyes lighting up as she recalled the gallop on Beacon Hill. "We—that is, Jamie and I took Piper and Snowdrop up to the hill fort. Piper went like the wind! He'll be impossible to beat in the race, won't he, Jamie?"

Jamie looked around from where he was unfastening Oriel's hitching rein. "Yes, my lady," he agreed. "He's galloping strongly, my lord, an' was hardly winded at the top," he added.

"Good work, Jamie," said Lord Roseby, smiling. "I shall have to ride him for myself in the next couple of days. Now, sort this horse out, and make sure my daughter doesn't get any more soaked. Come on, Will." He turned and strode out of the yard, his head bent to one side as he listened to Will chattering about his morning ride on Bumblebee.

Helena ran over to the tack room and picked up a thick woolen rug for Oriel. When she came out again, Jamie was leading the stallion over to one of the individual stables, rather than into the long stable block where the horses were kept in rows of stalls. The horse walked soundly but seemed too exhausted to lift up his hooves cleanly, and he stumbled when his toe clipped the cobbles.

"Easy, lad," murmured Jamie, reaching up to stroke Oriel's forelock. Startled, the horse snorted and threw his head up, his hooves clattering on the wet stones.

Jamie dropped his hand and waited until Oriel was standing still again, his flanks heaving and his eyes wide in alarm, so that the whites showed. Then Jamie swung open the stable door and let Oriel walk ahead of him through the narrow gap.

Helena stepped carefully across the slippery yard and looked through the doorway. "Is he all right?" she asked in a low voice.

"Oh yes," replied Jamie, his voice muffled as he bent down to unbuckle Oriel's noseband. "He's bound to be unsettled, being in a strange place. Did you bring a rug for him?"

"Yes, here it is," said Helena, slipping through the door and unfolding the blanket. At the sight of the bright yellow rug, the stallion's head shot up again and he swung his hindquarters around so that he was facing Helena.

Jamie hopped out of the way and placed his hand firmly on Oriel's shoulder. "Come on now, steady down," he murmured. He glanced at Helena and raised his eyebrows. "He's a lively one. Maybe we won't worry about a rug for now. He'll need to settle down a fair bit before someone rides him, that's for sure."

"He'll be fine," Helena replied, half to herself. In the pale late afternoon light, the stallion looked like a gaunt brown shadow, his mane and tail black with rain and hanging in limp tangles. There wasn't a white hair on him anywhere. Helena's fingers tingled with longing to brush his neglected coat until it shone. The horse snorted again, but more gently this time, and lifted his head to look straight at Helena.

She held the intelligent dark-eyed gaze, trying to read his thoughts. Where had he come from, this mahogany-dark stallion? The fine lines of his head spoke of noble breeding and his legs were clean and slender, suggesting he too could run like the wind. Helena could understand Jamie's concern, for the stallion had shown himself to be easily startled and unpredictable compared to the other horses in her father's stable yard. But then she remembered the way Oriel had blown softly onto her outstretched hand, and the expression in his eyes now was cautious rather than mistrustful. Whatever had happened to him in the past to make him so wary of strangers, Helena was determined to prove to him that he had nothing to fear in his new home.

HELENA'S FIRST THOUGHT ON waking the next morning was of the dark brown stallion, and as soon as possible after breakfast she excused herself and hurried down to the stable yard. Her father was already there, watching Jamie tighten Piper's girth. His rough-coated deerhounds, Salome and Batista, padded restlessly around the yard, sniffing the flower tubs as they waited for their master to call them.

Lord Roseby turned as Helena walked across the cobbles. "Good morning, Helena. Are you going to ride this morning?"

"Yes, Papa. Are you taking Piper out?"

"I am indeed," declared Lord Roseby. "How could I not, after you gave such a glowing report of him yesterday? Would you like to come with me?"

Helena hesitated, glancing at Jamie's back. She had hoped to ride with him this morning, and perhaps challenge him to another race. Even if he didn't ride Piper, there were other horses she was equally willing to try if he rode Snowdrop for her.

Lord Roseby clearly noticed her reluctance, for he smiled and started to pull on his gloves. "Maybe tomorrow instead? After all, Piper is nearly ready, and I need to go to the quarry this afternoon."

Helena relaxed and patted Batista, who had trotted over to press her thin body against Helena's skirt and push a long gray nose into her hand. "Thank you, Papa," she said. "Are you going to take Piper up to Beacon Hill again? The slope will do him good, although I think he should go to Eggardon at least once before the race. There's a track there which is almost as long as the racecourse."

Lord Roseby nodded gravely. "That sounds like an excellent idea, Helena. You make a very good trainer. It's a shame you can't ride in the race yourself!" He caught Helena's eye and grinned. For a brief moment, Helena wondered if her father suspected that she swapped horses with Jamie, but that couldn't be possible—he was usually out on business all day, either inspecting his quarries on Portland or overseeing court cases in Dorchester.

Jamie led Piper over to the mounting block so that Lord Roseby could climb on. The gelding looked none the worse for his hard ride the day before; in fact, Helena thought he looked better than ever. His chestnut coat gleamed in the low November sun, and his ears pricked up with interest as Lord Roseby strode over, settling his hat more firmly on his head. Sensing that he was about to leave, Salome and Batista circled the horse impatiently, keeping a cautious distance from Piper's heels.

"Excuse me, my lord!"

Helena spun around to see who was addressing her father. She smiled when she recognized the broad-shouldered frame of Samuel, Jamie's father. Samuel Polstock was the village blacksmith, much in demand for his gentle handling of horses as well as his skill with metal. He was wearing his heavy leather apron, so thick that it seemed to fold upward on a hinge when he walked. His errand must be urgent, Helena guessed, if he had left the forge without taking off his apron.

"Yes, Polstock, what is it?" asked Lord Roseby, turning to face the visitor.

Jamie leaned around Piper's head, his eyebrows raised in surprise. "What are you doing here, Father?" he asked. "Everything's all right at home, isn't it? The girls haven't had an accident?"

Helena smiled to herself. Jamie was tirelessly protective of his seven-year-old twin sisters, Meg and Lizzie.

Samuel Polstock glanced over at Jamie, his forehead creased in a frown. "Nay, lad, it's nothing like that," he said. "I just wanted to speak to his lordship, if you have a moment, sir."

Helena's father narrowed his eyes, then nodded. "Very well, Polstock. We can speak in the summerhouse." He gestured to the far corner of the yard, where a narrow passage led to the garden. Beneath the spreading branches of a cedar tree stood a small stone room that Lady Roseby used for entertaining guests in the summer. Samuel turned without another word and walked across the cobbles to the passage.

Lord Roseby handed his riding crop to Jamie and was pulling off his gloves when there was the crunch of hooves on the graveled drive and a sweating dun cob cantered into the stable yard. The rider was Roger Chapman.

"Lord Roseby?" he called to Helena's father, raising his hat as he reined the cob to a halt. Watkins ran forward to hold the horse's bridle. "My name is Roger Chapman. I am the new supervisor of Riding Officers for West Bay. Lady Roseby may have mentioned that I called to see you yesterday."

Lord Roseby looked up at the rider, his hazel eyes thoughtful. "Chapman? Yes, my wife did tell me of your visit. Congratulations on your new post."

"Thank you, sir," said Mr. Chapman, swinging his leg over the cob's neck and jumping lightly to the ground. He handed the reins to Watkins, who led the dun into the open-fronted barn and tied him to a rail. "I wonder if I might speak to you now about an urgent matter?" the Riding Officer asked.

Helena's father frowned for a moment. "Of course. Come into the house and we can discuss this further. Jamie, perhaps it would be better if you rode Piper this morning. I am sure Helena will accompany you on Snowdrop. And, Polstock," he called across the yard to where Jamie's father stood at the mouth of the passage, "I'll send word to the forge when I have finished with Mr. Chapman."

"Aye, very well, Lord Roseby," said Samuel Polstock, dipping his head respectfully.

Lord Roseby nodded to the Riding Officer and led the way toward the house. The deerhounds followed, their claws ticking against the cobbles.

"Good morning, Lady Helena," said Roger Chapman, raising his hat and nodding to her as he passed.

"Good morning, Mr. Chapman," Helena replied.

When the Riding Officer had followed Lord Roseby out of the yard, Jamie led Piper across the cobbles to Helena. "What urgent matter?" he asked.

Before Helena could reply, Piper skittered sideways as Samuel Polstock emerged from the passageway. "That's the new supervising officer from West Bay," said the blacksmith, laying a massive hand on the gelding's neck to calm him. "Old Jessop's been sent out of the way to some inland post, I reckon."

"Samuel, have you heard anything about the wreckers?" Helena asked, suddenly realizing that might be what Mr. Chapman had come to discuss with her father.

"Wreckers?" repeated Samuel. "Yes, I did hear a rumor that some gang was moving west from Poole."

Jamie's face darkened. "That's bad news, especially along Chesil Bank. No wonder Jessop's been sent somewhere else.

He couldn't have caught a wrecker if he sat on the beach all winter."

"Maybe, but he weren't so crafty with smugglers, either," replied his father. "Seems to me that Mr. Chapman is just the keen fellow the customs men have been looking for." He lifted his hat and ran a hand through his thinning black hair. "Anyhow, lad, I'm going back to the forge now. I left young Jacob Powell in charge of the bellows, an' I'll be lucky if there's enough heat left to make a nail."

"Shall I tell my father you'll come back to see him later?" Helena offered.

Samuel frowned, then shook his head. "Thank you, Lady Helena, but I'll catch up with him some other time. No need to worry him today. You take care on that horse, now." He nodded toward Piper and winked, and Helena realized with a jolt that Jamie must have told his father about their race on Beacon Hill.

As Samuel walked out of the yard she turned to Jamie, her hands on her hips and her eyebrows raised questioningly.

Jamie grinned, looking sheepish. "Don't worry, Nell, he won't tell anyone," he promised. "An' anyway, he seemed impressed. Your father isn't the only one who thinks you should be riding Piper in the race."

Helena shook her head, smiling. "Well, that's impossible, but at least I've got another chance to ride him today." She reached up and smoothed a lock of Piper's soft chestnut mane. "Watkins!" she called over her shoulder.

The head groom appeared from the tack room, carrying a box of brushes. "Yes, Lady Helena?"

"Please could you saddle Snowdrop for me? I'm going to ride out with Jamie."

"Of course, my lady," replied Watkins. "I'll have her ready for you in a couple of minutes."

While she was waiting, Helena crossed the yard and looked over Oriel's stable door. There was a faint crackle of straw, and a dark shape detached itself from the shadows at the back of the box and stepped into the light. His ears pricked, the stallion studied Helena with limpid eyes.

"Hello, Oriel," Helena whispered, reaching over the door with one gloved hand.

The horse stayed where he was but stretched his head forward until the long whiskers on his muzzle brushed against Helena's fingers. The fine skin on his shoulder twitched. Helena held her breath, willing him to come closer, then jumped as his head shot up and he skittered backward. Watkins was leading Snowdrop into the yard, and the sound of the gray mare's hooves on the cobbles had startled the stallion.

Helena took her hand back over the stable door. "All right, Oriel," she murmured. "I'll come and see you after I've ridden."

"Come on, Lady Helena," Jamie called from the other side of the yard. He had already mounted Piper and was waiting for her, his body twisted around expectantly in the saddle. "We don't want to get a soaking like yesterday," he added.

"Coming!" Helena replied. She smoothed down the skirt of her habit and walked over to where Watkins was holding Snowdrop, ready to lift Helena into the saddle. But part of her mind lingered in the warm shadowy stable, puzzling over the stallion that seemed longing to trust her but was so easily startled into suspicion and fear.

THE SUN HAD VANISHED behind thick dark clouds by the time Helena and Jamie returned from their ride, and the wind carried the sharp sting of raindrops. Helena's brother, Will, was playing outside, watched by Charity while he trundled his little four-wheeled cart up and down the drive and through the stable yard. His knees worked furiously and his mouth was set in deter-mination as he hurtled around the circuit.

Jamie frowned up at the sky when he had dismounted. "We hardly need more rain," he remarked.

Helena leaned down from the saddle to look at Snowdrop's muddy legs and her own spattered skirt. "You're right," she agreed. "The racecourse will be like a ploughed field if the ground gets much wetter."

"It's not just the ground," said Jamie, ducking his head under the saddle flap as he unbuckled Piper's girth. "Father told me that the cellar at the Black Feathers has flooded, an' the whole stock of ale nearly floated away last night." The Black Feathers was the village inn, standing on the bank of the River Bredy just before it flowed through a dip in the cliffs and down to Freshwater Bay.

"That would confuse the customs men." Helena laughed, slipping off Snowdrop's back. "Barrels of ale drifting out to sea with no one to claim them!"

Jamie led Piper into his stable and came back to fetch Snowdrop. "Maybe the customs men had better set to finding the wreckers rather than waste time chasing smugglers just now," he observed, his face clouded with concern. "The murder of innocent folk has got to be more important than a few kegs of brandy, don't you think?"

Helena felt a bit taken aback at the strength of feeling behind his words. After all, the smugglers had to be caught as well. Then she recalled the intensity of Roger Chapman's expression when he told her about the wreckers. "I think we can be sure that Mr. Chapman is going to do everything he can to find these villains," she pointed out. She reached up to pat Snowdrop's rump as Jamie led the mare past her. "I'm going to groom Oriel now," she told him.

"Be careful," Jamie warned. "He'll likely feel a bit more sparky today after a decent feed an' a night in a warm stable."

"I'll be fine," Helena promised. She picked up a box of brushes and walked over to Oriel's stable.

The horse was standing at the back, facing the door with his ears pricked and his eyes wide. Helena looked over the door and smiled. "Hello again," she said. "Would you like to be groomed?"

Oriel snorted gently, then took a step toward her. The fine wrinkled skin above his eyes twitched as if he were inviting her in with a delicate lift of his eyebrows.

Helena laughed and unbolted the door. She slipped into the stable, putting the grooming box on the floor in the corner. "You know you don't need to be afraid of me, don't you?" she murmured, straightening up and looking critically at the dark stallion.

After a night on thick, clean straw and with two good meals inside him, his coat already looked less dusty, and Helena could see the horse's muscles flexing on his shoulder as he walked hesitantly over to her. She held her breath, her heart pounding with excitement, while he lowered his head and sniffed softly at her hair, twitching his velvety lips. His breath was hot and hay scented on Helena's neck, and the tips of his front hooves just touched the skirt of her riding habit. Helena stayed absolutely still. Was the stallion beginning to trust her at last?

Suddenly from outside the stable there was a clatter of wheels and a piercing yell from Will. Oriel's head jerked up and his eyes rolled in terror. Helena ducked and held out one hand in an attempt to calm him, but it was too late. Startled beyond reason, the stallion let out a piercing whinny. He reared up and then plunged down again, his metal-shod hooves heading straight toward Helena as she crouched helplessly in the straw.

CHAPTER

HELENA HELD HER BREATH and forced herself not to cry out as one of Oriel's hooves struck her shoulder. The stallion landed heavily and wheeled away from her to stand stiff legged at the back of the stable, snorting. Helena stayed where she was, not daring to lift her head in case she startled him again even though her shoulder stung inside her thick riding coat, and her bodice was digging uncomfortably into her ribs.

"Nell! Are you all right? Where are you?"

Helena felt dizzy with relief as she heard Jamie's voice calling urgently from outside Oriel's stable door. She uncurled enough to call back in a low voice, "I'm in here, Jamie."

She listened to the sound of the door being unbolted, and the stable flooded briefly with light as Jamie opened the door and slipped inside. "Steady there, lad," he murmured to Oriel, who was shifting restlessly in the straw.

There was a loud rustle as Jamie knelt down beside Helena, and she felt his hand on her shoulder. "Nell, are you all right? What happened?"

Helena lifted her head, wincing under the pressure of Jamie's hand where Oriel had struck her. "I'm fine," she assured him, pushing herself up to her knees. Her black felt riding cap lay beside her, and she reached out stiffly to pick it up. She was alarmed to notice that her hand was trembling, and she busied herself for a few moments replacing her hat and checking the pins in her hair before turning to look at Jamie.

His brown eyes were wide with concern and his face was pale. "What happened, Nell?" he repeated, standing up and helping Helena to her feet.

"Oriel was startled when Will shouted, that's all," Helena told him, struggling to keep her voice steady. She was determined not to let Jamie know how much the accident had shaken her. Hot tears stung behind her eyes, from shock rather than the pain in her shoulder. "He jumped, and I fell over. I'm fine, really."

Jamie narrowed his eyes and stared at the dusty hoofprint on Helena's riding jacket. "Are you sure he didn't hurt you?"

"Yes, honestly." Helena straightened her coat and forced herself to look at the stallion. To her dismay, her heart was racing and her palms felt clammy with sweat. There was nothing to be afraid of, she told herself. The horse was watching her carefully, his head high and his neck muscles tense. His flank rose and fell with quick, shallow breaths, and a sheen of sweat glistened on his mahogany coat.

Helena held out one hand toward him, clenching the muscles in her forearm so that her arm didn't shake. "Silly old lad," she whispered, the words dragging like thistles over the lump in her throat. "Nothing to be scared of now."

Oriel snorted and tossed his head disbelievingly. Jamie touched Helena lightly on her arm. "Perhaps we should leave him for today," he suggested. "I'll give him a feed an' we can let him settle. He still looks pretty spooked to me."

Helena let her hand fall back to her side. "Yes, I suppose you're right." Shaken and sore, she tried to ignore her growing doubt that the stallion would ever settle down in his new home. There was a wildness in him, a wariness of spirit that seemed determined to keep everyone at a distance. And he had frightened her by rearing up like that, Helena couldn't deny it, although it would need more than a glancing blow to her shoulder before she would admit such a thing to Jamie.

Behind her, Jamie bent down and collected the grooming brushes, which had spilled into the straw. "Come on, Nell," he said, straightening up with the grooming box under his arm.

Helena started to walk through the straw toward the door. Tears of disappointment blurred her eyes and she reached up to wipe them away. There was a snort behind her and she turned to look over her shoulder.

Oriel was looking steadily back at her, a wisp of dried clover dangling from his lips from where he had been pulling at his hayrack. He blinked at her, his eyes gleaming like tiny moons in the dim light of the stable. His scare seemed to have been forgotten, and for a moment he looked like any other of Lord Roseby's well-bred horses enjoying the fragrant meadow hay.

Helena was not fanciful enough to imagine that the stallion was trying to apologize, but as she forced herself to breathe evenly and hold the horse's dark brown gaze, she couldn't help thinking there was a new gentleness in his expression. Everything's all right now, he seemed to be saying. It was just an accident.

Jamie's hand on Helena's arm interrupted her thoughts. "Let's leave the horse in peace," he said, opening the stable door and standing aside to let her go through.

Oriel's ears flicked back and forth, and he idly stamped a foreleg before turning back to tug another mouthful of hay from the rack.

Once outside the stable, Helena remembered the noise that had startled Oriel in the first place. "Is Will all right?" she asked anxiously.

Jamie slid shut the bolt on Oriel's door and smiled down at Helena. "Oh yes," he assured her. "He ran his cart into the water butt. Charity dusted him down an' took him indoors. He had a knock to his pride, that's all." His smile faded and his forehead creased in a frown. "I think it's you that came off worse, Nell," he said seriously. "Are you sure Oriel didn't strike you?"

Helena reached up involuntarily to touch her stinging shoulder. "His hoof just brushed against me, honestly," she said. Above her head, the stable clock puffed out three rasping chimes, each one accompanied by an ominous thud of machinery. Helena and Jamie had often joked that the clock was like a little old man in the way it grudgingly counted out the hours with a painful wheeze.

"Is it three o'clock already?" Helena exclaimed. She grimaced at Jamie, gesturing at her disheveled habit. "I suspect Mama would have something to say if I turned up at the dinner table like this."

"Aye, an' rightly so," Jamie replied. "Go on in an' change."

Helena nodded, privately hoping that she would be able to keep her injury from the curious eyes of her maid. "I'll see you tomorrow afternoon," she told Jamie. "Faith is coming in the morning so I won't be able to ride." Helena liked her gentle, good-humored governess; and although she begrudged any time away from the stable yard, at least Faith's lessons were more interesting than the endless samplers she labored at under her mother's critical eye. Needlework was Helena's least favorite pastime, and she failed to see how the ability to embroider hummingbirds on a cushion cover could possibly help her manage a household more effectively.

"You get on in, then," said Jamie, as Helena shivered in a sudden blast of salt-laden wind. "Don't worry about Oriel," he added, seeing Helena glance once more into the shadowy stable. "He'll get used to us soon, I'm sure."

Helena smiled gratefully at him and turned to climb the steps to the house. They seemed steeper than usual today. Her coat pulled painfully against the scrape on her shoulder and her legs still felt weak from shock. When she reached the house, she went straight upstairs to her bedroom, hoping to change into a clean gown before her maid came to help her get ready for dinner. She shrugged off the jacket of her riding habit and stepped out of the skirt before pushing her undershift off her right shoulder to see if Oriel had left any mark. A dark red crescent-shaped bruise bloomed on the top of her shoulder, faintly outlined in tiny beads of blood where the tip of Oriel's shoe had broken the skin.

The memory of the horse rearing over her made Helena's head swim and she took a deep breath. It was just an accident, she told herself firmly.

She was struggling to undo the laces that fastened her bodice when there was a knock at the door and the maid appeared, carrying a folded shift.

"Lady Helena, I've brought—" The maid stopped in the doorway, her eyebrows raised in confusion at the sight of Helena undressing without her. "Is everything all right, my lady?"

Helena flushed. "Yes, thank you, Louise," she said. "I just wanted to get changed after my ride."

Louise laid the clean shift on the oak chest at the foot of Helena's bed and walked across the room. "Here, let me help you," she said. Helena turned to let the maid reach the stiff knots, hoping that her hair covered the alarming bruise on her shoulder.

"It's this damp weather, my lady," Louise muttered as she picked at the laces. "I've been having the devil's own job with my stays, too." She broke off and glanced uncertainly at Helena, as if afraid that she had spoken too familiarly.

Helena felt a pang of sympathy. Louise was barely a year younger than she and had been at Roseby Manor for only a few months. "Then we must pray for dry weather, mustn't we?" Helena said with a smile. "I'm sure the horses would be grateful too. Poor old Snowdrop was sinking up to her hocks in the mud today."

Louise relaxed and returned Helena's smile. She finished untying the stays, laid the bodice on the bed, and picked up a hairbrush from Helena's dressing table. As she straightened out Helena's heavy coil of brown hair, she uncovered the crescent-shaped bruise and let out a gasp. "My lady, what have you done?"

"Oh, it's nothing," Helena said quickly, twisting away. "Don't worry about my hair now. I need to dress for dinner." She tried not to wince as she lifted her undershift over her head.

Louise pursed her lips and handed Helena the clean shift. "It doesn't look like nothing," she observed. "There's blood and everything."

"It's fine, really," Helena said, pulling the shift over her head. When she emerged from the neck and shook back her hair, she saw Louise studying her with narrowed eyes. Both girls were distracted for a few minutes by the task of squeezing Helena back into her bodice, and Helena hoped that the subject of her bruise would be dropped. But she clearly had not satisfied Louise's curiosity yet.

"Was it that new horse?" the maid asked with unexpected boldness as she held out a gown for Helena. "I heard Watkins telling Mrs. Gordon it was a mean old devil. Kicked him clean across the stable when he went to feed it last night."

Before Helena could rush to Oriel's defense, there was a soft tap at the door. "Come in," Helena called, threading her arms through the lace-trimmed sleeves of the heavy silk gown.

Sarah, Lady Roseby's maid, stepped into the room. "Your mother was asking if you were ready to come down to dinner, Lady Helena," she said. "Your father wishes to dine early because he is meeting some gentlemen tonight."

"Tell Mama I'm just coming," Helena said, lifting her chin to let Louise fasten the hooks in the front of her gown. Sarah bobbed a curtsey and slipped out of the room, leaving Helena to wait while Louise gave a hasty brush to her hair. There was no time to discuss Oriel now, and Helena just hoped Louise wouldn't think the angry hoofprint on her right shoulder was worth mentioning to anyone else in the household.

HELENA WOKE THE NEXT morning feeling stiff and sore, but she struggled into her underclothes alone before Louise arrived to help her dress. The bruise on her shoulder was even more pronounced now, a dramatic scarlet semicircle fading to purple and black at the edges. Her right arm felt heavy and uncomfortable, but Helena thought that she could hide the injury as long as she didn't use her right hand too much.

She was surprised to find both her mother and father in the dining room. When he wasn't due in court, Lord Roseby usually left early to visit the quarries on Portland, two hours' ride away.

"Good morning, Helena," said her father, lowering the sheets of his newspaper to smile at Helena as she sat down and let Hawk pour her some tea. "Did you sleep well?"

"Yes, thank you, Papa," Helena replied, lifting the cup carefully in her left hand. "Are you going to Portland today?" she inquired.

Lord Roseby shook his head. "Two of the cottages at the bottom of Church Lane have had some thatch washed away. I'm meeting Robert Clark this morning to see if he can repair them before any more rain gets in."

Robert Clark was the local thatcher. Like most of the villagers, his house was owned by Lord Roseby; and it often seemed to Helena that there was no area of village life that her father did not have some responsibility for, from paying for cottage repairs to providing work on the estate or in the manor house.

On the opposite side of the table, Lady Roseby put down the knife she had been using to butter a slice of toast and looked at Helena, her blue eyes grave. "I understand you had an . . . an accident with Oriel yesterday," she said.

Helena replaced her cup in the saucer with a clatter. "But that's all it was—an accident," she protested, wondering how on earth her mother had found out.

As if reading her daughter's mind, Lady Roseby said, "I heard Louise telling Mrs. Gordon that the stallion had kicked your *shoulder*, Helena. Please, could you explain to me how that happened?"

Lord Roseby looked up sharply. "Is this true, Nell?" he demanded.

"Yes, but Oriel didn't mean to hurt me," Helena insisted, feeling her stomach twist into a painful knot. "I had gone into the stable to groom him when Will crashed his cart into the water butt and made him jump. I fell over and one of his hooves just touched me. There's hardly a bruise . . . ." She trailed off as she saw her mother's face darken.

Lady Roseby turned to her husband. "You heard that he kicked Watkins as well?"

"Yes, Watkins told me," Lord Roseby admitted. "But it's not unusual for a horse to kick out when he's being fed, especially if he's as hungry as Oriel seems to be."

"Being hungry is no sort of excuse!" Helena's mother cried.

Lord Roseby frowned. "I'm not suggesting for one moment that we make any more allowances for Oriel than we would with any other horse."

"William, I really think that stallion is dangerous," Lady Roseby insisted. "We can't take this sort of risk with a horse we know nothing about."

Helena held her breath. Surely her mother wasn't going to make her father get rid of Oriel?

"I mean it, William," Lady Roseby went on. "I'm sure you don't want the grooms to be hurt, let alone your own daughter! I'm sorry, but the horse will have to be sold."

HELENA STARED AT HER mother in dismay. She was about to protest when her father held up his hand.

"One moment, Jocelyn," he said to his wife, with a glance at Helena that warned her to stay silent. "Don't you think we ought to give the stallion a chance to settle in before we judge him too harshly? From what Helena says, it does sound as if what happened to her yesterday was an unfortunate accident."

Helena felt her shoulders sag with relief. But her father hadn't finished. "However, I agree that we shouldn't take unnecessary risks. Until we can be a bit surer about the horse's temperament, I think Helena should leave his grooming and exercise to the stable lads." He turned to Helena, his hazel eyes serious. "Does that sound fair?"

Actually, it didn't, not to Helena. She remembered the gentle expression in Oriel's eyes when she had entered his stable yesterday and the way he had walked over to greet her of his own accord. Her shock at the thought that her father might sell

Oriel because of what happened had driven away the doubts she had felt straight after the accident. Remembering the way the stallion had seemed after the accident, Helena was more sure than ever that she would be able to win his trust in the end. But she noticed that her mother looked undecided, as if she might still insist on getting rid of Oriel altogether, so she said quickly, "Of course, Papa."

"And is that acceptable to you, Jocelyn?" asked Lord Roseby.

Lady Roseby nodded slowly. "Very well, but if the horse doesn't settle down, you will have to sell him, William. It is sheer good fortune that Helena has not been badly hurt." Her blue eyes met Helena's. "You do promise to stay away from the stallion, Helena?" she said. "There is really no reason for you to get involved with any of the stable work, but I think it's a little late for me to start telling you to leave the other horses to Watkins and Jamie as well." Her gaze softened with a glimmer of amusement.

Helena smiled back. "Thank you, Mama. And I understand about Oriel. I'm sure he'll settle down soon."

"I hope you're right," said her father, placing his napkin on the table and pushing back his chair. "Now, I must be off. Enjoy your morning with Faith, Nell." He smiled at Helena and bent to kiss his wife before sweeping out of the room, swinging his hat in one hand.

"WHY DO YOU THINK it was so important for Mr. Crusoe to tame the wild goats, Helena?"

"Goats?" Helena echoed, turning to look at her governess in surprise.

Faith Powell sighed. "Yes, Helena, goats," she repeated. She tapped the leather-bound book that lay open on the writing desk. "We have reached the chapter in Mr. Defoe's book in which Robinson Crusoe captures and tames some wild goats."

Helena flushed and looked down at the page. The heavy black print seemed to dance in front of her eyes, and she realized that she couldn't remember a single word of the scene she had just read aloud. In her mind, she had been back in Oriel's shadowy stable, endlessly replaying yesterday's scene. Could she have done anything differently—talked more firmly to him, or stood closer to his shoulder perhaps?

"I'm sorry," she apologized to her governess. "I was miles away."

"Even farther than Mr. Crusoe's desert island?" teased Faith.

Helena smiled. "Well, perhaps a little closer to home than that." For a moment, she was tempted to confide in Faith her fears about Oriel being sold before she had a chance to prove that he was safe. Even though the governess was several years older than Helena, Faith had grown up in Roseby and Helena had known her all her life. Faith's father, Elijah Buckle, owned the village inn, and her, sister, Charity was Will's nursemaid.

Then Helena paused. As far as she knew, Faith had not even seen Oriel, so could hardly be expected to sympathize with the troubled horse if she heard about Helena's injury. No, for now Helena decided to be silent about Oriel and force herself to concentrate on Robinson Crusoe's goats.

"Did he need them for food and milk?" she ventured, wrinkling her nose as she recalled the only goat she knew, the sexton's stinking and bad-tempered nanny. Helena felt a pang of sympathy for Mr. Crusoe if he had to drink goat's milk, which always smelled and tasted as if it had been standing in the sun for several days.

"Well, yes," Faith agreed. "But the goats have a wider significance too, don't you think? They could represent the way in which Robinson Crusoe is managing to tame his surroundings, to turn the island into a model of an English farm."

Helena shifted position on her chair to ease her stiff shoulder. The parlor was beginning to feel uncomfortably stuffy, although she was grateful to Mary Polstock for ordering a fire to be lit. It had rained steadily all morning, and Lady Roseby's new rose-patterned carpet was fighting a losing battle against the damp-laden drafts that whistled up through the floorboards. "It seems a shame that animals have to be tamed to have any value," she observed, thinking not of goats but of a mahogany-dark horse with intelligent, shining eyes.

Faith looked closely at her. "An interesting debate, but not one for today," she said, reaching over to close the book. From the hall, a clock chimed twelve, each note echoing along the stone-flagged corridor outside the parlor. "I see that it has stopped raining and I expect your mother would like you to have some fresh air before dinner, so shall we leave Mr. Crusoe on his island until next time?"

Helena flashed her governess a half-guilty smile. "Thank you, Faith."

She pushed back her chair and was about to replace the book in the glass-fronted bookcase when Faith added, "And perhaps you could read the next two chapters before then?"

Helena nodded. When she was less distracted, she enjoyed Daniel Defoe's story of the shipwrecked sailor, and having more chapters to read would give her a perfect excuse to avoid her needlework for another evening. One of her embroidered hummingbirds had gone very wrong, with a strangely misshapen wing that made it look more like a fat green fish swimming beside some heavy-headed roses.

She slotted *Robinson Crusoe* into its place in the bookcase, said good-bye to Faith, and ran upstairs to change into her riding habit. There was just time to ride Snowdrop before dinner and, most important of all, with her mother's ominous words ringing in her ears, find out how Oriel was today.

THE STABLE YARD WAS quiet when Helena arrived. Isaiah Buckle, Faith's seventeen-year-old brother, was carefully forking manure onto one of the tubs of flowers that stood at the edge of the yard. Isaiah was the undergardener at Roseby Manor, a long-shanked, skinny lad with high cheekbones and small, pale gray eyes that gave him the appearance of a hare.

"Good a'ternoon, Lady Helena," he greeted her, straightening up and blinking nervously.

"Good afternoon, Isaiah," Helena replied. "Have you seen Jamie?"

Isaiah gestured awkwardly toward the stable block with one long-fingered hand. "He's in there, my lady. Shall I fetch him for you?"

Helena shook her head. "Don't worry," she said. "I can find him myself." Isaiah nodded and bent over his barrowful of manure again.

Helena started to cross the cobbles to the stable block, tucking the ends of her shawl more securely into the neck of her jacket. She paused when she reached Oriel's stable and looked over the door. Inside, a shadowy brown shape rustled the straw.

"Hello there," Helena murmured, resting her gloved hands on the door. She glanced down at her fingers to reassure herself they weren't shaking. There was an unfamiliar tightness in the pit of her stomach, and she knew it was apprehension after yesterday's accident. But she was not about to let herself lose confidence in the horse after a single episode.

Another rustle, and Helena held her breath as the stallion stepped delicately toward her and stopped just beyond the light cast through the door. He stretched his neck forward and blew softly through flared nostrils, brushing her fingers with the lightest of touches.

Helena stayed completely still. "You know I won't hurt you, don't you?" she whispered.

Footsteps sounded in the arched entrance to the stable block, and Helena heard Jamie call something to Isaiah. She tensed, waiting to see if Oriel would react with alarm, but the stallion merely pricked his ears and turned his head toward the sound.

Jamie crossed the yard toward Helena and waited until he was standing right behind her before speaking in a low voice. "He seems a bit less jumpy today, doesn't he? Watkins said he even stuck his head over the door to look for his feed this morning."

Without taking her eyes off the stallion, Helena smiled. It sounded as if Jamie was as hopeful as she was that Oriel would be fine. "He just needed a bit of time to get used to us, that's all," she said. She turned to face Jamie, feeling a surge of excitement. "Shall I try brushing him again?"

Jamie looked uncomfortable. "Nell, your father doesn't want you to go near Oriel for a while, not until we can be sure he's safe."

"But I know he's safe," Helena protested. "Just look at him! Yesterday was an accident. Even my father said so."

Inside the stable, Oriel snorted gently as if in agreement.

Jamie shook his head. "Lord Roseby gave orders this morning to all of us: You're not to go into Oriel's stable until he is satisfied the horse isn't dangerous. I'm sorry, Nell, but you can understan' why he's worried."

Helena stepped away from the stable door and banged her hands together in frustration. "I know Papa is worried, but really, Oriel is fine now. And he's never going to get used to me if I'm not allowed near him." She returned to the door and studied the horse for a moment.

Oriel looked calmly back at her, a wisp of hay clinging to his velvety muzzle. Helena felt a fresh burst of impatience. If her father could see the stallion now, he would know that Oriel meant them no harm. And at the back of Helena's mind, she couldn't help worrying that if she didn't prove that he was safe very soon, her father might be persuaded that the horse should be sold.

There was a clatter of metal-shod hooves on the cobbles as Watkins went by on his way to lunge Monument, one of Lord Roseby's carriage horses. A long rein was clipped to the dark gray gelding's leather head-collar. They were heading for one of the paddocks where Watkins sent the horses around in wide, steady circles to stretch their legs and keep them fit on the days

Lord Roseby didn't use them.

"Don't you think we should be lunging Oriel too?" Helena asked, turning to Jamie.

"Maybe later on," Jamie replied guardedly. "After all, we don't know if he's been lunged before an' we don't want to upset him with too many new things all at once."

"Don't be such a coward!" Helena retorted, only half joking. Fear of losing Oriel lent sharpness to her tongue. "If you won't lunge him, I will. I bet he'd love to get out of that stable, anyway."

Jamie frowned. "I told you, your father doesn't want you handling Oriel yet."

"Then I'll just have to make sure he doesn't find out. We could lunge him tonight, couldn't we?" Helena defiantly held Jamie's gaze, her head high. Even Oriel pricked his ears at Helena's tone. "There's more than half a moon, and it should be clear enough," Helena went on, glancing up at the calico autumn sky. The rain clouds had cleared from the valley, scurrying away over Eggardon Hill like thick-fleeced black sheep. "I'll meet you down here at midnight."

Jamie looked taken aback, and Helena admitted that she had even surprised herself with her rebelliousness. After all, she had never suggested visiting the stable yard in the middle of the night before. But it was essential that her parents didn't find out what she was planning to do, because they would stop her without a doubt.

"I can't do that, Nell," Jamie said quietly, looking down at the cobbles.

"Oh Jamie, there's no need to be frightened of Oriel," Helena argued. "Just look at him! He's fine, and the sooner we start treating him like any other horse, the better." She couldn't help feeling puzzled by Jamie's reluctance. She'd never known him to be afraid of a horse before.

Jamie shrugged. "I'm not afear'd," he told her. "But your father has given an order, an' I don't intend to go disobeying him."

Helena lifted her chin, her green eyes sparkling. "And as *my father's* stable lad," she replied, choosing her words carefully, "what if I were to order you help me with Oriel tonight?"

Jamie met her gaze steadily, a smile twitching at the corners of his mouth. "You know me better than to try something like that, Nell. I can't meet you tonight an' that's that." His eyes suddenly turned serious. "If your father found out, I could lose my job."

Helena nodded despondently. She knew she was being unfair. She just wished she could have had her friend's support if she tried to lunge Oriel that night. Would she be able to manage the stallion on her own? But if she didn't, and if no one ever trusted Oriel enough to let him prove he was safe, the stallion might be sold.

Jamie didn't seem to notice Helena's anxiety. "You could be right about lunging Oriel," he went on. "I'll suggest it to Watkins. The horse'll certainly need exercising soon, with all the oats he's eating!" He grinned at Helena.

Helena smiled back. Oriel needed her to be brave on his behalf, even if Jamie couldn't help her. Reaching over the stable door with one hand, she stroked the stallion's warm neck. "Good-bye, Oriel," she murmured. The stallion responded by nodding his head and blowing hot damp breath onto her sleeve. His gentleness strengthened Helena's resolve and she felt her heart lighten.

She turned to Jamie, straightening her hat and smoothing down the jacket of her riding habit. "Please will you saddle Snowdrop for me?" she asked. "I'd like to ride her this afternoon."

Jamie nodded, apparently relieved that their brief argument was over. Helena replayed the conversation in her head and told herself that she hadn't actually lied to Jamie. He had just assumed that if he wasn't around to help her, then she wouldn't try to lunge the stallion. Forcing away the doubts that lurked like storm clouds at the edge of her mind, Helena watched him walk away to fetch Snowdrop. Excitement was already making the tips of her fingers tingle at the thought of taking Oriel out that night.

HELENA WAS CAREFUL TO TAKE A TINDERBOX to bed with her that night, so that she could rekindle her rushlight after everyone else had gone to bed. She listened to the stable clock strike eleven, and then midnight, before she heard the distinctive creak of her father's polished leather boots as he walked up the staircase and past Helena's door to his dressing room.

Once his door had closed, Helena forced herself to count to two hundred before pushing back her eiderdown and swinging her bare feet down to the floor. The floorboards felt like ice, a small price to pay in Helena's mind for the cloudless night that let the three-quarter moon shed a thin frosty light through her window. There was no need for the rushlight to get dressed, she thought, reaching for the riding habit she had left on top of her clothes chest. As she hooked the heavy woollen skirt around her waist, Helena wished for the thousandth time that she could wear breeches like Jamie that would let her walk freely and ride astride without chafing her knees. At least this riding habit had a skirt that wrapped around her so that she could divide it on either side of the saddle when she and Jamie swapped horses.

Hardly daring to breathe, she opened her bedroom door and crept along the landing, carrying her boots in her hand so that she could step more softly in stockinged feet. The rushlight and tinderbox were in the pocket of her skirt in case she needed more light once she got down to the stable yard. The wooden stairs felt perilously slippery, but she made her way safely down to the stone-flagged hallway and slid open the massive iron bolts on the back door.

Outside, the frosty air made her gasp. She stooped to pull on her boots, then ran down the steep stone steps that led to the stable yard. As Helena neared the corner of the house, she paused. Instead of the heavy midnight silence, sounds of movement were coming from the stables. A door swung open on protesting hinges, followed by a low murmur of words that Helena couldn't quite make out. Then there was a series of odd shuffling sounds, like soft drumbeats stopped short. More rustling, and the drumbeats came closer.

Helena peered around the corner, her heart pounding. Two dark shapes loomed toward her, bay carriage horses even more perfectly matched in the gray moonlight. Cloudy breath rose from their nostrils as they lifted their legs with slow uncertain steps. There was just enough light for Helena to see that their hooves had been muffled with strips of cloth tied around their fetlocks.

Fear and fury raced through Helena in equal measure. Someone was stealing Apollo and Jupiter!

She shrank back as the horses went past, the stone wall rough and cold beneath her gloved fingers. She had to wake up Watkins from the grooms' quarters or Hawk, who slept at the top of the house.

Suddenly Apollo balked, his head shooting up in alarm as a black-and-white shape darted across his path.

"Dratted cat!" hissed the slender figure holding the lead rope. He turned, raising one hand to soothe the startled horse. A shaft of moonlight fell across his face, and Helena felt her knees buckle with shock.

The horse thief was none other than Jamie Polstock.

6

HELENA OPENED HER MOUTH to call out, but a gust of icy wind took her breath away. As she struggled to find her voice, Jamie reached up to grab a handful of black mane and vaulted onto Apollo's back in one smooth movement. He kicked the gelding into a canter, clicking his tongue over his shoulder to encourage Jupiter to keep up. Two sets of muffled hoofbeats thudded down the drive and out of the gate before Helena had caught her breath again, leaving her staring in disbelief.

Where was Jamie taking her father's horses? He wouldn't steal them, Helena was sure of that. But what on earth could he be doing with them at this time of night? There was only one way to find out. Gathering the skirt of her riding habit in one hand, Helena ran over to the tack room. The door scraped on the flagstones as she pushed it open, and she held her breath, expecting angry shouts from the grooms' loft at any moment. But there was no movement and, leaving the door open, she tiptoed in and unhooked Snowdrop's bridle. After a moment's thought, she picked up a handful of cloths that were drying over one of the saddle racks before slipping out again.

She walked in the shadows beside the wall and crept into the stable block, breathing in the soft nighttime smells of quiet horses and hay. Snowdrop was standing in her stall at the far end of the passage, a ghostly pale shape with her head hanging low as she dozed. She pricked her ears when Helena approached, puzzled but not alarmed by the unusual hour.

"Hello, sweet girl," Helena whispered, shrugging the bridle from her shoulder and slipping the reins over Snowdrop's head. The metal bit clanked treacherously, but the mare soon muffled the sounds with her velvety lips. Helena buckled the throatlatch and noseband, then picked up Snowdrop's hooves one after the other and tied a stable cloth over each one, knotting the ends firmly in the crook of the pastern. The mare dropped her head to sniff curiously at her unconventional footwear.

"Come on, lass," Helena urged the mare quietly, leading her out of the stall and along the passage. Snowdrop's hooves made soft thudding sounds on the cobbles, but she lifted her feet carefully and didn't stumble as they made their way into the yard.

Helena led Snowdrop over to the mounting block and, with a final glance at the loft to make sure no accusing lights had been kindled, jumped onto the mare's broad, warm back. It was a long time since she had ridden bareback, but as children she and Jamie had often cantered around the orchard on Bumblebee with neither saddle nor bridle, and Helena knew that Snow-drop's gentle pace would make it easy to stay on. She scooped up the reins and urged Snowdrop down the drive and left into the road that led through the village, in the direction Jamie had cantered just a few moments earlier.

Behind her, the coach house clock wheezed out a single chime, and a dog barked in one of the cottages behind the Black Feathers. But everything else was still and silent, the lights in the inn long since snuffed out and the massive oak front door barred and bolted. Helena trotted past the inn and out of the village, gripping with her knees to stop herself from slithering off Snowdrop's back. There was no sign of Jamie and the carriage horses now, but there was only one road in this direction, leading toward the cliffs. The field gates on either side of the lane were shut and the dewy grass in each gateway looked undisturbed, so Helena felt confident that she was still following Jamie's route.

Ahead of her, the land folded into a steep-sided gully that led down to Freshwater Bay, as if a giant swimming ashore had leaned on the cliffs to steady himself. On either side of the gully, sheep-cropped turf sloped up to rejoin the cliffs. Just before the land fell away, the village lane met the main road that ran from Abbotsbury to West Bay. The River Bredy flowed under the main road here in a steady brown channel that followed the gully down to the shore. A narrow stony track ran beside it.

Helena reined Snowdrop to a halt in a spinney of beech trees next to the main road and looked down at Freshwater Bay. The angle of the gully as it sloped up from the beach was too steep to be able to see anyone on the track. But Helena could just see a narrow strip of shore at the edge of the bay, the sea glowing dull silver in the dim moonlight.

To her surprise, the cove was not empty. A long low-hulled boat rocked on the foam where the waves rolled onto the stones. Half a dozen shadowy figures were trekking across the beach toward the bottom of the gully, the noise of the sea muffling their footsteps as they crunched over the pebbles. Their steps looked awkward, their silhouettes grotesquely hunched, until Helena realized that they were carrying heavy loads away from the boat, round-sided barrels and softer bundles of something that looked like cloth.

She froze. These men must be smugglers!

Suddenly Helena realized that the boat was slipping away from the shore, propelled by six long pairs of oars that scooped noiselessly at the silver sea. The beach was empty now, with no sign of the smugglers who had been unloading the boat. But above the hiss and suck of the waves, a new sound could be heard. Muffled hoofbeats, the creak of a wooden cart as it climbed the steep slope up from the shore, and the pad of men walking quietly over hard-packed stones.

Helena drew back into the shadows under the trees, her

heart thudding painfully and her hands clammy with fear. What would these villains do if they found her spying on them? And where was Jamie? Helena just hoped that, wherever he had been taking Apollo and Jupiter, he would not cross paths with the smugglers. What terrible luck that they should all be out on the same night!

A single figure appeared at the top of the slope, where he paused and looked from side to side along the main road. Then he turned and raised one hand in a silent signal to the unseen men behind him. Almost at once, a horse loomed over the crest of the hill, its head nodding with effort as it dragged the heavy cart over the stones. A slim silhouette walked beside the horse's shoulder, urging it on with quiet words. Another horse and cart followed, less heavily-laden than the first, with men walking beside to steady the pile of barrels.

Helena felt a cold hard knot of dread in her chest. In less than a heartbeat she had recognized those horses and the slender figure walking beside the first cart. Jamie's path had more than crossed with that of the smugglers. He had provided them with her father's carriage horses!

The first cart reached the main road, and Jamie led the horse straight across toward the lane that led to Roseby and to the beech trees where Helena was standing. She held her breath and willed Snowdrop beside her to do the same. The fact that she knew one of this desperate band of criminals made no difference to her terror—in fact, it made things worse because she feared Jamie's reaction if he found out she had followed him. She felt as if she were dealing with a stranger now, not her childhood friend who swapped horses with her and knew all her secrets.

Then, to Helena's horror, Snowdrop snorted and shifted her weight noisily from one back leg to the other. The carriage horse pulling the first cart—in the dim light, Helena could not be sure if it was Apollo or Jupiter—leapt sideways in alarm and, made clumsy by the cloths on its hooves, stumbled onto its knees. There was a muffled curse from the figure at the head of the procession, who turned and ran back to the cart.

In her alarm, Helena couldn't help realizing that there was something familiar about this smuggler's light-footed gait and his long neck half-hidden under the broad black hat. She was almost certain it was Hawk, one of the footmen from Roseby Manor. Her mind reeled as it dawned on her that if this was a company of Roseby smugglers, she probably knew every single one of these men. But she wasn't dealing with her father's trusted workers and tenants now, who depended on the manor for wages and a roof over their heads. These men were pursuing their own dark purpose and had no need of the Rosebys. Helena didn't want to test their loyalty to her father—or to her—by letting them know that she had seen them.

Over at the cart, Jamie had calmed the startled horse—

Helena could see now that it was Jupiter, with a longer nose and narrower face than his stablemate—and had stooped to examine his knees. The carriage horse was standing up again but rested the tip of one front hoof on the ground as if reluctant to bear any weight on that leg. Jamie muttered something to Hawk and straightened up, rubbing the back of his neck as he always did when something was troubling him. Helena flinched as she recognized the familiar gesture, then felt her breath catch painfully against her ribs. Hawk was looking around and pointing at the beech trees, whispering something to Jamie. They were trying to work out what had frightened Jupiter, and Helena knew that there was nothing she could do except wait to be discovered.

Time seemed to stand still as Jamie jogged over to the trees. Halfway across the road he stopped dead, a low whistle of amazement escaping from his lips, and Helena knew that he had recognized Snowdrop's pale gray shape. Peering past Snowdrop's head, she saw Jamie lift one hand to reassure the men behind him that he was all right. The blood roared in her ears as she watched Jamie walk to the edge of the shadows and stand there, the moonlight gleaming on his pale knuckles as he clenched his fists by his side.

"Helena!" he hissed. "I know it's you. What the devil are you doing here?"

A sudden rush of anger gave Helena courage. She stepped

forward, one hand resting on Snowdrop's neck to calm the mare, who had lifted her head at Jamie's fierce tone. "I might ask you the same thing," she retorted. "How dare you steal my father's horses? And for *smuggling*?" She stopped, unable to give any more words to her fury and aware that Jamie's brown eyes were narrowed with an anger of their own.

"Don't be a fool, Nell!" he told her through clenched teeth. "I haven't stolen the horses. We just borrowed them for the run tonight. Normally we use farmer Powell's horses, but he's got a Riding Officer lodging with him just now. Look, I haven't got time to argue. Get back home with you, before you bring the customs men down on us."

"What makes you think I won't go and call the customs men myself?" Helena challenged him. "After all, you're no better than common thieves. What you are doing is against the law, you know, Jamie."

In one swift movement, Jamie stepped into the shadows and gripped her wrist with his hand. Helena flinched and tried to pull away, but he held her fast, his face so close to hers that she could feel his breath in her hair.

"We're a long way off being common thieves, Nell," he murmured, his eyes blazing into hers. "These goods are paid for fair and square, save for what the government would put on their value in taxes. All we're doing is findin' some way of feeding and clothing our families. But what would you know about not being able to afford a packet of tea or a roll of cloth? This isn't theft, Nell. It's just a different way o' buying things. None of us would hurt a soul. We don't even carry weapons, see?" He thrust open his coat with his free hand, revealing his stained white undershirt but no brace of pistols or stout stick, which was what Helena had been half expecting.

With an exasperated hiss, Jamie let go of Helena's wrist and turned away. "Now, get home before you have the rest of the company to answer to," he ordered. "Don't worry, we won't harm you," he added dryly, seeing the look of fear flash across Helena's face. "It's just that you're holding us up, an' by the look of Jupiter's knee, you've caused us more 'n enough trouble already tonight."

Helena felt a pang of concern for the carriage horse. "Is he lamed?" she asked, trying to look over Jamie's shoulder.

"Aye," Jamie nodded grimly. "Not badly, but he won't be pulling the cart again tonight. But that's our problem, not yours."

Just then, a broader shadow loomed up behind Jamie, and a deep voice asked, "What's going on here, lad?"

Helena bit her lip to stop herself from gasping out loud. It was Samuel Polstock, Jamie's father.

The blacksmith waited for a moment as his eyes adjusted to the dim light under the beech trees. Then he stared at Helena in disbelief. "Lady Helena! What are you doing out here at this time o' night?" His voice was quiet but thick with scarcely veiled anger, and Helena shrank back toward the trunk of the tree.

"I . . . I was following Jamie," she confessed in a rush. "I saw him take the horses, and—"

Suddenly Samuel stiffened, and Helena heard the sound of running footsteps, their speed and lack of caution revealing the urgency of the errand. A gangly figure came hurtling down the main road, a long-spouted metal lantern swinging madly from one hand. Pale harelike eyes were wide with alarm in a gaunt, flushed face as the messenger skidded to a halt beside Helena and Samuel.

"Coming from West Bay! Three of 'em at least," Isaiah Buckle blurted out, his ribs heaving under his thin dark blue jacket.

Samuel Polstock frowned, his expression dark.

Helena felt a chill run down her spine. "Who is coming?" she whispered.

Isaiah was too distracted to show any surprise that Lord Roseby's daughter had joined the company of smugglers. He drew in another ragged breath. "Riding Officers, my lady! 'Tis the customs men!"

7

SAMUEL POLSTOCK TURNED AT once to the men by the carts, who were staring curiously at the group under the trees. "Right, let's get this load up to the village."

He was interrupted by a low voice. It was Hawk, running softly across the road toward them.

"Sam, this horse isn't going to be any use to us now—" The footman broke off when he caught sight of Helena. "What the devil is she doing here?" he demanded, his eyes widening with alarm. He glanced over his shoulder as if expecting dragoons to come bearing down on them at any moment.

Polstock shook his head impatiently. "There's no time to worry about her now. Are you sure the horse is lamed?"

Hawk nodded. "We'll have to turn 'im loose an' use th' other to pull both carts. Not that we've much time for that, but if we hurry we might stay ahead of the patrol."

Samuel frowned. "Well, if that's the only way we'll get this haul done tonight, we'd better get goin'. Go an' unhitch the lame horse, Richard," he ordered the footman. "We'll shift the cart out of the road until we can come back for it."

Helena had been listening in silence, biting her lip to stop herself from interrupting Samuel and Hawk with apologies for startling Jupiter. Behind her, Snowdrop snorted and butted her gently in the back. Almost before she had a chance to measure her words, she blurted out, "Why don't you use Snowdrop instead? She's easily strong enough to pull that cart and it would save time, wouldn't it?"

Even as her words hung in the frosty air, she was aware of just how extraordinary her suggestion was. The daughter of Lord and Lady Roseby had offered to help a company of smugglers! But she found it impossible to stay afraid of these men. Helena had known them as loyal friends for all her fifteen years, and as smugglers for barely fifteen minutes. In spite of the nighttime and the secrecy, they were her father's villagers.

Jamie looked shocked. "Don't be daft, Nell," he whispered. "This is none of your business, nor Snowdrop's."

Samuel Polstock laid one massive hand on Jamie's shoulder. "Hold on, lad." His brow furrowed and his expression was unreadable as he studied Helena for a few moments. She held his gaze steadily, hoping he understood that she could not stand by and watch her friends and neighbors be captured by Riding Officers, whatever they had done. Her offer was genuine, and she didn't see how else they would manage.

At last Samuel Polstock nodded. "All right, we'll use Lady Helena's mare."

"But what if she tells the customs men about us?" Jamie objected, wrenching away from his father's grasp. "She oughtn't to be out here, an' you know it."

Helena had had enough of being squabbled over. She straightened her riding jacket and led Snowdrop forward, brushing past Jamie as she emerged from the shadows under the trees. The rest of the smugglers were huddled around the first cart, muttering to one another with tension visible in every stiffened fiber of their bodies. They stopped talking when Helena appeared and stared in amazement and, in some cases, panic. Glancing swiftly along the line of men, Helena felt oddly calm as she recognized Hugh Weaver, one of the gardeners at the manor, and Robert Clark, the thatcher. There was no time for civilities, so she said nothing but led Snowdrop briskly over to where Jupiter stood, still holding up his front leg.

Hawk was wiping away a trickle of blood that ran down the carriage horse's cannon bone. He looked up when Helena drew near and his eyes registered alarm for a split second, then relaxed as Samuel came up behind Helena.

"We'll use the gray mare instead of this one," said the blacksmith in a low voice that invited no argument. "Unhitch quickly—the patrol will be along soon."

Hawk jumped up and started undoing the harness at once.

Jamie appeared at Helena's elbow. "I'll take Snowdrop now," he murmured, his face hidden in the shadows beneath his broad-brimmed hat. He reached past Helena and took hold of Snowdrop's reins. "Come on, lass."

Helena stepped back and watched as Jamie expertly backed the gray mare into the traces where Jupiter had been. There was something strange about this hitching up and it took Helena a moment to work out what it was. She missed the creak of leather that usually accompanied straps being buckled into place, and when she peered closer at the harness she realized with surprise that it was made of rope. Almost unconsciously, she reached out one hand to feel the trace that lay along Snowdrop's flank.

"Rope harnesses make no noise," Jamie explained over his shoulder. He pointed to the wheels of the cart, and Helena saw that the wooden rims were covered with close-fitting strips of leather. "We let no curious ears hear us if we can help it," he said.

Helena nodded.

Jamie's father touched her lightly on the shoulder. "Get into the back cart, Helena. Be quick, now."

"What about Jupiter?" Helena asked, looking around for the carriage horse.

"I've let him loose in yon field." Hawk came up to them, his hands full of muffling cloths and Jupiter's bridle hooked over one shoulder. "He'll be all right there till morning, an' Jamie can fetch him back before anyone notices he's gone."

Jamie finished slipping neat felt hoof covers onto the gray mare's shoes instead of the knotted rags, and beckoned to Helena. She followed him past Snowdrop's cart, which was piled high with dark wooden barrels and shiny oilskin bundles that gleamed with saltwater, to Apollo's cart, where the men were climbing silently aboard.

"Here, my lady." A large rough hand reached down to her, and Helena grasped it and allowed herself to be pulled up into the back of the cart. The owner of the hand shifted along and patted a barrel beside him. "You can sit 'ere," he urged her.

Even in the darkness, Helena knew that voice. It was Diggory Hardcastle, the church sexton. "Thank you, Diggory," she murmured, gathering her skirt and carefully lowering herself onto the unsteady seat. Jamie had already gone back to lead Snowdrop. Helena looked at her companions. Of the five or six men crouched on barrels and bundles around her, most of their faces were in shadow, but there was something familiar about the shape and bearing of each one. Helena was sure that the burly, long-legged figure at the far end of the cart was Harry Savage, the tenant of the home farm, Roseby Manor, who looked after her father's dairy herd.

The cart moved off with a jerk, and Helena was nearly jolted off her barrel. Diggory grasped her arm to steady her.

"All right, my lady?" he grunted.

"Yes, thank you," Helena replied, bracing her feet on the floor of the cart. A small voice at the back of her mind asked her exactly what she thought she was doing, but she silenced it firmly.

Apollo pulled the cart steadily between the moonlit hedges, the only noise the creak of barrels and the soft breathing of men, The leather-covered wheels made barely a whisper over the stones, and Apollo's hooves padded like a cat in velvet slippers. As the lane started to climb to the outskirts of the village, something sharp and metallic rolled along the floor of the cart and came to a stop against Helena's ankle. She bent down and picked it up, turning it curiously in her hands. The moonlight glinted on a strange pewter lantern, with a long thin spout extending from the gap where the light would shine out. Helena had seen it in Isaiah's hand when he came running down from his lookout on the main road.

Diggory leaned closer to her, his bushy gray whiskers tickling Helena's cheek and his breath wheezing in her ear. "'Tis a spout lantern, my lady," he whispered. "The light shines out to sea but nowhere else. Young Isaiah wants to signal to just the one ship out there, an' not to any customs men further along the cliff, you see."

Helena nodded. With a boldness that surprised her she asked, "What's in this load, Diggory?"

She felt his watery blue gaze rest on her for several long seconds. "Brandy in the barrels," he told her at last. "An' in them oilskin bundles, tea, lace, an' silk. Mostly tea, my lady."

It sounded to Helena like the shopping list Mary Polstock took with her to Dorchester on market day. She wasn't sure what she had been expecting, but this seemed like extraordinary lengths to go to for the sake of a pot of tea and some fabric. Was it true what Jamie had said, that this was the only way most people could afford such everyday things? Helena dug her fingers into the stiff woollen cloth of her riding habit, suddenly aware of how little she really knew about the lives of the villagers.

The first cottages loomed out of the darkness on either side of the lane. Not a light flickered in any window as the carts rolled softly past, and Helena wondered if the occupants were busy "watching the wall," so there could be nothing to tell the customs men if they came asking awkward questions. The thought made her glance back along the lane, half expecting to hear hoofbeats in pursuit and see the glint of horses' bits appear around the corner at any moment.

Diggory followed her gaze. "They'll be a while yet," he assured her. "Isaiah's got good eyes an' fast feet, which is why we make him lookout. He'll have spotted 'em along the cliffs as soon as they left West Bay, an' that's a good hour's ride off."

Helena felt her heart begin to pound with a new and much

sharper fear. What would happen if they had been too slow in changing horses on the front cart? Would she really be arrested by Roger Chapman's men? Oh Lord, what would her father say? Surely the Riding Officers would know that she wasn't a real smuggler!

Suddenly the cart jolted to a stop. Hawk left Apollo's head and came around to the back. "Here, Lady Helena," he said, holding out his hands to help her down. Helena stood up and let the footman lift her onto the ground. Then she moved quickly out of the way as the men behind her slid off the cart like eels and began to unload the bundles. Looking around, Helena realized that they had come to a halt outside the churchyard next to Roseby Manor. Thoughts of her parents' horror if they knew where she was crowded Helena's mind as she saw the familiar bulk of her home looming behind the square bell tower.

Samuel Polstock appeared among the men, his hatless head of thick black hair standing above most of the other smugglers. "Make it quick, lads," he ordered in a low voice, reaching over the side of the cart and lifting out a stout wooden barrel as if it were a piece of kindling.

Robert Clark thrust an oilskin bundle toward Helena. "Can you carry this, my lady?" he asked.

Helena wrapped her arms around the awkward package. It was cumbersome and slippery but not heavy. "Yes, I think so," she replied.

The thatcher pointed toward the lych-gate. "Take it up there after Diggory," he ordered.

The sexton was disappearing into the shadows under the roofed gateway that led into the churchyard. Helena felt her way carefully up the uneven steps, the oilskin bundle threatening to slip out of her grasp at any moment. She followed the sexton along the verge beside the gravel path that led around the side of the church. A sinister black doorway yawned at the foot of the south wall. Helena knew that this was the entrance to the crypt, although she had never been down there. It was the church cellar where her Roseby ancestors lay buried. The thought of all those skeletons crumbling to dust in their stone coffins made Helena step back a few paces until she was standing among the gravestones on the grass.

Diggory stood beside the black hole, his sea-drenched bundle dumped on the path at his feet. He had opened a small pewter tinderbox and was striking a sharp-edged flint against the steel. A burst of sparks flared into a tiny flame as they caught hold of the strip of linen that had been folded into the tinderbox. Helena watched in silence as the sexton shielded the flame with one hand and coaxed an open-sided lantern into giving out a pale yellow light. Then he held the lantern out over the entrance of the crypt, its beams barely reaching as far as the first stone step.

"Is this where the . . . the cargo is to be stored?" Helena asked hesitantly.

"Aye, lass." Diggory grunted. He ducked down and climbed into the gaping hole, the lower part of his legs swallowed up at once by thick shadow. He stopped abruptly, and Helena heard him curse under his breath. Without thinking, she dropped her oilskin bundle and ran over to the crypt entrance. The sexton was standing a few steps below her, gazing down into the darkness.

Helena held up her skirt and started to feel her way down toward him. She had only descended as far as Diggory's step before she halted in alarm. The icy cold that wrapped itself around her feet and shins was not the damp musty air of a tomb. The crypt was flooded. Helena was close enough to the surface of the water to see the light from the lantern reflected in a faint gold sheen, ruffled by the folds of her skirt as it floated around her.

A noise from above made Helena twist around and look up. Samuel's head was framed in the doorway, his expression unreadable in the shadow. "Is something wrong, Diggory?" he demanded in a low voice.

Diggory turned and sloshed back up the steps. "Aye," he said shortly. "River Bredy must have risen undergroun', like it did twen'y year ago. We won't be using this place tonight, that's for sure."

"Blast!" muttered Samuel. Then he jumped as the beam from Diggory's lantern fell on Helena's face. "What are you doing down there, Helena? Come on, lass, no point in you soaking your feet."

"But where will you put the cargo now?" Helena asked as she made her way back out of the crypt, allowing Samuel to steady her with one hand for the last step.

"We have other places," Samuel answered quietly.

"Not so many this time," Diggory warned the blacksmith. "You know the cellars at the Black Feathers are flooded too, an' we filled Master Powell's hayloft last week."

Samuel frowned at Diggory as if warning him to guard his tongue. Several of the other smugglers had joined them by now, standing quietly with their loads resting on the dew-soaked grass. Helena had noticed that they all kept off the treacherously loud gravel path, stealth coming as naturally to them as cats stalking prey, it seemed. There were a few murmurs at the news of the flood but still the same calm that had greeted Isaiah's warning of the customs men. This was no desperate band of criminals ready to fight their way out of trouble, Helena was increasingly sure of that. She searched the shadowed faces for Jamie and smiled when she met his solemn, dark-eyed gaze. He had removed his jacket for the unloading and his shoulders looked almost as broad as his father's as he stood in his shirt with one hand steadying the barrel at his feet.

Helena found herself filled with a strange confidence, as if it was up to her to find a new place to store the cargo. After all, she reasoned with dazed, sleepless logic, the smugglers wouldn't have made it to the village if she hadn't lent them Snowdrop. If she had done that much for them, it was only natural that she should help keep their cargo safe from the customs men as well. She took a deep breath and turned back to Samuel Polstock. "You could use the hayloft at Roseby Manor," she told him. "I think there would be enough room for this load and it's close enough to unload before the Riding Officers arrive."

Behind her, she sensed Jamie stiffen with alarm, but she ignored him and gazed steadily at Samuel. The blacksmith nodded slowly, his eyes fixed on Helena's. "First a spare horse, now space for our cargo," he murmured, his mouth curving upward. "'Tis unlikely an' unlooked for, but tonight we have no choice. Thank you, Lady Helena. Right, lads, let's get this stuff 'round to the stable yard. No need to put it back on the carts— we can take it through the side gate." He bent down and shouldered his barrel, then led the way through the gravestones to the wrought-iron gate that opened into the grounds of the manor. None of the men objected, although a few shot uneasy glances at Helena, their eyes faintly gleaming under their hats.

Helena knew there was no time to defend her actions out loud, not even to Jamie, who stood like a statue at the edge of the group. She heaved up her oilskin bundle once more and began to pick her way across the uneven turf toward the gate. She glanced back when she reached the entrance to her own garden and saw Jamie nudge his barrel toward Isaiah Buckle, indicating that he should take care of it while he went back to see to the horses. A broad shadow loomed up behind Helena, staggering under the weight of two bundles of cloth, and grunted at her to keep going. She turned quickly and followed the line of men along the stone path that led to the stable yard.

No one spoke. The path was barely twenty yards from the house, and if Helena had thought the smugglers moved quietly before, now they walked like ghosts, in spite of their heavy burdens. By the time she turned the corner into the stable yard, the first of the loads was being heaved through a narrow hatch into the hayloft above the horses' stalls, just inside the main archway. She waited in line until she reached the archway, and a pair of hands reached down to take the bundle from her. A tall figure stepped up to help her hoist the awkward load high enough, before it was hauled into the darkness above them. Breathless with effort, Helena turned and found herself looking into the round, friendly face of Harry Savage. He nodded briefly, stalling her attempt to thank him, and slipped into the shadows again.

Suddenly the activity around her froze into wary stillness. Two sets of hoofbeats could be heard on the road through the village, growing nearer and nearer. The group of men in the archway turned as Jamie ran into the yard, dragging Apollo and

Snowdrop behind him, their necks stretched against the taut reins.

"Customs men!" he gasped. "They were just coming into the village when I was taking the carts back to the Black Feathers."

Samuel looked around at his men, his eyes narrowed. "We'll have to hide here," he decided. "Into the loft, all of you."

The last barrel was heaved up, quickly followed by its bearer, Hawk the footman. Once inside the hayloft, he knelt at the edge of the hatch and reached down to haul up the next man. Helena stood in the shadows at the edge of the archway, watching them.

Jamie led Snowdrop over to her and thrust the rein into her hand. "Here, take the mare back to her stall," he said. "Don't worry about the felt shoes. There's no time to take them off an' the straw should hide her hooves if the customs men go looking."

Helena nodded and led Snowdrop along the passageway to her stall. Quickly swapping her bridle for the head-collar that hung down from the ring in the wall, Helena squeezed out past the mare's warm gray flank and ran back to the yard. Jamie was just heaving himself into the hayloft, his legs kicking to propel himself upward. Only Samuel Polstock was left.

"Come on, Helena," he said. "There's no time for you to get back into the house."

Sure enough, Helena could hear the rapid drumbeat of cantering hooves much more clearly, the hollow thud on packed stones switching to the crunch on gravel as they swung into the drive that led to the stable yard.

Helena's mind raced. Was she about to be caught with a company of smugglers in her father's own stable yard? But somewhere amid her growing panic she felt a small icy core of calmness take over. Because whatever her fears for herself, there was only one person who might have any legitimate reason to be there in the middle of the night as far as the customs men were concerned.

Helena turned to Samuel. "Get into the hayloft," she told him. "This is my father's land. I can deal with the customs men when they arrive."

Samuel frowned. "I can't let you do that," he began.

"We don't have time to argue," Helena cut him short. She motioned with her hand toward the hatch where Jamie's face peered down anxiously, a pale disk in the gloom. The hoofbeats grew louder, and now she could clearly hear the jangle of metal bits and the quiet words exchanged by the customs men. Samuel reached up and gripped the sides of the hatch. With a tiny grunt, he heaved his body up into the loft and disappeared. The door to the hatch was slid into place by unseen hands, and Helena was left alone in the archway.

CHAPTER

8

"WHO GOES THERE?" ROGER Chapman's voice rang out
across the stable yard, echoing around the moonlit cobbles.

Helena stepped forward out of the shadows. Her wet skirt
clung uncomfortably to her shins and she tried surreptitiously
to shake it free with one hand. Then she lifted her head and
looked up at the dark-cloaked rider on the dun cob. "Mr.
Chapman!" she exclaimed. "Is there something wrong?"

"Lady Helena!" The Riding Officer looked startled. "What
are you doing here? It is not safe for you to be out here. My
men and I are pursuing a company of smugglers."

"Smugglers? In Roseby?" Helena tried to echo the same
tone of fascinated concern with which she had greeted Mr.
Chapman's news of wreckers two days before.

"I'm afraid there are." Roger Chapman swung his leg over
the cantle of the saddle and leapt down to the ground. His
eyes were narrowed and his forehead creased with something
Helena feared was suspicion. She straightened her back and
concentrated on keeping her face expressionless. This was her

father's stable yard, she told herself, and she had every right to be here, even at this unusual hour. And she forced herself not to think about the men breathing silently in the hay-scented darkness above her head.

Behind Chapman, the two other customs men reined their horses to a halt. Sitting lightly on the bony gray horse was the young man with sandy hair who had visited the manor previously. Helena guessed that he was the officer who was lodging with the Powells at Upbredy Farm. The third officer was a stocky, red-faced man whose dark blue jacket fitted a little too tightly across his chest. His bay gelding stood with his head hanging low and his flanks heaving, streaked with sweat and mud from the gallop along the cliffs. With a jolt of alarm, Helena realized that she knew this man. He was Tom Clark, the brother of Robert the thatcher, who was at that very moment hiding in the hayloft barely ten yards away.

Feeling her heart pound so loud she was sure the men would hear it, Helena met Roger Chapman's blue gaze. "I have seen nothing that would concern you tonight," she told him carefully. "Nor have I heard anyone pass in the street."

But Chapman was not so easily dismissed. Tapping the side of his boot with his riding crop, he peered past Helena into the shadowy archway. "May I ask what you are doing out here at this time of night, Lady Helena?" he inquired.

"I was concerned that my father's new stallion would not

settle. He was upset by an incident yesterday, and I wanted to check that he was all right." Helena glanced across the yard to the dark rectangle of Oriel's door. There was no movement from within, and she hoped the stallion would not look calmly out to belie her description of a troubled horse that required nighttime visits.

Roger Chapman studied Helena for several long seconds. At last he nodded and raised his hat politely to her. "I take it that all was well with the stallion, Lady Helena?" he said. When Helena nodded, he went on, "In that case, we shall leave you in peace. But you will of course inform me if you do see anything I should know about?"

"Of course, Mr. Chapman," said Helena.

Roger Chapman swung himself into the saddle and wheeled the cob around, turning to look down at Helena once more. His eyes were like pale shards of ice in the gray moonlight, burning with cold fire into Helena's green-eyed gaze. "No doubt we shall speak again," he murmured, raising his whip in a salute. "Good night, Lady Helena."

He touched his spurs to the dun's sides, and the cob cantered out of the yard. The other officers followed, Tom Clark drumming his heels against the flanks of his tired horse.

Helena stumbled back two paces and leaned with relief against the wall of the archway. She suddenly felt exhausted, her legs unable to support her weight any longer. The softest of noises above made her look up. She saw the hatch slide open, and Samuel Polstock lowered himself down.

"Thank you, Lady Helena," he said quietly. "Now get yourself inside. It's been a long night for all of us."

Jamie dropped onto the cobbles beside his father. He looked at Helena for a moment, his brown eyes wary and assessing, as if he was seeing her in a new and unfamiliar light. "Thanks— for everything," he muttered.

"All right, Jamie," his father interrupted him. "Let Lady Helena get off to bed now. Go on, lass."

Tired beyond words, Helena nodded and stumbled across the stable yard toward the steps that led up to the manor. She was dimly aware of more figures sliding out of the hayloft behind her, and into her dazed thoughts came the question of what was going to happen to the cargo hidden in her father's stables. But she was too weary to puzzle over that now. As she recalled Samuel's quiet control of his company of smugglers, she hoped she could trust the blacksmith to sort everything out without anyone else finding out about the illicit use of the hayloft.

A GUST OF WIND rattling the window jolted Helena out of a confusing dream about goats and lame horses and long-nosed lanterns. Through the gap in the curtains, she could see that the sky had only just begun to lighten. It was too early to get up, but she knew she would not go back to sleep now. Her head throbbed and her heart was pounding, and she lay still for a few moments under the comforting weight of the blankets before she remembered what was wrong.

Jamie was a smuggler! And not just Jamie but half the men of Roseby, it seemed. The events of the previous night flooded her mind, cast in moonlit shades of gray—Jamie taking the carriage horses, the silent boat in Freshwater Bay, Snowdrop pulling the cart back to Roseby, the flooded crypt, and finally speaking to the customs men with their prey hiding above their heads.

A fresh wave of horror swept over Helena as she realized how close she had come to being arrested, and she let her head sink into the soft feather pillow until the dizziness had passed. When her head cleared, she realized with an uneasy prickle of guilt that she had been a hundred times more afraid of capture by the Riding Officers than of anything the smugglers might do to her. Even now, back in the safety of her father's house, she found it impossible to connect the black-hearted criminals described in newspaper reports with the friends and neighbors she had lived among all her life.

The men had clearly been shocked to see Helena last night, but they had made no attempt to conceal what they were doing or scare her into silence. Instead, they had trusted her—to the extent of letting her help them and even keep their hiding place secret from the customs men. Recalling their quiet sense of purpose, Helena guessed that smuggling was part of their way of life—albeit a muffled, midnight way of life—that somehow sat easily with their daylight routine. She wondered if it was possible that the other villagers were unaware of what was going on; her governess, Faith Powell, for example—did she know that her husband, Jonathan, provided the horses to pull the carts? And the carts themselves belonged to Faith's father, Elijah Buckle, innkeeper of the Black Feathers.

Helena shook her head in confusion. It looked as if the only villagers who did not know about the smugglers were the Rosebys themselves. Downstairs, the clock chimed eight. It was still early for breakfast, but Helena decided to get up. She felt her stomach tighten at the thought of encountering the smugglers in their daytime roles—not just Jamie, but Hawk the footman and Samuel Polstock—but she could hardly hide in her bedroom forever. And if they had trusted her to keep silent last night, they would trust her today.

Rinsing her face in the basin of cold water that Louise had brought to her room the evening before, Helena dressed in a clean riding habit and went downstairs, feeling every muscle in her body protest from the jolting midnight cart ride and insufficient sleep afterward. An elderly footman, his neatly curled wig dazzling white against his dark green jacket, was crossing the hall with a silver teapot. "Good morning, Lady Helena," he greeted her.

"Good morning, Mansbridge," she replied. She smiled her thanks as the footman opened the door to the dining room and stood back to let her go in.

Her father was sitting at the breakfast table, studying some papers. "You're up early, Nell," he remarked as she slipped into the chair opposite him.

"I couldn't sleep," Helena told him truthfully. She watched Mansbridge pour her some tea and couldn't help feeling a guilty pang of relief that Hawk wasn't serving them this morning.

"Shall I fetch your eggs now, my lord?" Mansbridge asked Helena's father.

"Yes, please. And could you see if Mrs. Gordon has any ham as well?"

"Of course, my lord." The footman bowed and left Helena alone with her father in the dark-paneled room.

"Are you going to Portland today, Father?" asked Helena, wrapping her cold hands around her teacup.

Lord Roseby shook his head. "I had intended to, but another magistrate has been called to London unexpectedly, so I have to go to Dorchester to take over his cases."

Helena felt her stomach churn with something that felt like dread. "Do any of the cases concern smugglers?" she asked, hoping that she sounded only mildly interested.

"No, not this time," replied her father distractedly, his attention on one of his papers as he squinted at the cramped print. Frowning, he held the sheet up to the window. "This clerk's handwriting looks more like Greek!" he muttered.

"But sometimes you try smugglers, don't you?" Helena persisted, unsure where she wanted this conversation to go but equally aware that her mind was buzzing with unanswered questions.

Lord Roseby looked at her with raised eyebrows. "Well, yes," he said. "Why the sudden interest in smugglers, Nell?"

Because I think I have become one! Helena replied silently. Aloud, she said, "I'm just curious, that's all. After Mr. Chapman's visit, I realized that I—I don't know much about smugglers and wreckers. And perhaps I should, since we live so close to the sea, and it's obviously going on around us. . . ." She trailed off as her father's expression turned to one of puzzled amusement.

"What is it that you want to know?"

"Why is it so wrong, what they do?" Helena asked in a rush, feeling the blood rise to her cheeks. "Not wreckers, I mean. I know what they do is terrible—theft and murder of all those innocent sailors. But smuggling, well, I don't really understand, that's all," she finished lamely, lifting her cup and swallowing a mouthful of tea to hide her awkwardness.

Lord Roseby looked down at his papers and tidied them for a few seconds, straightening their edges. "Do you understand about taxes, Helena?" he asked at last.

She nodded. "When things are brought to this country from abroad, we have to pay more for them and the extra money goes to the government."

"That's right. And at the moment, because of the war we are fighting in France, the government is in need of more money than usual. So it has put higher taxes on certain goods like tea and brandy and lace."

Helena shut her eyes for a moment, picturing the sea-soaked barrels and oilskin bundles heaved one by one into her father's hayloft. "And does this make them too expensive for people to buy?" she asked, opening her eyes and meeting her father's gaze.

"Well, yes, sometimes," he admitted. "Tea in particular is very expensive just now, but it could be argued that the government is fighting the war on behalf of the people of Britain so it is only fair that they should have to pay for it."

A black speck floated to the surface of Helena's tea. She studied it, wondering if this particular tea leaf had funded a soldier's wages. "But if the government put lots of tax on tea, they'll end up losing money because people will smuggle it instead, won't they? I mean, everyone drinks tea. It doesn't seem fair that people can't afford it."

Her father smiled. "You sound like a dissenting politician, Nell. But, yes, that does seem to be what is happening. Hence the arrival of Mr. Chapman and his Riding Officers. They certainly seem determined to stop any smuggling that's going on around here."

"Do you think there is? Smuggling in Roseby, I mean."

Lord Roseby narrowed his eyes, the expression in his hazel eyes guarded. "I am a magistrate, Nell," he said. "I know as well as any man how many unseen things there are going on around us. It is my job to supervise the trials of those who are caught, not hunt them out myself."

The door opened and they both jumped. Mansbridge came in bearing a silver tray with a dish of eggs and folded slices of glistening pink ham.

"Thank you," said Lord Roseby as the footman placed the dish in front of him.

Mansbridge turned to Helena. "Will you be wanting anything, my lady?"

"Just some more tea, please," she said. She waited until the footman had left the room, then turned back to her father. "But smugglers aren't as bad as wreckers, are they?"

Lord Roseby swallowed his mouthful of ham before replying. "That would depend on your point of view, Helena," he said calmly. "As far as the government is concerned, the smugglers have avoided paying tax on their goods, which is against the law."

"But they haven't actually stolen the things in the first place, have they?" Helena persisted.

"No, that's not how they work. If you really want to know—"
Lord Roseby raised his eyebrows at Helena as he wiped his lips
with a napkin, and she nodded "—then it's my understanding
that the master of the smuggling ship buys his cargo in France
and brings it across the Channel. When he reaches England,
the cargo is unloaded by a different group of men led by someone called a lander. He decides where the smuggled goods are
hidden and how they are sold."

That meant Samuel Polstock was Roseby's lander, Helena
thought. "Who pays for the goods in the first place?" she
asked.

"It varies. Sometimes the master of the ship, sometimes
the lander, and sometimes someone who is willing to finance
the operation but doesn't want to get directly involved. Once
the first lot of goods has been sold, the lander gives that
money to the master of the ship to pay for the next trip."

"So it really is just a different way of buying things," Helena
murmured, echoing Jamie's words from the night before.

Her father frowned. "Mr. Chapman wouldn't agree with
you. Whether you approve of the taxes or not, smugglers are
breaking the law, and that can drive them to take desperate
measures such as shooting customs men to avoid being captured. There's little to choose between smugglers and wreckers
then, I'm afraid."

His face was grim, and Helena wanted to blurt out that the

Roseby smugglers weren't like that. Jamie had promised her that they never carried weapons and she believed him. It wasn't just his word that she trusted—the men she had seen last night were the same villagers she had known all her life, and she couldn't imagine them causing harm to anyone, even a customs man. Everything her father had said told her that her instinct to protect the smugglers had been right.

On the other side of the table, Lord Roseby slid his papers into his leather document case and stood up. "You look a little pale, Nell," he observed. "You've not been having nightmares about smugglers, I hope?"

Helena shook her head. "Oh no," she told him. *Not exactly*, she added silently. "But I do have a slight headache. I was hoping a ride on Snowdrop might clear it."

"Good idea," said Lord Roseby. "Now, I must be off or I won't be finished by this evening. Your aunt Emma is paying us a visit tomorrow and I promised your mother that I would join her for afternoon tea." He went over to the door and opened it just as Mansbridge entered with a fresh pot of tea. "Have a pleasant day, Helena. I'll see you this evening."

"Good-bye, Papa," said Helena. She drank another cup of tea and decided against any toast. She wanted to go down to the stable yard as soon as possible.

As she ran down the stone steps, her pace slowed and a pang of nervousness about seeing Jamie clutched at her stomach.

Would he treat her differently now that she knew about the smuggling? He might feel awkward around her—not just because Helena had seen this secret side of his life, but because the smugglers had been forced to rely on her to deal with the Riding Officers. Helena didn't want Jamie to feel in her debt. If anything, she had more reason to be grateful to him and to the other smugglers for trusting her to stay calm and keep their secret.

Helena cautiously entered the stable block, her steps sounding unnaturally loud on the cobbled floor. Jamie was grooming Piper in the stall nearest the door, whistling softly between his teeth as he ran the soft-bristled brush down the chestnut's gleaming shoulder. He glanced over his shoulder as Helena approached, and to her relief she saw that he was smiling, his brown eyes as warm as ever. She suddenly realized that Jamie had always had to cope with the division between her roles as childhood companion and young lady of the manor; she would have to show the same respect for the two very different aspects of his life: stable lad and smuggler.

Helena slid into the stall and stroked Piper's nose. "Has Jupiter come back?" she asked softly.

Jamie frowned at her to keep quiet, nodding his head toward the other end of the stable block. Helena peered down the passageway and saw Watkins emerging from the carriage horse's stall.

"Just a scrape on his knee, like you said, Jamie," he called. "Oh, good morning, Lady Helena. Looks like Jupiter banged his knee last night. It's a bit swollen but there's nothing to worry about. I'll tell Lord Roseby we'll have to use Monument and Fleet for the next few days."

"Very well," Helena said faintly. She glanced sideways at Jamie, but he was busy untangling Piper's amber tail with gentle strokes of the brush.

"Will you be riding today, my lady?" Watkins asked.

Helena saw Jamie give a tiny shake of his head. Of course, she thought, Snowdrop would be tired after pulling the smugglers' cart and deserved a day off. "Er, no, thank you, Watkins," she replied. She smiled at the head groom, hoping he couldn't see the scarlet flush that she could feel creeping up her cheeks.

He nodded and went out of the stable block. Helena heard him call across the yard to Harding, the coachman, about Jupiter being lame. She turned to Jamie. "When did you bring Jupiter back? Is his leg really going to be all right? Didn't anyone notice he was missing?"

Jamie straightened up and looked at her, his brown eyes guarded. "Not too many questions, Nell," he warned. "Jupiter's fine, like Watkins said. What you saw last night—" he paused, running his fingers through the bristles of the brush in his hands, "—an' all that, it's our business, not yours. You do know that, don't you?"

Helena felt a sudden flare of anger. "How can you say that?" she demanded. "It was thanks to me that you got the load back last night. And as it's now hidden right above our heads, I think it is still very much my business. I gave you my word that I wouldn't say anything. Do you doubt me now?"

Jamie shook his head, his eyes softening. "Of course not, Nell. But it's better that you don't know too much, honestly. The less you know, the less you don't have to tell if the customs men come asking. See?"

"Yes, I suppose so," Helena admitted. "Will you be needing to use my father's horses again? How long will the Riding Officer be staying at Upbredy Farm?"

"Evan Price? No one knows." Jamie pulled a face. "It makes things more difficult, that's for sure." He winked at her, and Helena felt faintly surprised that he could be so cheerful after such a near miss with the Riding Officers.

"Jamie, I didn't come down to the stable yard last night to follow you," she confessed. "I mean, I didn't even know you were taking Apollo and Jupiter until I got here. I came to see Oriel. To . . . to lunge him."

The stable lad frowned. "Nell, I told you not to. Your father doesn't want you near him, an' we still don't know that he's really safe."

"Of course he's safe!" Helena argued. "And I'm going to

come and see him again tonight, even if you won't help me. If I can keep secrets for you, then I think you can keep a secret for me."

Jamie narrowed his eyes, and Helena said hastily, "I didn't mean that the way it sounded. I'm not going to say anything, I promise. But I'm just so afraid that my father will sell Oriel if we don't start working him soon. How else are we going to prove that he's settling in?"

Jamie sighed and started to pack away the grooming brushes. "You're as stubborn as a mule when you want to be, Nell." But he was smiling, and his eyes danced as they met Helena's. "All right, I s'pose I'd better come an' help. I must say, I think you're right about the stallion. He was quiet as anything when I gave him 'is breakfast this morning. What time do you want to meet?"

Helena returned his smile. "Midnight?" she suggested. "After my father has gone to bed. Hopefully there'll be enough moon to see by. We managed last night, didn't we?"

"Aye, we did. Now, I must take this fellow out for a leg stretch in the paddock." He clipped a coiled lunge rein to Piper's head-collar and turned the chestnut to face the doorway, then glanced over his shoulder at Helena. "I'll see you tonight."

"Yes, tonight," Helena echoed. She watched Jamie lead Piper out through the archway, and let her gaze travel across the yard to Oriel's stable. The dark brown stallion was looking over his door, his ears pricked as he watched Piper step gracefully over the cobbles. Then Oriel's head turned and his eyes rested on Helena. His ears flicked and he nodded his head very slightly, as if he sensed that she had been talking about him. Helena felt a bubble of excitement swell inside her. She could hardly wait for nightfall.

9

THE COACH HOUSE CLOCK was just summoning enough breath for its twelfth chime when Helena walked quietly into the stable yard. She went over to Oriel's stable and peered into the warm shadows, her fingers closing around the carrot that she had brought from the pantry. It felt cold and hard through her thin leather gloves, and Helena wondered if anyone had brought this horse a treat before. His wariness made that seem unlikely.

There was a rustle of straw as the stallion moved toward the door. Helena saw his eyes first, reflecting the pale moonlight with the faintest of gleams. Then Oriel gave a snort of curiosity and pushed his head over the door, his muzzle brushing against Helena's arm.

"Hello, Oriel," she greeted him, reaching up to run her free hand down the length of his nose. His eyes widened but he didn't flinch away, and Helena felt her heart leap. There could be no doubt that the stallion was beginning to trust her. Slowly she raised her other hand and offered Oriel the carrot. He sniffed at it hesitantly, almost knocking it off her flattened palm, then flicked his velvety lips over it and picked it up with his teeth. It stuck out of one side of his mouth like a stumpy orange pipe, and Helena smiled. "Go on, boy, it's for you," she reassured him.

The stallion blinked at her and began to crunch noisily, flipping the end of the carrot into his mouth until it had disappeared, leaving just a few orange shreds on his muzzle.

"He's enjoying that," said a quiet voice.

Helena jumped and turned around to see Jamie standing behind her, a bridle hooked over one shoulder. "I don't think anyone's given him a carrot before," she told him.

"You could be right," Jamie agreed. He opened the stable door. "Come on, let's get him out while he's still in a good mood." He slipped the bridle over Oriel's head, and the stallion opened his mouth willingly for the bit. "We'll lunge him in his bridle, I think," Jamie whispered to Helena.

She nodded in agreement. The bit would give them more control than an ordinary head-collar. But she couldn't believe that Oriel would put a hoof wrong. His coat rippled like liquid mahogany in the dim light from the lantern that Jamie had hung inside the stable door, and when his eyes met Helena's she thought that his former wariness had been replaced by a look of intelligent curiosity.

Jamie clipped the lunge rein to the side ring of Oriel's bit and looped the coiled rein over his arm. Then he pushed open the stable door. "You go out first, Nell," he murmured.

Helena walked out into the silent yard. The sky was clearer than the previous night, and the moonlight had turned the cobbles to pewter. She turned to see Jamie standing back just inside the stable door, to let the stallion make his own way out. Oriel hesitated in the doorway, stretching his head forward with his nostrils flared. Then he stepped out onto the cobbles, giving a nervous snort as he left the warmth of his stable and felt the cold night air on his flanks. Jamie walked quietly out at his shoulder and let the horse stand for a moment. Oriel looked around the yard with his beautiful head raised and his ears pricked as if he had been carved from dark bronze, and Helena felt her breath catch in her chest.

An owl hooted in the copse behind the stable block and Oriel swung his quarters around in alarm, his hoofs clattering on the cobbles.

"Hush, lad," Jamie soothed, jumping out of the way and placing one hand on Oriel's neck to quiet him. He raised his eyebrows at Helena as if to make sure that she wanted to carry on. Helena nodded determinedly. They'd got this far; there was no point in taking the horse back to his stable without trying him on the lunge now.

Jamie led the horse along the path that led through the kitchen garden to the fields. As they neared the first paddock,

Stone Jack, the elderly bay gelding that had been Lady Roseby's wedding present to her husband, loomed out of the shadows and stuck his head curiously over the railings. Oriel stopped dead, lifting his head so abruptly that the rein was nearly jerked out of Jamie's hands. Helena bit her lip as she watched Jamie calm the stallion and urge him on again.

They reached an empty paddock, and Helena ran forward to open the gate. Oriel walked in, his hooves thudding hollowly on the turf.

"You stay by the fence, Nell," said Jamie. "Just for now, then you can have a go."

Helena longed to stand with Jamie while Oriel circled at the end of the rein, but she knew that her friend had more experience lunging horses, so it made sense to watch this first time. Wrapping her skirt warmly around her legs, she pulled herself up onto the fence and perched on the top rail. Behind her, the fields sloped up away from the village to the Knoll, an old coast guard's lookout on top of a wooded hill. To the east lay Beacon Hill, a flattened black shadow against the indigo midnight sky. A tiny orange light flickered halfway along the length of the hill, casting its silent warning to sailors out in the Channel. Passing ships would be safe tonight, with the beacon to guide them and a breeze to carry them away from the hidden reefs.

Jamie led Oriel into the center of the paddock and walked away from him, uncoiling the lunge rein to give Oriel enough room to move in a comfortable circle. Then he flicked the rein at the stallion's flank to send him forward. But instead of walking around Jamie, Oriel snorted and bucked, plunging into the air with his back hunched and his head tucked between his knees. Landing with a jolt, he swung around to face Jamie, his legs braced and the whites of his eyes glowing with mistrust.

"Easy, lad, easy," Jamie murmured. He took a couple of paces toward Oriel, coiling the loose rein over his arm, and clicked his tongue encouragingly. "Come on, now, walk on."

Oriel tossed his head and broke into a ragged canter, his hooves slipping on the smooth turf to leave dark scars in the grass. Jamie quickly uncoiled enough rein to allow Oriel a larger circle, keeping the rein just short enough so that the slack didn't drag on the grass and tangle in the thudding hooves. He swiveled on his right heel and held the rein with both hands, following the horse with his eyes and talking softly to him in an attempt to calm him down.

But the stallion took no notice and galloped faster and faster around the paddock, his mane and tail flying like black silk in the cold air. He was going too fast to keep his balance and every so often he skidded, his hooves sliding sideways underneath him. To regain his footing, he stuck his head out and dug up clods of earth with the tips of his hooves, scrambling with his powerful hindquarters until he could race forward again.

Helena gripped the top rail of the fence, feeling a hard anxious knot form in her stomach. Jamie had been right: Oriel was nowhere near calm enough to be lunged yet. If he carried on like this, he might even injure himself.

In the center of the paddock, Jamie started to reel in the lunge rein, looping it over his arm and forcing the stallion to canter in smaller and smaller circles until he dropped into an uneven trot. At last, exhausted, Oriel slithered to a halt. He snatched at the rein and rolled his eyes nervously as Jamie walked up and ran his hand down the sweat-streaked brown shoulder.

Helena jumped down from the fence and walked over to them, forcing herself to move slowly so as not to startle Oriel even more. "That didn't go very well, did it?" she muttered.

"Aye, well, he's not been out of the stable for a few days so there's bound to be a tickle in his toes," Jamie pointed out, sounding breathless. "But I don't think there's much point carryin' on tonight. He'll only start to upset himself, an' we don't want him to slip over any more on this wet grass."

Helena shook her head, too disappointed to speak. She reached out to stroke Oriel's nose, and the stallion jerked his head away, scattering foam over Helena's sleeve. To her dismay, she felt hot tears sting her eyes. She had been so certain that she and Jamie would have been able to prove to her father and to Watkins that the horse was safe enough to stay at Roseby. It looked like she had been expecting miracles.

"Come on," said Jamie. "Let's take him back to the yard." He glanced at Helena and read the concern in her face. "There's no harm done, Nell. But it looks as if your pa may be right. I don't know that we'll ever tame this one."

Helena clenched her fists in frustration as she remembered the way Oriel had taken the carrot from her hand. "You can't give up!" she burst out. "We'll just have to try again. Come on, Jamie, you said yourself that it's not surprising if he's a bit lively first time out."

Jamie frowned and said nothing, but Oriel snorted and tossed his head as if agreeing with her. His flanks rose and fell in quick bursts, and sweat trickled down his ebony legs and dripped onto the grass. He seemed willing enough now to walk beside Jamie out of the paddock and back along the track to the stable yard. Helena latched the gate and followed them, suddenly hollow with exhaustion after two disrupted nights.

The lantern in Oriel's stable was still throwing out a pale yellow glow that sent thick black shadows into the corners. Jamie led the stallion inside and started to unbuckle the bridle. Helena slipped in after them and reached up to lift the bridle over Oriel's ears. He didn't flinch away this time, but stood with his head low, his lips snuffling at her wrist as she carefully let the bit drop out of his mouth.

"You need to help me with this," she whispered, resting her cheek against Oriel's smooth warm face. "You'll be all right next time, won't you?"

Suddenly Oriel lifted his head with a jerk and shifted so that he was facing the door. Helena stumbled, her skirt dragging in the straw, and Jamie reached out to steady her.

"Shh," he hissed. "Keep still." With his other hand, he closed the shutter on the lantern to extinguish the flame.

"What's going on?" Helena whispered in alarm.

Jamie said nothing, just nodded toward the yard. Helena crept closer to the stable door and looked out, feeling Oriel's shoulder warm beside her. In the dull pewter moonlight, she could just make out a line of shadowy figures moving across the yard, the hunched silhouettes and uneven gaits oddly familiar after last night. It was the smugglers, come to retrieve their cargo from the hayloft.

Helena turned back to Jamie, about to ask him where the barrels and bundles were being taken. But he shook his head at her, stalling her questions, and they waited in silence. Helena leaned against the wall and closed her eyes, feeling sleep tug at the corners of her mind.

The sound of Oriel shifting in the straw roused her. The stallion was snuffling at her hair, his breath warm and hay scented against her neck.

"Come on, Nell." Jamie stepped out of the shadows, the bridle slung over his shoulder and the lunge rein coiled in his hand.

Helena looked out over the door. The yard was empty, with no sign of the men who had carried off two cartloads of smuggled cargo. "Do you know where it all goes?" she asked quietly.

"Most of it stays in the village," Jamie answered. "It's not like we're bringing in big cargoes to sell inland. Once it's been out of sight for a couple of days, my dad sends it on to places where it can be collected more easily. I guess he didn't want to leave it here for too long, seeing as this isn't one of our usual places."

"Why did we have to hide just now?" Helena couldn't understand why Jamie had insisted on staying in the stable with the lantern extinguished, when she had already met the smugglers.

"Tonight was different people," Jamie explained, staring at a piece of straw that he was twisting between his fingers. "I'm part of the landing team—that's what you saw last night. But the next stage, the distribution, well, that's down to other folk."

"Does your father organize them as well?"

Jamie looked up at her and narrowed his eyes as if assessing how much he should tell her. Then he nodded. "Aye, but I don't know who they are. Not for sure, anyway. An' I know better than to ask questions. It's like I said—the less you know, the less you can tell."

Helena understood. There was a quiet code of honor among these men—among all the villagers, she suspected—that depended on accepting that some things couldn't be known or told. Suddenly she yawned, and Jamie smiled.

"Go on, Nell. There's nothing more to be done here."

Helena slipped out of the stable and ran across the damp cobbles. When she reached the corner, she paused and glanced back at Oriel's stable. The stallion was watching her, his ears pricked and his eyes like liquid black glass. In spite of her tiredness, Helena felt a surge of determination inside her. She would show her father that Oriel belonged at Roseby Manor, whatever it took. The horse was as big as any challenge Helena had faced, but she was not going to give up now.

HELENA SLEPT LATE THE following morning and was only woken when Louise brought hot water to her room. The maid set the jug on the nightstand and walked over to the window, flinging back the curtains to let in the soft gray light. Helena pushed aside her heavy eiderdown and sat up, running her fingers through her sleep-tangled hair. A faint stab of pain reminded her of the bruise on her shoulder, which had faded to a dull purple crescent.

"Good morning, my lady." Louise turned back from the window and bobbed a curtsey. Her smile vanished as her eyes fell on Helena's riding habit, which lay wet and crumpled on the chest at the foot of the four-poster.

"Whatever have you been doing, Lady Helena?" she exclaimed, scooping up the heavy woollen skirt and frowning at the dew-stained folds.

Helena swung her feet over the edge of the bed and jumped down, wincing at the icy cold floorboards. "'Tis November," she pointed out to her maid. "You cannot expect me to ride and stay dry all the time."

Louise tutted under her breath. "Aye, an' that's two riding habits you've muddied in as many days, my lady," she scolded. "Susan Clark won't thank me when I take this one down to the laundry. She's busy enough with your mother's new gown." She glanced up at Helena, her brown eyes dancing with excitement and the damp skirt temporarily forgotten. "Have you decided on the color of your gown yet, Lady Helena?"

With everything that happened over the last few days, Helena had almost forgotten that her mother had offered to have a new outfit made for her to wear to the Bridport race. "I haven't given it a moment's thought," she confessed. As Louise started to look disappointed, she added quickly, "Perhaps you'd like to help me?"

"What about dark green, to match your eyes?" Louise suggested. "An' Mrs. Clark has some nice yellow-sprigged cotton for the petticoat."

"That sounds lovely," Helena agreed absently. She walked over to the tall leaded window which looked across the lawns to the paddocks. Jamie was leading Jupiter out, and Helena was relieved to see that the carriage horse was walking evenly with no sign of favoring his injured foreleg.

Behind her, Louise opened the chest and took out a full-skirted lilac gown and a clean cotton shift. "Just as well you won't be riding today, my lady," she remarked. "Not with both habits dirty like they are."

Helena spun around, frowning. "Not riding?" she echoed. She had been hoping that she and Jamie could take Piper and Snowdrop to Beacon Hill again, or even Eggardon. With the race barely a fortnight away, Piper needed as many training gallops as they could give him.

"Aye, 'tis today that Lady Windlesham comes to visit," Louise informed her.

Helena felt her heart sink uncharitably as she remembered her father's telling her about Aunt Emma's visit the day before. Lady Roseby's sister was married to Sir Henry Windlesham, who owned banks in Weymouth, Dorchester, and Lyme Regis. They lived in a town house in a fashionable part of Dorchester, which Lady Emma insisted was the only bearable place to live if one had to be this far from London. Helena knew that her mother would not choose to live anywhere but Roseby; she guessed that it was only politeness that prevented Lady Roseby from pointing this out to her sister in no uncertain terms.

Louise went on. "Lady Roseby told Sarah that she hopes to arrive by eleven o'clock, in time for late breakfast. Though what the rain has done to the Dorchester road, Lord only knows. 'Twill be a miracle if her ladyship's carriage makes it through in one piece from what I hear."

Helena slipped off her old shift and held out her arms for the clean one. "I'm sure my aunt will be fine," she said. *And if she isn't, then we'll hear every detail of her terrible journey for the rest of the day,* she told herself silently.

She ran down the main staircase as the hall clock chimed eleven, and wondered if there was time to slip down to the stable yard and see how Oriel was after last night's disastrous attempt to lunge him. Disappointment dragged at her stomach as she remembered how he had bolted around the paddock at the end of the lunge rein, oblivious to Jamie's steady hands and soothing words.

A glance into the front parlor told her that Lady Windlesham had not yet arrived, and Lady Roseby was nowhere to be seen, so Helena fetched a thick woollen shawl from the chest by the back door and wrapped it around her shoulders. She was saved from having to make her escape when the door swung open to reveal Jamie carrying a basket of leeks and parsnips.

"Good morning, Lady Helena," he said. He frowned as his eyes traveled from the rough shawl to her full-skirted indoor gown. "Were you on your way out?"

"I was hoping to visit Oriel before my aunt arrives," Helena confessed. "But since you're here, you can tell me just as well how he is this morning. There's no heat in his legs, I hope, after last night?"

Jamie shook his head. "None at all, an' he ate all his breakfast straight off. Honestly, Nell, you wouldn't think he'd been out at all. I thought I'd ask Watkins if we could put him in the paddock with Stone Jack for a leg stretch this morning. It seems like he's fit enough to go out of the stable, at least."

"And that should make him calmer for the next time we lunge him," Helena agreed. She saw Jamie's eyes darken. "We are going to lunge him again, aren't we?" she insisted. She felt frustration well up inside her and added, "Oriel means us no harm, and I won't have you or my father tell me otherwise!"

Jamie held up his hand, just as if he were soothing a troubled horse. "I know that, Nell, but you must admit he's a handful. I may be able to explain Jupiter's scraped knee, but I'm not sure I could so easily face your father if you got hurt trying to work Oriel. Especially when we all know you've been told not to."

Helena unwrapped the shawl from her shoulders and folded it up into a neat square. "Let's see how he is after a day in the paddock," she said, tight-lipped. The rattle of carriage wheels outside the front door made her jump. "That will be my aunt arriving," she told Jamie. "I won't be able to ride today, so would you be able to lunge Snowdrop, do you think? I don't want her thinking she's only to be used as a cart horse from now on!"

Jamie grinned, clearly relieved at the lightness that had returned to her tone. "Aye, I'll make sure she gets some fresh air. Now, I must take these vegetables to Mrs. Gordon, an' you had better go and greet your aunt." He nodded toward the wide passageway that ran the length of the house from the back hall to the magnificent front entrance.

Helena pulled a face at him, then straightened her shoulders and smoothed down her petticoat as she heard Mansbridge opening the front door. "See you tomorrow," she whispered to Jamie. "Tell Oriel and Snowdrop that I haven't forgotten about them."

AUNT EMMA'S VISIT PROVED as trying as Helena had feared. From her vivid descriptions of the ruts and the jolting carriage and the floundering horses, it seemed as if Lady Windlesham had endured the most uncomfortable journey ever suffered by a human soul. Privately Helena thought that if the road was as bad as her aunt claimed, she should have turned back at the first puddle and stayed in Dorchester. But Aunt Emma seemed to regard her visits to Roseby as a charitable mission to relieve her sister from the tedium of rural life. When she had exhausted the last horrific detail of her mud-spattered journey, she summoned Helena to sit beside her on the padded settle in the front parlor and raised her spectacles to study her niece closely. Helena flinched, startled, when her aunt exclaimed out loud at her wind-flushed cheeks.

"Proper young ladies have a complexion like porcelain," she told her niece. "And what on earth do you do to make your poor hands like this? It looks like you have been washing bed linen! Surely your mother can find a decent laundrywoman, even in this remote place?" She let out a peal of shrill laughter at her joke, and Helena smiled politely.

Then Lady Windlesham frowned, her forehead creasing into plump folds that shed heavily scented powder in a sooty white waft. "Helena, I suspect this is all because of too much riding. You should know by now that young ladies need to ride only enough to meet the right sort of people and show off a handsome figure in a habit. Once a week maybe, but any more time spent outdoors than that, and, well, this is what becomes of your poor face and hands." She sat back against the cushion and fanned herself weakly, as if the thought of so much fresh air made her feel faint.

Lady Roseby came unexpectedly to her daughter's defense. "Helena is a fine horsewoman. William and I are very proud of her." She flashed a warm smile at Helena. "We have been thinking that she has outgrown dear old Snowdrop and that it will soon be time to buy her a younger hack of her own."

"Really? Mama, that would be wonderful!" Helena exclaimed, forgetting for a moment that her aunt would disapprove of such unladylike enthusiasm. Much as Helena adored Snowdrop, the thought of a new horse was irresistible, and her mind raced with pictures of striking bays and high-stepping dappled grays.

And then another horse cantered into her imagination, mahogany dark with a jet-black mane and tail, and Helena knew what she really wanted. There was no need to buy another horse. Oriel would be perfect!

Lady Emma hadn't finished pointing out her sister's deficiencies in raising her daughter. "Horsemanship is all very well, Jocelyn," she commented through pursed lips, "but it won't win Helena a husband. She's fifteen now, quite old enough for a suitable engagement. Have you really had no offers for her yet?"

For goodness' sake, Helena thought indignantly. Aunt Emma made her sound like a prize sow, to be prodded and haggled over by suitors, with no concern for her own feelings! She opened her mouth to object but was forestalled by her mother, who had clearly guessed what Helena was thinking.

"There's plenty of time to find Helena a husband," Lady Roseby said smoothly. "And you'd be surprised at how many eligible young men we meet, even out here in the middle of nowhere!" Her blue eyes shone with mischief and she shot an amused glance at her daughter.

They were saved from further debate by the staccato rap of small feet along the passage. A moment later, Helena's little brother, Will, appeared in the doorway, his round face flushed scarlet and his hair sticking up in unruly blond tufts.

"Mama, I had the most brilliant fencing lesson this morning," he burst out, running across the room and laying his small damp hands in Lady's Roseby's lap. "I can't wait to tell Papa all about it. Mr. Benedict said I'll be a better swordsman than him if I practice enough!"

Lady Roseby gently ran her hand over her son's wild hair. "And Mr. Benedict is right." She smiled. "If we practice hard, we can be good at anything. Now, Will, your father will not be home from Portland until this evening, but go and find Charity to wash your hands and then come and tell your aunt Emma all about your lesson."

Helena glanced sideways at her aunt. Lady Windlesham's expression showed distinct alarm at the prospect of being entertained by a small boy. As Will raced off down the passageway in search of Charity, Helena heard him call out, "Papa! What are you doing back here?"

Lord Roseby said something in low tones that obviously satisfied his son's curiosity before entering the front parlor and bowing politely to Lady Windlesham. "Good afternoon, Emma. How kind of you to visit us," he greeted her.

Helena's aunt smiled condescendingly. "Come now, William, just because I'm used to socializing in Dorchester—and more commonly these days, London—doesn't mean I can't make the effort to see my poor dear sister, you know. Although, as Jocelyn will tell you, I had the most dreadful journey this morning. Sir Henry will be horrified when he sees the state of the new carriage, horrified!"

Lord Roseby arranged his face into a suitable expression of concern.

Helena's mother put down her teacup and looked up at her

husband. "We weren't expecting you back from Portland for another hour at least," she said.

"I've had word that Judge Trimble will be arriving in Dorchester tomorrow for the assizes and wishes me to sit with him in court. I shall need to go over some papers this afternoon."

Helena felt a shiver run down her spine. The assizes were a series of trials that took place twice a year under a judge that traveled especially from Bristol or Bath. All the most serious cases were reserved for these sessions because only a circuit judge had the authority to pass the death sentence. As a magistrate, Lord Roseby was sometimes invited to sit alongside the circuit judge to help oversee the trials. Helena didn't envy her father for having to enforce such strict penalties. For crimes that were not punished by hanging, the prisoners could face transportation to the British Colonies in Virginia and Barbados, where they faced a life of slavery on the plantations, far from their families in the hostile environment of the New World.

Helena was jolted out of her thoughts when she heard her father's next words.

"That Riding Officer, Chapman, will be calling here this afternoon," he explained to Lady Roseby. "I've told Hawk to bring him straight to my study."

Helena felt the blood roaring in her ears and the room

seemed to sway around her. Roger Chapman? Would he say anything to her father about seeing her in the stable yard two nights ago?

And then a new and even more dreadful thought struck her. Could it be possible that Mr. Chapman, mindful of the forthcoming assizes, was coming here with evidence of the Roseby smugglers?

11

"IS MR. CHAPMAN INVOLVED in the assizes?" Helena asked, her voice sounding strangely high-pitched.

Aunt Emma looked shocked. "Really, Helena," she fussed. "It is not seemly for young ladies to worry about the law."

Lord Roseby held up one hand. "It's all right, Emma," he said. "Jocelyn and I have always encouraged Helena to take an interest in what goes on around her. Surely awareness is preferable to sheltered ignorance?" He went on before Lady Windlesham could react. "Yes, Nell, Mr. Chapman is involved with these assizes."

Helena held her breath, hoping her father hadn't noticed the blood drain from her cheeks.

Lord Roseby continued, his hazel eyes serious. "The Riding Officers in Lyme Regis caught a gang of wreckers three days ago," he explained. "They will be brought to trial at these assizes."

Helena shut her eyes for a moment, relief making her head spin. Lyme Regis was a town ten miles west along the coast, with its own company of Riding Officers. For now, the Roseby smugglers were safe.

She opened her eyes again. "Are they the wreckers that Mr. Chapman came to warn us about?" she asked.

"I fear not," her father admitted. "The gang that has been arrested are all local men. Mr. Chapman had news of a gang from further east, toward Poole."

Aunt Emma drew in her breath sharply. Lady Roseby observed her sister's discomfort and smoothly changed the subject. "Shall I tell Mrs. Gordon that you will be having dinner with us, William?"

Lord Roseby shook his head. "No, thank you, Jocelyn. I'll ask Mansbridge to bring me something in my study." He bowed again to Lady Windlesham. "Good day, Emma. Have a safe journey home."

Lady Windlesham inclined her head. "Thank you, William. Good day to you too."

Lord Roseby walked out of the parlor, leaving Helena breathing deeply as she waited for her heart rate to return to normal. She still felt a trickle of unease about what Roger Chapman would say to her father about his most recent visit to the manor, when he had found Helena in the stable yard long after midnight. Just then, she heard the front door being opened, and Hawk's murmuring tones welcoming the guest. There was the chink of spurs as booted feet walked across the stone-flagged hall and Hawk's softer footfalls leading the way along the passage.

Helena jumped up from the sofa, suddenly determined to speak to Mr. Chapman before he saw her father.

"Are you all right, Helena?" asked her mother.

"Yes, thank you, Mama," Helena replied, feeling a guilty flush spread up from her neck. "May I be excused for a moment?"

"Of course." Lady Roseby nodded.

Bobbing a polite curtsey to Aunt Emma, Helena smoothed down her petticoat and hurried out of the parlor. Mr. Chapman was following Hawk to her father's study, and she almost collided with the Riding Officer as she darted into the passage.

"Good day, Lady Helena." The customs man bowed to her, his blue eyes giving away nothing. "I trust you are well?"

Helena stopped, flustered. "Thank you, Mr. Chapman, I am very well."

Behind her, she could feel that Hawk had stopped too and was watching the pair of them closely, his eyes burning into Helena's back. The footman knew as well as Helena the circumstances of her last meeting with the Riding Officer, and she wondered if Hawk thought she was about to confess everything.

"And how is the stallion? Calmer now, I hope?" Chapman inquired.

"He is much better, thank you," Helena answered.

"You've heard about our latest acquisition, then?" said Lord Roseby, making Helena jump as he emerged from his study to overhear their conversation.

"Yes, indeed," replied the Riding Officer. "He sounds very interesting."

"I don't know about interesting." Lord Roseby frowned. "He's a good-looking animal, that's for sure, but he's been too much of a handful to ride so far. Still, we're going to give him a while longer to settle in. Is everything all right, Nell?" He suddenly seemed curious about what Helena was doing in the passageway.

Helena flushed. "Yes, Papa." She nodded politely to the visitor, silently thanking her father for confirming that it might have been necessary for her to visit Oriel at night. With luck, Roger Chapman would see no reason to mention the encounter to her father after all. "Good day to you, Mr. Chapman."

The Riding Officer returned her bow. "And to you, Lady Helena."

As Helena hurried toward the back hall, she was so lost in thought that she didn't see Eliza Clark, one of the housemaids, crossing the back hall with her arms full of bobbins of thread. The two girls collided at the foot of the stairs and the bobbins clattered noisily onto the stone floor.

"Oh, Eliza, I'm so sorry!" Helena exclaimed. "Here, let me help you pick them up."

"Thank you, my lady," said Eliza, her cheeks scarlet.

One of the bobbins had rolled along the passage as far as the door to the study, and when Helena went to retrieve it, she heard her father inside, discussing the assizes with Mr. Chapman.

"Have you a list of the defendants?" he asked the Riding Officer.

"Yes, my lord." There was a rustle of paper. "Joseph Nickle, Peter Baggs, Nicholas Bennett, and Timothy Harkness, all charged with wrecking. The Riding Officer at Lyme Regis asked me to bring these papers to you today, sir. He apologizes that he was unable to come himself."

Suddenly the bobbin slipped out of Helena's fingers and rattled treacherously against the stone flags. She scooped it up and hurried back along the passage before her father came out and found her eavesdropping. "Here you are, Eliza," she said, handing it to the maid.

"Thank you, my lady," said Eliza, flashing a shy smile at Helena. She disappeared toward the laundry room, leaving Helena alone in the back hall.

The list of wreckers' names echoed in her head, and Helena suddenly wished that she could go to the assizes herself and watch the trial. She wanted to know exactly what it was her father did when he was in court, what went on behind the massive studded oak doors at the top of Dorchester High Street.

And she couldn't deny a bit of curiosity about seeing the gang of wreckers in the dock. The illustrations in the newspapers always depicted them as mean-eyed, shifty-looking fellows, as if thieves and murderers didn't look like ordinary folk but were somehow changed visibly by their wicked ways.

Helena shook her head, dazed by more frightening thoughts. She wanted to believe what Jamie had told her—that what smugglers did was not a malicious crime but simply buying things in a different way. But it was still against the law. And if they were caught, they would end up in the Dorchester courthouse, facing her father with the full weight of the law behind him.

HELENA WOKE EARLY THE next morning and slipped downstairs before Louise came to help her dress. She had put on an indoor gown, knowing that she had lessons with Faith that morning, but she wrapped a thick shawl around her shoulders and put on her outdoor boots so that she could go out to see Oriel before breakfast. She wanted to find out how he had behaved when Jamie put him in the paddock with Stone Jack the day before. Dinner with Aunt Emma had gone on so long—they sat down at three and didn't leave the table until nearly six—that there hadn't been time to visit the stables.

For once, the autumn sky was clear blue and the air was still. The stone steps glistened with pearly frost, and when

Helena reached the stable yard, Isaiah was scattering soil on the icy cobbles, his eyes screwed up against the sun. He looked up as Helena appeared and to her surprise, a shy grin flashed across his face. She smiled back, acknowledging the secret they shared.

There was a clatter of hooves behind her, and Helena turned to see Jamie leading Snowdrop out of the stable block. The gray mare arched her neck and snorted dramatically as she stepped onto the soil-covered cobbles.

Helena laughed. "Don't be silly, Snowdrop! It's only to stop you from slipping."

"It must be the sunshine," Jamie remarked. "They're all actin' like yearlings this mornin'. Jupiter nearly pulled my arm off when I took him out to the paddock."

"Is Oriel going out today?" Helena glanced over at his stable door, but the shadows inside gave nothing away.

Jamie halted Snowdrop next to her. "He's just finishin' his breakfast," he said. "But I think we'll put him out with Stone Jack again afterward." His brown eyes looked serious for a moment, and Helena felt her heart sink as she waited for him to go on. "Watkins had quite a job leading him out to the paddock yesterday. Jumpin' about like a trout on a line, he was."

"Did he settle down once he was in the field?"

Jamie nodded. "Only after he'd chased Stone Jack around the field a couple o' times, mind you. It didn't do the old boy any harm, but I think Watkins is going to want to see Oriel looking a good deal calmer before he tries to lunge him."

"When will that be?" Helena protested. She didn't know how much time her father was going to give Oriel to prove himself, and she couldn't help feeling frustrated by Watkins's lack of urgency. But the head groom didn't have any particular reason to want to keep the stallion. As far as he was concerned, Oriel had caused nothing but trouble so far.

Jamie clicked his tongue to make Snowdrop walk forward. "I don't know, Nell," he said. "There's a lot to be done with the other horses just now, with the race coming up an' your father in Dorchester every day this week."

Helena watched him lead the gray mare across the yard, her hoofbeats muffled by the earth on the cobbles. As they passed Oriel's box, the stallion thrust his head over the door, his nostrils flared.

"Good morning, Oriel," Helena called softly. To her delight, he turned his head in response to her voice. She ran over and reached up to smooth his forelock. There was a wisp of hay caught in the silky black hair, and Oriel stood patiently, blowing hot damp breath onto Helena's shoulder while she untangled it.

"You've got a knack with that stallion, Lady Helena," said a low voice behind her. Harding the coachman had just emerged from the door in the corner of the yard that led to his quarters. As the most senior member of staff in the stables, he had his own set of rooms, separate from the loft where Jamie and the other grooms slept. The coachman walked briskly over to Helena, puffing out his thick white mustache as he felt the chill morning air. "At least the road'll be harder with this frost," he remarked. "The horses have been sinking up to their hocks the last few weeks."

Helena nodded, remembering Aunt Emma's martyred description of her journey from Dorchester. Behind her, Oriel snorted, spattering her hair with flecks of wet hay. Helena ducked away, laughing.

Harding narrowed his eyes until they almost disappeared among the folds of his tanned, wrinkled face. "It's good to see him lookin' more settled. You keep on like that, miss, an' your father will be happy to keep him."

Helena raised her eyebrows, sensing an unexpected ally in the wise old coachman. "I'd be glad to see Oriel stay at Roseby," she agreed carefully.

The coachman nodded. "Aye, he's a fine fellow." He shivered and fastened the top button on his greatcoat. Above their heads, the coach house clock chimed half past eight. "Time I was getting the carriage out for his lordship," said Harding. He lifted his hat. "Good day, my lady."

"Good day to you, Harding," Helena replied. The mention of the coach reminded her that her father was going to be in court today. Her curiosity about the assizes hadn't diminished, and she wondered if her father would let her watch one of the trials from the public gallery. If she hurried, she might catch him still at breakfast. She turned back to Oriel, who was watching her with his ears pricked. "You behave today," she whispered to him, rubbing his long nose. "Harding doesn't think you're dangerous. You just have to convince Watkins and Papa too."

The horse tossed his head and snorted. Helena paused for a moment, admiring the sheen on his dark brown coat, as smooth as a polished conker. Then she wrapped her shawl closely around her shoulders and ran back across the yard and up the steps to the back hall.

Her father looked up as she entered the dining room. "You're up early this morning, Nell," he commented, laying down his butter knife and taking a bite of toast.

"I just wanted to visit Or—the horses before Faith arrived," Helena told him, suddenly remembering that she wasn't supposed to have anything to do with Oriel.

Lord Roseby nodded and folded his napkin, pushing back his chair ready to leave. Helena was just wondering if she should ask him about going to the courthouse when there was a soft knock at the door and Mary Polstock appeared.

"Faith Powell is here, my lord," she said. "Shall I ask her to come through? Perhaps she'd like a cup of tea while you finish your breakfast, Lady Helena?"

"Excellent idea, Mary," agreed Lord Roseby. "It's a bitter morning. She'll be glad of something to warm her up. And please could you send Mansbridge to tell Harding that I'll be ready to leave in fifteen minutes?"

"Yes, my lord," said Mary, curtseying before standing back to let Lord Roseby walk out of the dining room ahead of her.

Helena concentrated on squashing some butter onto her toast with her knife, trying to soften the yellow lump that had set like stone after a night in the cold pantry. She was just about to give up and ask Mrs. Gordon for some fresh toast when Faith entered the room with a rustle of her crisp black gown.

"Good morning, Helena," she said with a smile.

Helena put down her knife and beckoned her governess to the chair next to her. "Hello, Faith," she said. "I won't be a moment. Would you like some tea? I'm just considering a more effective way to melt this frostbitten butter!"

Faith laughed and sat down. "'Tis so cold this morning, you might have to settle for slicing it like cheese. Now, how would you like to go on an outing? There's an exhibition of waxworks at Dorchester Town Hall all week, representing the kings and queens of England for the last seven hundred years."

"That sounds interesting," Helena said.

"I thought so too." Faith smiled. "And you'll be pleased to hear that we can go today. I mentioned the exhibition to your father just now and he kindly said we may share his carriage to

Dorchester, so we must be ready to leave very shortly."

Helena laid down her butter knife and stared at her governess, her heart pounding as a daring plan pushed its way into her mind. Something even more interesting than the waxworks exhibition was taking place in Dorchester that day. It all depended on Faith considering a visit to the courthouse as important to her education as a display of kings and queens. But the fact that they were traveling in the very same carriage as her father seemed like an opportunity too good to waste.

12

HELENA DECIDED TO SAY nothing to Faith until they arrived in Dorchester, just in case her governess canceled the outing altogether. She climbed into the carriage beside her, grateful for the thick woollen rug to tuck over her knees and the steel foot warmer under the seat. The journey to Dorchester would take a couple of hours at least, and the leather curtains at the glassless window were already fighting a losing battle with the icy air. Her father sat opposite her, his greatcoat buttoned all the way to his chin and his top hat pulled low over his ears. He smiled at Helena as she got in, but his hazel eyes were somber and distracted. Helena guessed that he was preparing himself for the day in court.

She leaned forward and looked through the gap at the edge of the window. The door to Oriel's stable was open and she guessed that Jamie was leading the stallion out to the paddock. Narrowing her eyes, she saw that the thin layer of soil on the cobbles outside Oriel's stable had been scuffed by restless hooves, leaving long scars that uncovered the glistening gray stones. Helena sighed inwardly. It looked as if Oriel had side-stepped impatiently when Jamie led him out of the stable—hardly the sort of behavior that would make Watkins any more eager to try lunging him.

The carriage lurched as Harding heaved himself into the driving seat. The coachman flicked his long whip over the backs of the stone-gray horses in front of him and the carriage rolled out of the stable yard with a creak of harness and a soil-muffled rumble of wheels. They took the road that led north out of the village and climbed steeply up the ridge of hills that led to Dorchester. The deeply rutted mud that had made Aunt Emma's journey so uncomfortable had frozen into sharp brown waves that sent shudders jolting through the carriage, and Helena had to brace her feet on the floor to stop her head from banging painfully against the window frame.

She pushed aside the curtain and watched the fields slip by, silvery-green under their thick coating of frost. When they reached the main road on top of the ridge, she shaded her eyes with her hand and let her gaze travel back over the village of Roseby and out to sea. The water was a thousand shades of blue and silver, the surface sending out sparkling flashes like diamonds. A tall-masted ship was pulling away from the harbor at West Bay, its sails curved like a plump-breasted seagull.

Faith touched Helena's arm, making her jump. "Shall we practice the irregular French verbs we have been learning recently?" she suggested. Her smile acknowledged the fact that she knew Helena would rather spend the journey gazing out of the window.

"Of course," said Helena, mindful that she needed to keep her governess's goodwill until they arrived in Dorchester. She buried her gloved hands under the woollen rug and tried to keep her teeth from chattering as she conjugated each verb for Faith's critical ear. Opposite them, Lord Roseby traveled in silence, his head bowed over the sheaf of closely printed papers that he took from his document bag.

After two hours, by which time the foot warmers had cooled and Helena was beginning to wonder if she would ever feel her toes again, they reached the outskirts of Dorchester. The town was growing rapidly now that the road to London had been improved, and the carriage rolled past a row of elegant half-built terraced houses before coming to the top of the High Street. Ahead, the road sloped down past the Town Hall and the Corn Exchange, magnificent gray stone buildings with ornate gables that extended out over the street. A chestnut seller had set up his stall beside the road and a tempting smell of roasted nuts wafted into the carriage, making Helena's mouth water. She listened to the rumble of carriage wheels and the shouts of people outside, and felt a thrill of excitement at being somewhere so different from Roseby.

Harding reined the horses to a halt outside the courthouse and held them steady while Lord Roseby stepped down from the carriage. "Have a good day, Helena, Mrs. Powell," he said, raising his top hat to them. He ran up the steps to the massive double doors, unbuttoning his greatcoat so that it flared behind him like a peacock's tail.

Faith opened the door, ready to instruct Harding to drive on to the Town Hall.

Helena took a deep breath. It was time to put her plan into action. "Would you mind if we didn't visit the waxworks exhibition today?" she asked.

Her governess looked back at her with a puzzled frown, one gloved hand resting on the door handle.

"It's just that I would rather attend the assizes," Helena went on.

"Whatever for?" asked Faith, surprised.

"I haven't been into the courthouse before," Helena explained hesitantly. "I am curious to know what my father does as a magistrate. And 'tis the trial of a wrecking gang today. Since Mr. Chapman warned us about a gang coming from Poole, I . . . I was interested to hear that arrests had been made."

"Mr. Chapman?" Faith echoed.

"He's the new Riding Officer at West Bay."

"Oh, yes." The governess's expression darkened. "I should have thought he'd have better things to do than scare young ladies with tales of wrecking gangs," she remarked. "But I agree that it would be educational for you to watch a trial. The law 'tis not some mysterious holy thing but the work of a few mortal men, no more divine than you or I. And I suppose that since we are here, it makes sense to take advantage of the timing." She narrowed her eyes at Helena. "Am I right in thinking that you have not asked your father's permission?"

"No," Helena confessed, shaking her head.

Faith looked thoughtful for a moment. "Well, I'm sure Lord Roseby would have no quarrel with your taking an interest in the way the law works, but we shall be discreet, nevertheless. Come along, we must be quick or the session will start without us."

Helena barely had time to feel relieved that her request had been granted so easily before Faith had taken her hand and helped her out of the carriage.

"Thank you, Harding, that will be all for now," she called up to the coachman. He touched the brim of his hat and nodded, the narrow portion of his face that was visible above his scarf bright red with cold.

Faith rested her hand beneath Helena's elbow and steered her across the crowded pavement and up the steps to the courthouse doors. Helena felt her heart begin to pound. She was actually going to watch the trial of the wreckers!

Inside the doors, the entrance hall was empty except for a few cloaked figures hurrying to take their places before the start of the session. Faith led Helena to a small door in the corner that opened on to a narrow staircase, enclosed by the wall on one side and a tall wooden partition on the other.

"This leads to the public gallery," she explained quietly.

Helena paused, about to ask how Faith knew her way around so well, but the young woman clearly guessed what Helena was thinking and smiled at her over her shoulder. "I have been to watch a trial before," she added.

Helena followed her governess up the steep stairs, gripping the handrail tightly with one hand. The public gallery consisted of several rows of wooden benches, packed with people fidgeting and muttering to one another and occasionally standing up to call to someone on the other side of the room.

"Where shall we sit?" Helena whispered.

Faith put her finger to her lips and, gathering her skirt in one hand, led the way between two rows until they reached a corner at the back of the gallery. Helena sank down onto the uncomfortable hard bench, feeling the wall cold and damp against her shoulder. In front of her the rows sloped steeply down so that the spectators could look onto the heads of the prisoners. The dock stood in the center of the courtroom, a small wooden cubicle enclosed by high railings. On either side were two tiers of long high-backed benches. The people sitting here were hidden from the public gallery by tall wooden screens.

Faith touched Helena's arm and pointed to the right-hand benches. "That's the jury," she whispered. "On t'other side is the lawyers and the gentlemen of the press, and on the top row, businessmen and gentlefolk who want to watch the trial."

"Where does the judge sit?" Helena asked.

Faith nodded toward a magnificent canopied chair that stood beneath the windows in the wall directly opposite the public gallery. Two smaller chairs stood on either side.

Just then, a dark-suited lawyer stood up from the left-hand bench and walked forward to a waist-high desk that reminded Helena of a pulpit. "All rise for Justice Robert Trimble," he ordered, banging a small wooden hammer on the desk.

The people around Helena heaved themselves to their feet, muttering under their breath as elbows banged uncomfortably and skirts and greatcoats tangled together. At the far end of the court, a short man, dressed in bright scarlet robes and a vast white wig that curled down his back, walked slowly out and lowered himself onto the canopied chair. He was followed by two men in black frock coats and shorter wigs, who took their places on the chairs on either side.

Helena swallowed. The tall man on the left of the judge was her father! He looked different somehow, an expression of stern concentration creasing his forehead and making his eyes look dark and fierce. Helena's heart began to pound, and she pressed herself tighter into the corner, suddenly afraid that her father would see her and demand to know what she was doing there.

The people in the gallery sat down again with no less rustling and shuffling. To Helena's surprise, the gray-haired woman in front of her produced a russet apple from somewhere under her shawl and started to munch loudly, settling herself on her many layers of petticoats as comfortably as if she were beside her own hearth. Her companion, a younger woman with curly red hair escaping from a dirty lace cap, sneezed violently, making Helena jump.

"Bring forward the defendants," ordered the man with the wooden hammer.

A broad-shouldered, ruddy-faced man, who looked to Helena more like a farmer than a court officer, nodded and let himself into the dock through a small wooden gate. To Helena's surprise, he bent down and opened a tiny narrow door just visible in the corner of the dock. Ducking his head, he squeezed through the door and disappeared down some unseen stairs. Helena looked questioningly at Faith, but her governess did not lift her gaze from the now empty dock.

The tiny door opened again, and the court officer emerged, his face even redder after the climb. Puffing, he stopped at the top of the stairs and looked over his shoulder to beckon impatiently. Helena's stomach lurched. She was about to set eyes on the gang of wreckers!

The public gallery was completely silent as the first prisoner emerged. He was short and squarely built, and he kept his head bowed so that his pale curly hair fell around his cheeks and hid his face. Almost immediately behind him, so close that he seemed in danger of treading on the first man's heels, came an older man. He had long straggly gray hair and a deeply lined face that reminded Helena of Mansbridge, her father's elderly footman, and she felt a disconcerting pang of sympathy. She was surprised that the two men should have been made to negotiate the narrow staircase so close together, until the hush of the court allowed her to hear an unmistakable clank of iron, and she realized with a jolt that the prisoners were chained together. Then the third prisoner emerged, and a murmur spread through the gallery like the wind stirring a pile of fallen leaves.

Helena stared in disbelief. The third wrecker was barely older than she! He was taller than the other two men, scrawny framed with narrow shoulders, and his thick sandy hair stuck straight up, making his head look square. His eyes were stretched wide with fear, and Helena could see him trembling, each shudder sending a ripple through his sweat-stained shirt as if a breeze had found its way into the airless courtroom. She felt the hair prickle at the back of her neck. What was this terrified, harmless-looking boy doing in the dock, charged with destroying ships and murdering innocent souls?

The prisoners shuffled awkwardly to the front of the dock and stood in a row with their shackled hands resting on the wooden rail and their backs to the gallery.

Helena recalled the conversation she had heard between her father and Mr. Chapman. "Only three prisoners?" she whispered to Faith. "My father said there were going to be four."

Faith shook her head slightly, indicating that she didn't know where the fourth prisoner was.

In front of them, the gray-haired woman twisted around with a creak of protesting stays and looked up at Helena, her brown eyes bright like a bird's. "Haven't you heard, dearie?" she whispered dramatically. "One of them has turned King's evidence to save his own neck. He'll testify against these three an' send them to the gallows, for sure."

"How could anyone betray his friends like that?" Helena protested.

"Friends?" the woman's neighbor echoed with a scornful sniff. "These men aren't friends. They are greedy, murderous souls who use the sea for their own wickedness."

Helena shuddered and stared at the youngest wrecker. She still couldn't help thinking that he must have been there by mistake. The red-haired woman followed Helena's gaze. "Don't be fooled by a young face, m'dear," she said, as if she could read Helena's mind. "I've heard folk say that he was the worst of all."

Her companion nodded eagerly, flecks of apple clinging to her lower lip. "He may look scared now but that's nothing to what 'is victims felt. 'Tis easy to pity him when he's standing chained an' helpless, but never forget what he did on a cold beach to those poor shipwrecked souls."

Helena flinched as an image of the bloodstained scene forced its way into her mind. She buried her hands in her lap, suddenly chilled in spite of all the people around her.

Next to the judge's platform, one of the lawyers was confirming the names of each of the prisoners. "Timothy Harkness, aged thirty-one years, of Lyme Regis; Nicholas Bennett, aged forty years, of Lyme Regis; Peter Baggs, aged nineteen years, of Lyme Regis." Then the first witnesses were called, one after the other, local officers of the law who described how they had seen the wreckers carrying their stolen cargo along the cliffs. The men had fled when the officers raised the hue and cry, but the leader of the gang had been caught after he stumbled into a rabbit hole and broke his leg.

"Joseph Nickle!" called the court officer.

A hush fell over the public gallery, as if everyone were holding their breath. The gray-haired woman whispered helpfully to Helena, "This un's the fourth wrecker. He's more hated than the rest of 'em put together after 'e betrayed 'is own men."

The door at the back of the courtroom opened and a short, squat-framed man limped out on rough wooden crutches. He hobbled awkwardly into the witness box and stood with his head raised defiantly, his eyes raking the public gallery as if daring anyone to call out against him. He had thick black hair and a bushy, gray-streaked beard, so that when he spoke, his words came out muffled. In a gruff voice, thick with the local Lyme accent, he confirmed the identities of each man in the dock and their place in the gang of wreckers.

Helena listened, unable to take her eyes off the man who was willing to send his former companions to the gallows when his own hands were just as bloodstained. The women in front of her pursed their lips and hissed, prompting the court officer to glare at the public gallery and call for silence. The wrecker in the witness box looked up with a gleam of amusement in his beady black eyes, and Helena felt a jolt of horror run through her.

Then the lawyers began their speeches, their voices low and measured so that Helena began to feel sleepy and heavy headed in the stuffy gallery. She had only the vaguest idea of how much time had passed, although her early-breakfasted stomach told her it was approaching the middle of the afternoon. With all the rustling and coughing, it was hard to make out exactly what the lawyers were saying, and instead Helena stared at her father, trying to reconcile the hard-faced magistrate sitting next to the judge with the man she knew at home. From time to time he leaned over to murmur something to the judge, who was listening gravely to each witness, his small, soft-featured face nodding in agreement with some points and frowning at others. The last of the lawyers sat down and the sound of several pairs of feet echoing hollowly on floor-boards made Helena look around, puzzled.

"The jury's going out to make their decision," Faith explained quietly, nodding to the right-hand bench. The judge and the magistrates also left the platform, vanishing through the paneled door in the back of the courtroom.

Helena wondered if the people in the public gallery would go out for some air or refreshment. But they seemed content to wait where they were, passing hunks of bread around and chatting comfortably with occasional, quickly hushed bursts of laughter. The red-haired woman produced a pewter flask from her skirts and took a long swig, then wiped the neck of the flask with her handkerchief and offered it to Helena.

Helena shook her head. "No, thank you," she said, hoping that the woman wouldn't take offense. To Helena's relief, she just shrugged and handed it to her companion, who swigged cheerfully.

The footsteps sounded again as the jury filed back into the courtroom, followed by Judge Trimble and the magistrates. Everyone in the gallery seemed to stiffen in expectation, and the red-haired woman stuffed the cork back into her flask and hid it among her skirts again.

The judge sat on his canopied chair and smoothed out his scarlet robes. "Men of the jury, have you reached a decision?" he asked.

A middle-aged man stepped forward, his face almost as pale as his dove-gray wig. "Yes, my lord, we have."

"Do you find the defendants guilty or not guilty?"

There was a pause, the silence broken by the sharp metallic clank of a shackle as one of the men in the dock let his hand slip from the rail.

"Guilty, my lord," said the man from the jury.

"An' so they are," muttered the red-haired woman fiercely, and her companion nodded. Helena glanced around the gallery at the rows of grim faces. No one had challenged the verdict. The prisoners may have been betrayed by one of their own gang, but that didn't make them innocent.

Faith touched Helena's arm to get her attention. "The judge is about to pass sentence," she murmured.

On the platform, a court officer had brought out a small flat square of cloth on a red cushion. Helena watched as Judge Trimble solemnly placed the cloth on top of his wig. Then he looked at the men in the dock, his eyes narrowed. "Timothy Harkness, Nicholas Bennett, Peter Baggs," he declared in heavy, ringing tones. "This court finds you guilty of the charge of deliberately causing a ship to be wrecked and of the murder of innocent souls. I hereby sentence all three of you to be hanged by the neck till you are dead."

13

〰〰〰

"*DEAD . . . DEAD . . . DEAD . . .*"

The final damning word echoed around and around in Helena's head, and she struggled to her feet, suddenly desperate to escape the stuffy public gallery. Her legs felt cramped and weak after sitting for so long, and she staggered against the bench in front.

"Look out, dearie!" exclaimed the gray-haired woman, almost toppling onto the man below.

Faith grabbed Helena's arm to steady her. "Come, Helena, you look pale. Let's go outside."

Still holding Helena's wrist, she led her toward the stairs. There were a few disgruntled murmurs as Helena stumbled over knees and booted feet, but soon they were making their way down the steep staircase and emerging into the hall below.

"Wait here while I send someone for the carriage," Faith told her.

"What about my father?" Helena protested.

"I'll leave a message saying that we had to go home early because you felt unwell," said Faith.

Helena nodded and leaned against a cool stone pillar with her eyes closed, listening to her governess's footsteps fade across the marble floor.

A low voice beside her made her jump. "Lady Helena! I had not expected to see you here. Have you come to see your father?"

Helena turned around. Roger Chapman stood there, immaculately dressed in a dark blue coat and white breeches. He peered closely at Helena. "Are you all right?"

"She'll be fine, thank you, Mr. Chapman." Faith returned and rested her hand protectively on Helena's arm. "We were just leaving."

"Good afternoon, Mrs. Powell," said the Riding Officer, with a small bow. "Would you like me to tell Lord Roseby that you are here?"

"That won't be necessary," replied Faith. "I am sure he will be busy awhile yet."

Roger Chapman held her gaze for a few moments. "I trust Mr. Powell is well?" he enquired.

"Very well, thank you," said Faith.

Helena wondered how Mr. Chapman knew Faith and her husband, until she remembered that one of the Riding Officers was lodging at Upbredy Farm. And then a new fear flew into her mind on shadowed wings. Faith's husband, Jonathan, usually provided the horses to pull the carts that transported the smuggled cargo. Did Roger Chapman suspect that Faith might know about the Roseby smugglers?

Faith was looking steadily at the Riding Officer, but Helena knew her governess well enough to tell that she was feeling uncomfortable. Her anxiety was conveyed in the quickness of her breath and the way her knuckles were turning white, her fingers clutching her gloves.

Suddenly a familiar voice rang out, and Helena turned to look over her shoulder. "What are you doing here, Helena?" her father demanded, crossing the stone-flagged hall toward them.

Helena knew there was no point in lying. "We—we came to see the trial, Papa."

Lord Roseby looked taken aback. "What for? You've never asked to come here before."

"We thought it would be educational to see our legal system in operation, my lord," Faith put in. She had released her grip on her gloves and was breathing normally. Helena wondered if she was relieved at being saved from the Riding Officer's asking any more questions.

Lord Roseby's expression darkened for a second, then he glanced at Roger Chapman and Helena guessed that he was prevented from challenging the governess by the Riding

Officer's presence. "Well, in the future it might be better to ask me first which trials would be suitable. I take it you sat in the public gallery?" He raised his eyebrows at Helena, and she nodded.

"Next time I shall arrange for you to sit in the private spectators' bench, which should be more comfortable. Helena, you look pale. Do you feel well enough for the journey home?"

"Yes, Papa," Helena assured him. "I just needed some fresh air."

Roger Chapman stepped closer to Helena, his blue eyes searching hers. "Lady Helena, I hope you were not too upset by seeing those villains in the dock," he said. "'Tis but a drop in the ocean, and where they were, more gangs will come to take their place. My men and I will not rest until we have flushed out all the villains along this coast."

But the Roseby smugglers aren't villains! Helena wanted to tell him. *They do no harm to anyone.* She was saved from having to make a reply by a small dark-eyed boy who came running up to Faith and whispered to her that the carriage was waiting outside.

"Will you be traveling home with us, Lord Roseby?" Faith asked, pulling on her gloves.

"Yes, I will," replied Helena's father. "The session has finished for today, and I wish to dine at home. I shall see you again tomorrow, Mr. Chapman," he added, turning to the Riding Officer.

Roger Chapman nodded respectfully. "Good day to you, Lord Roseby. And to you, Lady Helena, Mrs. Powell. I wish you a safe journey home." He bowed to them before turning to run up the shallow steps and through the door that led to the private chambers of the courthouse.

Harding was waiting outside with Monument and Fleet, steam billowing from the horses' nostrils in the chilly afternoon air. Helena crossed the pavement behind Faith, pulling her cloak around her for warmth. It was nearly dark and a shop selling hot pies on the other side of the High Street was doing a brisk trade with people hurrying home, their faces swathed in mufflers and their heads low. All along the High Street, lights glowed welcomingly in the windows, and the sound of a fiddle playing and bursts of laughter came from the inn that stood next to the Corn Exchange. But Helena felt a chill inside her that had less to do with the frost and more to do with what she had seen and heard that afternoon.

After the hard wooden benches, the carriage's red velvet seats were soft and welcoming, and so was the heavy woollen rug that Faith unfolded across Helena's lap. As the horses pulled them steadily up the High Street and onto the road that led to Roseby, Helena braced herself for further questions from her father, but he was occupied with more papers from his document case. Faith seemed content to sit in silence too, leaving Helena to lean against the window frame and watch the darkening fields slide by.

She couldn't shake her mind free of the image of the boy in the dock. Whatever she had expected the wreckers to look like, it hadn't been that—a young village lad like any she knew from Roseby. And as the carriage rolled away from the town, scraping and bumping over the frost-bound road, Helena's mind started to play cruel tricks on her, substituting for the sandy hair and pale blue eyes of the youngest wrecker the brown hair and dark eyes of Jamie's face.

HELENA SLEPT BADLY THAT night, faceless prisoners shuffling in chains through her dreams. She woke late and went straight down to the stable yard, hoping that the icy wind blowing from the sea would drive out the ghosts in her head. She wanted to talk to Jamie about the trial, to see if he understood how serious it would be if the Riding Officers found out about the smuggling. No matter how much Helena believed that the Roseby smugglers wouldn't harm anyone, the law would treat them like any other criminals if they were caught; and she was suddenly very scared for the men she had grown up with in the village.

She looked for Jamie in the main block, but he was

nowhere to be seen. Only Watkins was there, whistling tunelessly as he saddled Calico, Lady's Roseby's dappled gray hack. A dark green rug lay over the mare's quarters to keep her warm until Helena's mother was ready to ride.

Helena nodded a greeting to Watkins and went out of the stable block. Oriel's stable door lay opposite, and she walked across the cobbles to see him. The top half of the door was in darkness, and at first she couldn't tell if the stallion was inside. But as she drew closer she caught the gleam of light on a mahogany flank and heard the soft crackle of straw as he shifted his weight from one leg to the other.

"Good morning, my lovely man," Helena murmured, resting her gloved hands on the stable door.

"And good morning to you!" called a voice from the back of the stable.

Helena jumped. "Jamie! I didn't see you in there. What are you doing? Is Oriel all right?"

Jamie emerged from the shadows, ducking under Oriel's neck and straightening up with one hand on the strong, shining neck behind him. "Aye, he's fine," he assured Helena. "I've been grooming him, that's all."

Now that Helena's eyes had gotten used to the dim light inside the stable, she could see that Oriel was wearing a head-collar that was tethered to the metal ring in the back wall. Helena let herself in and stood just inside the door.

She narrowed her eyes and looked critically at the stallion, who turned his head to look calmly back at her, his ears pricked and his eyes gleaming black pools.

"He looks fantastic," Helena observed quietly. "You can't even see his ribs any more."

"No, he's filled out nicely," Jamie agreed, beginning to sweep a soft-bristled brush over Oriel's hindquarters with long, even strokes. He paused and smiled over his shoulder at Helena. "He was calmer in the paddock yesterday too. Only chased Stone Jack around for a minute before he dropped his head an' settled down to grazing like he'd never seen grass before."

Helena stepped forward, her skirt dragging on the straw, and smoothed one hand down Oriel's warm shoulder. "Well done, Oriel," she murmured.

The stallion twisted his head around and blew softly into her hair, his lips nibbling at the velvet clasp at the base of her neck.

Helena laughed and straightened up, catching hold of the loosened clasp with one hand. "Careful, boy, you don't want to eat that," she warned him. Then she turned to Jamie. "Does Watkins know how well Oriel behaved yesterday? Is he going to lunge him soon?"

Jamie shook his head. "I think he'd like to put the horse in the paddock a few more times first, make sure he's got all the itch out of his toes."

"But there's no reason to wait any longer!" Helena protested. "Now that Oriel's had a chance to stretch his legs and see the paddocks by daylight, I'm sure he'd be fine."

"I agree it looks like Oriel is getting more used to us," Jamie admitted. "But I already told you, Watkins is very busy with the other horses just now, with the race coming up."

"Then we'll have to lunge him again ourselves," Helena decided. She sensed that Jamie was about to argue and went on quickly, "I know it didn't do much good last time, but you can see how much better Oriel is around us. Please, Jamie, just one more try."

Jamie glanced at the horse, who was watching them with an expression of interest in his dark, intelligent eyes. Then he nodded. "All right. Let's have a go tonight. There's enough of a moon to see by, an' he'll have been in the paddock all afternoon anyway." He flashed a grin at Helena, his teeth white in the shadows. "Don't worry, Nell. I've not given up on him yet."

Helena smiled back, but inside she felt her stomach clench with nerves. Would the stallion behave any differently this time? They had so much to prove before her father would let Oriel stay, and grazing quietly in the paddock was a tiny milestone compared with working on a lunge rein—not when he had leapt around so wildly last time. Helena watched Jamie turn back to grooming the horse. She was about to tell him about the other thing that was troubling her—the trial—when a clatter of buckets from outside warned her that Watkins was in the yard. She closed her mouth again and let herself out of the stable. She would be able to talk to Jamie tonight.

14

THE STABLE YARD CLOCK was chiming one by the time Helena slipped out of the back door. Her father had stayed up later than usual, going through papers in his study for the next court session, and Helena was on the verge of drifting off to sleep before she heard him come quietly upstairs. Shaking her head impatiently to clear away the stuffiness, she picked up her thickest cloak and crept down the wooden stairs to the back hall, holding her breath at every treacherous creak.

Jamie had already put a bridle on Oriel, and the stallion watched over his door as Helena crossed the yard, the rings of the bit glowing eerily in the moonlight against his velvet-brown nose.

Jamie's face appeared beside the horse, a woollen scarf wrapped tightly around his neck to keep out the relentless wind. "All set, Nell?" he whispered.

"All set," she replied. She drew back the bolt and held the door open so that Jamie could lead Oriel out. The stallion walked steadily out of the warm stable, his nostrils flared and his ears pricked. Helena felt the knot of tension in her stomach begin to relax. After several days of going out in the paddock, Oriel definitely looked calmer. But was he calm enough to work on the lunge?

Jamie led the horse along the path through the orchard, the long rein looped carefully in his left hand. With his right hand, he held the reins close to Oriel's bit, giving just enough slack to allow the stallion to stretch his neck and see the ground before putting down his hooves. Helena followed, trying not to flinch as the wind reached under her cloak with icy fingers and whipped strands of hair painfully across her cheek.

When they reached the paddock, Jamie beckoned Helena forward. "Would you like to have a go this time?" he offered. "He seems quiet enough, but I'll stand with you just in case."

"Yes, thank you," Helena said, breathless from the cold wind. Tucking her hair behind her ears, she took the rein from Jamie and led Oriel into the center of the paddock. Her heart was pounding and she could see the rein quivering where her hands were shaking. She took a deep breath and reminded herself that Oriel would be able to tell at once if she was nervous.

Jamie stood just behind her, his breath warm on her left ear. "Just send him on, an' let out the rein as he goes," he instructed quietly.

"Walk on, Oriel," Helena called to the stallion, unspooling a loop of rein and shaking it gently.

Oriel tossed his head with a snort and skittered forward, his back hooves slipping as the rein went taut and jerked him to a halt.

"Easy, boy, easy," Helena soothed. "Walk on, now."

Beside her, Jamie stretched out one hand as if to take the rein from her.

Helena shook her head. "I'm fine," she said. "Let's give him a few moments to settle down."

The stallion stood a few yards away from them, staring into the shadows at the edge of the field. The breeze pulled at his tail, making it stream across his flanks like a black ribbon. With a jerk, Oriel moved forward again, lifting his hooves high with stiff, uneven strides. Helena uncoiled more of the rein so that the horse could walk in a bigger circle. Oriel jumped as the slack rein sagged to the ground, and Helena quickly gathered it back in until the rein was taut again.

The stallion made his way around the paddock in a lopsided circle, snatching at the rein if he went too wide and the bit pulled against his mouth. Helena watched despondently. Oriel was moving like an unschooled yearling, with his back hunched and his weight on his forelegs so that his nose stuck out and his neck was hollow. Even though he was only walking, his strides were short and choppy; and every so often he stumbled, breaking into a ragged trot to regain his balance.

Jamie seemed to guess what Helena was thinking. "At least he's not leaping around like last time," he pointed out. "We can't expect him to come straight out of the stable an' look like Sultan or Snowdrop. How do we know if he's had any schooling at all afore now?"

Helena nodded. Jamie had a point, but she couldn't help feeling disappointed by the tense, unbalanced horse in front of her. Then she gave herself a mental shake. The whites of Oriel's eyes weren't showing now and he didn't seem to want to bolt like last time, which suggested that he wasn't scared. The only way to find out if he had been schooled before was to treat him as if he had and see how he reacted. With a surge of confidence, Helena realized that they couldn't possibly expect Oriel to behave like the other horses if they didn't treat him like one.

Instinctively she took a step forward and shortened the lunge rein so that she could feel the pressure of the bit against the stallion's mouth. If she had been riding him, she would have used her left leg and a touch of the whip on his right flank to bring his hindquarters underneath him. But from the ground, she would have to use her voice and the position of her body to urge him forward.

"Trot on, Oriel," she commanded, clicking her tongue.

The stallion threw up his head and jumped forward, but Helena braced herself, standing still so that the weight of her body helped steady the rein. As soon as Oriel stopped, she clicked him on again.

"What are you doing, Nell?" asked Jamie in a low voice.

Helena didn't take her eyes off the horse. "I think Oriel can do better than this," she explained. "He's not scared of us now. We just need to make him work a bit harder, that's all."

At the end of the lunge rein, Oriel flicked one ear at her as if admitting the truth in her words. Helena held the rein as lightly as she could in her left hand, feeling the horse nod his head with each step. Then she walked forward, making a smaller circle inside Oriel's tracks so that her own movement encouraged the horse to keep going.

"Trot on!" she told him again, and this time Oriel didn't snatch at the rein but kept his head steady, and the rein stayed evenly taut in Helena's hand. His hooves thudded in a regular, two-beat rhythm and he arched his neck as his hindquarters drove him forward so that Helena could feel the bit light and soft in his mouth.

She heard Jamie whistle softly behind her. "Well done, Nell!" he whispered. "He's really listenin' to you now."

Helena breathed out in relief. "Yes, he is, isn't he?" she murmured, unable to stop a delighted smile from spreading across her cold cheeks. "Good boy, Oriel," she said out loud, shaking the lunge rein to keep him trotting steadily. It was important that he did as many circles as he could to build up his muscles. But it was obvious that he had been well schooled before, wherever he came from.

Suppressing a yawn, Helena realized that now was as good a time as any to speak to Jamie about the assizes. She guessed that Jamie would have heard about the trial, especially as the wreckers had been caught just a few miles along the coast. "Jamie, did you know the men in the Lyme Regis wrecking gang?" she asked hesitantly.

She felt him nod in the dark behind her shoulder. If he was surprised by the abrupt change of subject, he gave no sign of it. "I knew of Tim Harkness," he replied. "His sister lives near West Bay. I heard he always had an eye for trouble. Wreckers are bad news an' 'tis as well they've been caught."

"And sentenced to be hanged," Helena reminded him, feeling her throat tighten as she pictured the three men in the dock. She was still haunted by the scared face of the youngest wrecker, and she felt her stomach turn over in terror at the thought that Jamie might one day stand in the same place. Helena realized that she wasn't sure what the penalties would be if the smugglers were caught. Suddenly transportation, even if it meant being sent to the other side of the world, seemed preferable to the possibility that the Roseby smugglers might be sentenced to the harshest punishment of all.

"Jamie, would smugglers ever be hanged?"

Her words hung in the air in a cloud of fast-dissolving breath. The silence stretched between them, broken only by the measured beat of Oriel's hooves and the creak of his bridle as he nodded his head in time with his footfall.

"Aye, they can be," Jamie said at last.

Helena gripped the lunge rein more tightly until she could feel her nails digging into her palms through her leather gloves.

"But not for smuggling alone," Jamie went on. "You'd have to fire a musket at a customs man first, so don't worry."

"Don't worry?" Helena echoed angrily. At the end of the rein, Oriel snorted and jerked his head, startled by her raised voice. Helena waited until the horse was trotting evenly before she spoke again. "What if one of you let off a shot in self-defense or to warn the others? You'd all be hanged!"

"That would never happen, because none of our men carry guns," said Jamie. "My father is very firm about that." Unexpectedly, he reached up and gripped Helena's shoulder, making her jump. "You have to believe me, Nell," he insisted. "We never hurt a soul, I promise."

Helena didn't reply. She watched Oriel instead, circling calmly around them. He carried his tail high so that it streamed behind him like smoke, and moonlight gleamed on the muscles that rippled on his shoulder and flank. Helena drank in his exquisite shape with thirsty eyes. But the excitement she had felt earlier had been tarnished by her fears for Jamie. With Mr. Chapman around, asking endless questions and watching, watching all the time, how long would it be before the Roseby smugglers were caught and handed over to the law?

15

THE WHOLE WORLD LOOKED as if it had been carved from ice when Helena awoke the following morning. She threw back the curtains at her window and gazed in delight at the frost-bound garden, each blade of grass and each leaf held motionless in a sleeve of delicate white crystals. The cushioned window seat was cold and damp under Helena's knees, but suddenly she remembered her success with Oriel the night before and felt a warm glow that even the frost could not chill. She just had to persuade Watkins to try lunging the horse, and then he would tell her father that Oriel deserved to stay at Roseby.

The jug of hot water that Louise had brought her was already cooling, so Helena washed hastily and put on her warmest shift underneath her riding habit. Last night, as she and Jamie had led Oriel back to his stable through the cold, quiet garden, they had decided that Piper should go to Eggardon Hill today for a training gallop. The long track stretched up the sheltered inland side of the hill where the frost would have been less fierce, so the ground should not be too hard.

Her mother and Will were at the dining table when Helena arrived for breakfast.

"Good morning, Helena," said Lady Roseby, looking up from the piece of toast she was spreading with butter for Will.

"Good morning, Mama," Helena replied. She sat down and smiled at Eliza as the maid poured her a cup of tea.

As Helena reached for some toast, she couldn't help yawning widely.

"Did you not sleep well?" asked Lady Roseby, sounding concerned. "You look a little pale."

"I'm fine, Mama," Helena assured her, taking a sip of tea.

"Watkins is going to take me out on Bumblebee this morning," Will announced through a shower of toast crumbs.

Helena smiled at her little brother. "Lucky you. You'll need to wrap up warm though."

Will stuck one leg out from under the table. "Look," he ordered Helena, pointing to his thick, knitted leggings.

"They look very cozy," Helena agreed.

"Will you be riding today, Helena?" Lady Roseby asked. "I know Faith isn't coming, but Susan Clark needs to measure you for your new gown. There's less than two weeks before the race, you know."

"Can she measure me this afternoon?" Helena asked. "I'd like to take Snowdrop out first."

Her mother nodded. "Very well. Shall I tell Susan to

expect you at two o'clock?"

Helena swallowed her last mouthful of toast. "Yes, Mama, thank you." She pushed back her chair and stood up. "Have a good ride, Will. Don't wear out poor old Bumblebee's legs!"

"I won't," Will promised her, his blue eyes round and serious.

In the back hall, Helena asked Hawk to fetch her a shawl to tuck inside her riding jacket. The footman returned in a moment, his feet padding softly over the stone flags, and handed the shawl to Helena with a polite bow. There was no trace of the smuggler in his bearing, the man who had dealt with the injured carriage horse and hidden from the customs men in his employer's hayloft while Helena faced the officer's questions. She tried to meet Hawk's pale gray eyes, searching for some trace of fear of the dreadful punishment that awaited all the smugglers if they were caught. But his expression was as calm and unreadable as ever.

Helena was brought back from her thoughts by a knife-edged blast of cold air as Hawk opened the back door for her. "Enjoy your ride, Lady Helena," he murmured.

"Thank you, Hawk," said Helena. She gathered the skirt of her riding habit in both hands and made her way carefully down the steep steps, made even more perilous by the sheen of ice that glazed the smooth gray stone. The air was so cold that she was flushed and breathless by the time she reached the stable yard.

Jamie was crossing the cobbles with Piper's saddle on one arm and the bridle hanging from his shoulder. His legs were clad in woollen leggings like Will's, and his breath puffed in steamy clouds above the thick scarlet muffler he had wound around his neck. "Good morning, Lady Helena," he greeted her, his brown eyes sparkling. "I won't be long. Perhaps you'd like to see the stallion before your ride?"

"How is he this morning?" Helena asked, knowing that they couldn't mention last night with Watkins bustling in and out of the stable block on the other side of the yard.

"Eating his head off, an' dying to get out in the paddock," Jamie replied. He nodded toward the stallion's stable. "See for yourself while I tack up Piper."

Helena crossed the yard, the soil-covered cobbles gritty under her feet. As she passed the coach house she noticed that the carriage had already gone. Her father must have made another early start for the assizes.

Oriel poked his head over the door as Helena approached and welcomed her with the softest of whinnies. She stopped and smiled at him, remembering how beautifully he had moved on the lunge, his long strides gliding effortlessly over the frosty grass. Walking over to the stable door, Helena reached out one hand to stroke Oriel's nose and jumped back when he suddenly threw his head up in alarm.

Turning, she saw Watkins coming toward her, a thick woollen

rug folded over one arm and a leather head-collar swinging from his other hand.

"Sorry, my lady," he puffed, his face red and his eyes streaming from the cold. "Didn't mean to make him jump like that. He's still a flighty one, isn't he?"

"No more than the other horses," Helena objected without thinking.

Watkins raised his eyebrows in surprise, and Helena went on quickly, "I mean, he's much calmer than when he first arrived, isn't he?"

"He does seem to be settlin' down, my lady," Watkins agreed. "I reckon he'll need a bit longer afore we start working him, though. An' your father still doesn't want you grooming him."

Helena decided not to argue. Instead, she asked, "Are you going to put Oriel out in the paddock this morning?"

"Aye, I thought he could do with some fresh air, an' he's eaten a good breakfast this morning so the grass shouldn't do him no harm."

Helena nodded. She knew that too much frosty grass on an empty stomach could give a horse colic. She stood back and watched as Watkins let himself into the stable and slipped the head-collar over Oriel's finely chiseled head.

The groom noticed Helena's admiring gaze. "He's quite a looker, isn't he?" he commented. "Let's hope he settles down soon an' we can start working him. He'll have a fair bit of speed in those long legs of his, even more than Piper maybe."

Helena's relief at hearing Watkins praise the stallion was overtaken by a rush of excitement. What if the groom was right, and Oriel turned out to be even swifter than the fastest racehorse her father had ever owned? Helena couldn't imagine galloping faster than she had done on Piper, but suddenly she felt her fingers tingle with the urge to swing herself onto Oriel's back and send him racing along the cliffs, to see just how fast he could run.

Just then, a clatter of metal-shod hooves on the cobbles made her look around. Jamie was leading Snowdrop out of the stable block, the mare's coat dazzling white in the wintry sunlight.

"Ready, my lady?" he called.

"Just coming," Helena replied. She glanced into Oriel's stable once more and reached in to stroke his warm, shining neck.

Watkins was buckling the outdoor rug onto the horse. "Have a good ride, my lady," he said, looking up and blowing on his fingers.

"I will," Helena assured him with a smile. She crossed the yard and allowed Jamie to lift her onto Snowdrop, then waited, twining her fingers in the mare's soft mane, while he led out Piper and swung himself into the saddle. The chestnut gelding looked magnificent, his muscles rippling like water underneath the smooth bronze coat.

Jamie bent down to adjust one of his stirrup leathers, then gathered up the reins and nudged Piper's flanks with his heels, sending the horse out of the yard and down the gravel drive.

They followed the lane that went straight across the valley, over the River Bredy as it wound its way through the Powells' farm, then steeply up the hill through Far Cheney, the next closest village to Roseby. The frost had sealed every noise into a heavy silence that lay like water over the white landscape. Both horses seemed glad to be outside, lifting their hooves high over the frozen ruts and tossing their heads in clouds of plumy breath.

After half an hour, as Far Cheney's church clock chimed mid-day behind them, they reached the bottom of the track that wound up the side of Eggardon Hill. The turf-covered ramparts above them looked soft edged and peaceful in the sun.

Piper swung his hindquarters sideways and snatched eagerly at the bit when his hooves touched the grass.

Jamie laughed and patted his neck, then looked up at Helena. "Want to swap?" he offered.

"I'm all right with Snowdrop," she told him, leaning down to rub her gloved hand under the soft white mane. She knew that the mare would find it easier to tackle the hill with Helena's lighter weight, and she would get almost as much pleasure from watching Piper run as in riding him herself.

Jamie nodded, flashing her a smile of thanks, and shortened the reins, his face suddenly serious. He turned Piper's head up the track and closed his heels against the chestnut flanks. Piper sprang forward at once, his front legs striking out with a flash of gleaming iron. Jamie crouched low over the horse's withers and let Piper stretch his neck, his whole body flattening closer to the ground as he settled into the gallop.

Helena scooped up the reins and kicked Snowdrop with her left heel. The mare may have been older than Piper, but she leapt forward just as keenly, her hooves drumming steadily on the frosty turf. Helena leaned over the strong white neck, pushing her hands forward to give Snowdrop her head and gripping the pommel tightly with her right leg. The cold air made her eyes stream, until the horse ahead was nothing more than a brownish blur gradually getting smaller as Piper's long strides ate up the ground.

Jamie and Piper had already reached the flattened summit by the time Snowdrop cantered through the break in the ramparts. The mare had slowed on the final stretch, but Helena let her choose her own pace. There was nothing to be gained by pushing the gentle horse too hard.

Jamie's eyes were shining and his face was flushed. "That

was brilliant!" he shouted, gathering up the reins as Piper skittered underneath him. "I can't see any horse beating him in the race."

Helena nodded, still breathless from the gallop. Snowdrop came to a halt beside the gelding, and Helena sat back, pushing the hair out of her eyes with one hand. "He goes really well for you," she agreed when she found enough breath to speak.

"Aye, but he'd go as well for anyone," Jamie pointed out loyally. "Like when you rode him on Beacon Hill last week."

"Don't be so modest!" Helena teased. Serious for a moment, she studied the way Jamie sat lightly in the saddle, his legs careful not to touch Piper's sides and his hands gentle on the reins. "You're by far the best rider of any at Roseby Manor, you know," she pointed out. "It's a shame you can't take him in the race yourself."

Jamie laughed. "Piper's your father's horse, Nell," he reminded her. "He's hardly likely to let a stable lad ride him. Not that I'd say no if he asked," he added. "But I know Lord Roseby's been looking forward to trying him out all year, an' the horse'll go just as fast for him as me. Now, come on, Nell, let's walk home before they catch a chill."

He turned Piper back the way they had come, leaving the reins slack so that the gelding could stretch his neck. Snowdrop followed without needing any command, leaving Helena to gaze across the gentle Dorset hills that unfolded all around her.

In her mind's eye, she could see a horse galloping over the ramparts, its neck stretched out and its tail flying out like spun silk. And its coat was not burnished bronze but dark brown, and its mane and tail were black as ebony.

HELENA'S HANDS AND FEET were numb with cold by the time they rode into the stable yard, and when she jumped to the ground it felt as if icy needles were sticking in her toes. Watkins led Snowdrop into the stable block and Helena limped over to the tack room, intending to warm her hands at the wood-burning stove. Damp air made the leather tack stiff and prone to cracking so the stove was kept lit all winter. The chimney ran up through the loft where the stable lads slept, and Helena guessed they appreciated its steady warmth even more than the saddles and harnesses below. She paused in the doorway, blinking as her eyes adjusted to the dim light inside.

Suddenly, someone loomed out of the shadows toward her, his footsteps echoing on the stone floor. Helena jumped backward with a startled cry.

"Sorry, miss," said the man, coming into the daylight. He was thin and narrow shouldered, half a head taller than Helena, with curly dark hair and gray eyes. "I didn't mean to frighten you." He grinned, revealing uneven white teeth, and he reached out with one hand as if to pat Helena on the shoulder.

"Uncle Mathias! What are you doing here?"

It was Jamie, walking toward the tack room with Snowdrop's saddle and bridle over one arm.

The stranger spun around and smiled even more broadly. "Well, you've grown, young Jamie!" he declared. "'Tis a few years since I clapped eyes on you, an' I can see you'll be catching your pa up soon." He winked at Helena. "I could tell you some tales about this lad, that's for sure."

Jamie frowned, as if uncomfortable at the familiar way his uncle was treating Helena. "Mathias, this is Lady Helena, the daughter of Lord and Lady Roseby."

Mathias raised his eyebrows, then grinned and bowed. "Honored to meet you, Lady Helena," he murmured.

Helena flushed and glanced at Jamie. "Thank you, Mr.—er—"

"Jarrow. Mathias Jarrow, master stonemason formerly of Weymouth, temporarily of Roseby," Jamie's uncle announced with a flourish.

"What do you mean?" asked Jamie. "Why've you left Weymouth?"

"Did your ma not tell you I was coming?" Mathias shrugged. "Well, 'twill be common enough knowledge once I've had an evening in the Black Feathers! The stone merchant's warehouse where I've been working this past twelvemonth burned down a week ago. No money coming in so no way to pay the rent, see? That's why I couldn't stay in Weymouth no longer."

"I'm so sorry," Helena said.

"I'll be all right," said Jarrow with a wry smile. "I brought my tools with me, an' I'm sure there's call for stone work 'round here." He opened his jacket to reveal a faded brown leather pouch slung across his chest, bulging with curious shapes.

"Thank goodness you didn't lose them in the fire," Helena remarked.

Jarrow reached into the pouch and drew out a short-handled mallet, its round metal head worn to a fine shine. He smoothed one hand over it and rested its weight lightly in his palm. Helena noticed a narrow gouge running across the top of the mallet as if it had been scored by a stray nail.

"I wouldn't leave my tools behind anywhere," Jarrow said quietly. "They're all a man needs for his trade, they are. Anyway—" he slipped the mallet back into the pouch and took out a small cloth bundle "—I reckoned my sister Mary would put me up for a few weeks, just till I find another place. Here, Jamie, 'tis some bread and cheese that your ma asked me to bring for your dinner."

"Thanks," said Jamie, taking the bundle.

Jarrow looked at them from one to the other, then smiled and raised his hat to Helena. "Good day to you, my lady. I won't get in your way no more, Jamie. I can see you've got important work to do." He thrust his hands into the pockets of his well-worn coat and walked away across the yard, nodding to Isaiah who was pushing a laden wheelbarrow out of the stable block.

"He seems very friendly," Helena observed, watching the man head down the drive.

"Aye." Jamie sounded doubtful. When Helena looked questioningly at him, he shrugged. "Oh, he's pleasant enough, but he stayed with us a few years ago an' kept the twins awake all hours with his friends calling 'round."

"Well, if he's thinking of staying for longer this time, perhaps he'll be more thoughtful," Helena suggested. "And he did say he would only stay for as long as it took him to find a new job. Poor man, it must have been awful when the warehouse burned down."

She broke off as Hawk appeared at the corner of the yard, a greatcoat thrown over his dark green livery.

"Lady Helena, your mother asked me to tell you that Mrs. Clark is ready to see you now," the footman informed her.

Helena nodded. "Thank you, Hawk. I'm just coming. I'll see you tomorrow, Jamie. And can you give Snowdrop a mash of hot bran this afternoon?" She flashed him a grin. "She deserves a treat after that gallop."

"Certainly, my lady," replied Jamie, returning her smile before disappearing into the tack room.

HELENA WENT TO HER bedroom to change out of her riding habit before going to see Susan Clark for the fitting. Louise helped her into an indoor gown with a quilted petticoat that would keep out the worst of the drafts in the old manor house. Even though the house walls were nearly a yard thick, the bitter salty wind still managed to find its way into every room, making smoke spew out of the fireplaces in gritty black puffs.

Mrs. Clark was in Lady Roseby's bedroom, pinning a length of silk for an evening gown around her mistress's waist. Helena's mother was wearing a fashionably wide wooden hoop under the skirt, which emphasized her narrow waist and made the lilac fabric hang in elegant folds. Susan Clark looked up when Helena appeared in the doorway and gave her a tight-lipped nod, unable to speak with her mouth full of pins.

Lady Roseby twisted around as far as the hoop would allow and smiled at Helena. "There you are, my dear," she said. "Do come in. Susan has some lovely new fabric for our gowns. Had you any colors in mind for your race-day outfit?"

Helena walked over to her parents' enormous four-poster, where several bolts of cloth lay in rows like shiny plump fish. As small children, she and Jamie had played pirates and shipwrecks on the high goose-feather mattress, bobbing around on top of the eiderdowns and using the heavy velvet curtains to swing themselves down to the floor. In their imaginations, the big oak linen chest at the foot of the bed had been a locked chest of rubies and emeralds and peacock feathers fit for an Indian prince. The colors of these jewels were echoed now in the swathes of fabric that covered the bed. Helena ran her hand lightly over them, enjoying the cool slipperiness of the silk and the ghostly cobweb feel of the lace.

"I like this one," she said, holding up the corner of a rich green damask, the color of yew tree leaves. It would go well with her eyes, as her maid Louise had suggested. And the thickness of the heavy silk meant it would keep her warm even when she was watching the race.

Susan Clark looked over her shoulder and nodded. "Aye, that's a lovely color, Lady Helena. I can make you a gown in that for sure. I'll take your measurements as soon as I've finished this skirt. And the petticoat?"

Unlike Helena's riding habits, formal gowns were left open in front below the waist to reveal the petticoat underneath. She spotted a bundle of soft creamy cotton at the end of the bed. "Will that be suitable?" she asked.

"Yes, dear, that will go perfectly with the green damask." Her mother smiled. The pinning of her evening skirt done, Lady Roseby undid the ties at her waist and let the heavy wooden hoop fall to the floor. Then she stepped carefully out and threaded her arms into the gown that Mrs. Clark held out for her. "Did you notice the lace?" she added to Helena. "Susan brought that specially to trim the neck and cuffs of our new gowns."

"It's beautiful," Helena agreed. She bent down to admire the intricate patterns, as delicate as sea foam. Helena thought it looked as fine as any cloth Aunt Emma brought down from London, even though Lady Windlesham protested endlessly about how impossible it was to find decent fabric in Dorchester.

Suddenly Helena froze, and the lace seemed to scratch against her fingers like sticky burrs. Where could Susan Clark have gone to find such exquisite cloth? Not to London, that was for sure. For the villagers of Roseby, even a trip as far as Dorchester was unusual. No, there was only one place this lace could have come from. And that was France, brought softly in at the dead of night on a smugglers' galley and stored in some crypt or inn cellar—perhaps even in Lord Roseby's hayloft—until it could be distributed throughout the village by silent, cloaked men. Susan's husband, Robert, had been among the company of smugglers the other night. Helena clearly remembered him among the men lifting bundles into the hayloft.

She ran her hand over the bolt of lace again, hoping that her mother couldn't tell how fast her heart was pounding. She was sure that Lady Roseby had no idea where her fine lace came from. But Helena knew and, what was more, had probably played a part in landing this particular cargo. She would be wearing smuggled goods to the race!

SOFT GRAY CLOUDS HAD spread across the sky since Helena and Jamie returned from their ride, and now she heard cold rain drumming on the stone paths around the manor and spattering against the windowpanes. The weather certainly wasn't good enough to lunge Oriel, and she couldn't help admitting that a night of unbroken sleep would be welcome. As soon as Mrs. Clark had finished pinning and tucking different lengths of cloth around her, she changed into her well-worn indoor gown and escaped downstairs. She believed her mother and Mrs. Clark when they told her that her new gown would look lovely, but she wished it could be practical as well as pleasing to the eye. Not for the first time, she envied her father and Will, who could wear breeches and soft calico shirts and warm, close-fitting jackets.

Throwing a shawl over her head and shoulders, she ran down to the stable yard to look for Jamie. He was in Jupiter's stall, tucking a thick rug over the horse's hindquarters to keep out the damp night air.

"How's his leg?" Helena asked, walking quietly up.

"It's fine now," answered Jamie. He squeezed out of the stall and brushed his hands together. "He an' Apollo will be taking Lord Roseby to Dorchester on Monday." He frowned as if puzzled by what Helena was doing in the stables so late. "Did you want something, Nell?"

"Only to tell you that I don't think we should work Oriel tonight," Helena said. "He won't thank us for taking him out in the rain, that's for sure."

"No, he won't," agreed Jamie. He looked down at the floor and scuffed the toe of his boot against one of the cobbles. "I won't be around tonight anyway, as it happens."

Helena stiffened. "Another landing?" she whispered.

Jamie nodded. "These clouds will cover the moon, an' 'twould be a pity to waste the sort of weather that'll keep the customs men indoors. High tide's at ten, so with luck we'll all be abed by midnight."

"Will you be using the carriage horses?" Helena asked.

Jamie shook his head. "No, there's only the one load coming in. We should be able to manage with Elijah's horse."

Helena pictured the innkeeper's famously bad-tempered cart horse, Duke, whose enormous hairy feet had kicked many a lad out of his stable. "Good luck." She grinned.

Jamie winked at her. "Thanks. With that old nag, we'll need it."

"And . . . be careful," Helena added, suddenly feeling her stomach twist with fear. She reached out and rested her hand on Jamie's sleeve.

"We always are, Nell," Jamie promised softly, his brown eyes warm. "We always are."

LORD ROSEBY ARRIVED BACK from Dorchester shortly before dinner, his greatcoat shedding raindrops like a massive dog shaking its coat dry. Helena was just coming down the stairs, having changed into a new gown after soaking the hem of her other one during her visit to the stable yard.

"How did Piper go this morning, Nell?" her father called up to her, standing still to let Mansbridge lift the dripping coat from his shoulders. "Jamie told me you were planning to take him to Eggardon Hill this morning."

Helena smiled, unable to hide her excitement. "He was wonderful, Papa," she told him. "I can't see any horse beating him if he stays as fit as he is now."

"Is this the gelding you were telling me about?" said a voice from the shadows by the door.

Helena jumped and leaned over the banister to peer into the gloom. A man stepped forward into the thin pool of light shed by the flickering candles. His dark blue coat was beaded with rain, and his boots and breeches were plastered with mud. "Good evening, Lady Helena," he greeted her.

"Good evening to you, Mr. Chapman," Helena replied.

"Mr. Chapman will be joining us for dinner," Lord Roseby explained. "I caught up with him on the way home and thought he looked in need of a bite to eat before going the rest of the way. Mansbridge, please could you tell Mrs. Gordon that we will need another place laid?"

"Of course, my lord. Would you like me to bring some refreshments to the front parlor before dinner is served?"

"Thank you," said Lord Roseby. He watched the footman disappear through the door that led to the kitchen and pantries, then turned back to Roger Chapman. "Yes, I've high hopes of this horse. He's only seven and this will be his first race, but he hunted well last season and as Helena says, he's swifter than any other horse in my stables."

Not exactly, Helena put in silently. Piper might be able to beat the other horses in the race, but she didn't think he could out-run Oriel.

"Then I look forward to seeing him race," Mr. Chapman told Helena's father with a smile.

Just then, Lady Roseby came along the passageway with a soft rustle of silk. "Mr. Chapman, I'm so glad you could join us for dinner," she greeted her guest, holding out her hand for the customs man to raise politely to his lips. "Please come through to the parlor. There's a good fire waiting for you. I'm sure you must be chilled to the bone after the journey from Dorchester."

"Thank you, Lady Roseby, a fire sounds most welcoming." The Riding Officer followed her along the passage, his spurred boots echoing on the stone flags.

"Come, Nell, keep us company," Lord Roseby invited, standing aside to let Helena walk ahead of him down the passageway.

Helena nodded obediently, hoping that her nervousness didn't show in her face. She was still afraid that Mr. Chapman would mention their midnight encounter in the stable yard in front of her parents.

Then another thought struck her and she straightened her back, a small smile lifting the corners of her mouth. At least if Mr. Chapman was here, dining at the manor, it meant that there would be one less Riding Officer to patrol the cliffs, while the Roseby smugglers landed their latest cargo.

THE CONVERSATION AT THE dinner table turned inevitably to the current assizes, and Helena asked what that day's trial had been about.

"A young fellow accused of sheep stealing," said her father, looking up from the apple that he was peeling into a single, deft curl with his knife. "It's usually a capital offence, which means it carries the death penalty, but Judge Trimble acknowledged that it was the first time he'd been in trouble and sentenced him to ten years' transportation."

"Thank goodness," murmured Lady Roseby. "I cannot help but be saddened when the death sentence is passed. What those wreckers did deserves no pity, but one can only feel sorrow for their mothers and wives and children."

Roger Chapman nodded and paused in his careful slicing of a pear. "In all my career, I've never yet understood what could drive a man to wreck ships deliberately for the sake of an unknown cargo."

"Have you caught the gang from Poole yet?" Helena asked.

The Riding Officer shook his head, his expression darkening. "Alas, no, Lady Helena. There's been not a sign of them the whole length of Chesil Bank, although that can only be a good thing. With luck, they will have been frightened off by the fate of the Lyme Regis men."

"God willing," agreed Lord Roseby, raising his glass and taking a long drink of wine.

Roger Chapman picked up his glass as well and drank, then sat for a moment turning the heavy goblet in his hands and watching the ruby liquid gleam and swell in the candlelight. "Wreckers or not, there's still plenty to occupy a Riding Officer," he remarked, so softly he almost seemed to be speaking to himself.

"Do you mean smugglers?" Helena said, her voice sounding loud and hollow in the wood-paneled room.

Mr. Chapman put down his glass and raised his eyes to hers.

In this light, they seemed dark blue, almost black, with tiny orange pinpricks where the candle flames were reflected. "Yes, smugglers," he said.

"Surely it's more important to catch the wreckers?" Helena argued, unconsciously lifting her hand to her throat as if to cover the guilty flush that had started there. "After all, they are responsible for the murder of innocent souls and the destruction of ships, while smugglers merely—"

"Merely?" Roger Chapman echoed. "Be careful not to believe sentimental stories, Lady Helena. Smugglers are not modern-day Robin Hoods, you know, risking life and limb for the sake of the poor. They are thieves, no more and no less, stealing from the government by avoiding import duties."

Helena wanted to protest that the villagers couldn't be blamed for finding some other way to obtain things as ordinary as tea and cloth when import duties made them impossible to afford otherwise. She remembered what Faith had said about the law being man-made, and she realized that in her opinion, the men who had created the laws about import duties were wrong. It wasn't even as if the taxes raised would benefit the people in any direct way. Her father had told her that the money was needed to pay for the war in France, a country nobody from Roseby had any interest in, that was for sure.

"At least the smugglers don't hurt anyone," she pointed out.

Mr. Chapman raised his eyebrows. "Don't they? 'Tis not

uncommon for customs men to be shot when they're carrying out their duties. And that's murder plain and simple, would you not agree?"

Helena looked down at the apple core turning brown on her plate and said nothing. She knew that any further argument would only attract suspicion from the Riding Officer.

Roger Chapman clearly took her silence for agreement, for he leaned forward and looked earnestly at her from under his thick dark hair. "Lady Helena, as an officer appointed by the government, it is my duty to rid this coast of lawlessness, wrecking, and smuggling alike. And it is everyone's duty to report wrongdoing, to help me and my men keep villages like this one safe."

"And have you found any evidence of smuggling in Roseby?" asked Helena's father, reaching down to smooth Batista's head. The deerhound was lying under his chair, her nose tilted up in the hope of catching a dropped morsel of food.

Helena froze and kept her eyes fixed on her plate. Underneath the table, she dug her nails into her palms until she felt them bite into her skin. Was Mr. Chapman about to tell her father that he had seen her in the stable yard in the middle of the night?

The Riding Officer paused before replying to swallow a piece of pear. "This village would be unusual if it did not have a company of smugglers, my lord," he said. "You will understand that I cannot tell you exactly what information we have received so far. But in my opinion, the best chance of catching them is to be in the right place at the right time. And if that means a few sleepless nights then so be it. Smugglers can't be lucky all the time. Sooner or later we'll be there when the tide is up and they have their hands full of cargo."

Helena looked up to see her father raising his wineglass to Mr. Chapman. "Then I wish you happy hunting." Lord Roseby smiled.

The Riding Officer nodded and took an answering sip of wine. His gaze met Helena's for a moment, and she thought she saw a faint gleam of amusement in his eyes. She flushed and told herself that if Mr. Chapman had truly suspected her of being involved with the smugglers, he would have mentioned it by now. He had admitted that customs men had to catch smugglers red-handed. As long as he was sitting in her father's dining room, Jamie was safe.

Lady Roseby beckoned to the footman to refill their guest's glass. "I heard you discussing my husband's prospects in the forthcoming race, Mr. Chapman. Will you be taking part yourself?"

The Riding Officer sat back and laughed, shaking his still damp hair out of his eyes. "Sadly not, Lady Roseby. My cob, Noah, is a brave old fellow and made no complaints about carrying me here tonight, even though he was up to his hocks in mud for most of the journey. A few years ago he'd have given the finest Thoroughbreds a good run for their money, but he's past the time for racing now." He smiled, affection for his horse softening the lines on his face, and Helena warmed toward him in spite of the tension of their previous conversation.

"Will you be looking for a new horse soon?" asked Lord Roseby.

Mr. Chapman shrugged and stabbed a slice of pear with the tip of his knife. "There's a few miles yet in old Noah," he said. "But if a particularly good prospect came along, who knows? I like a fine horse as much as the next man, after all." He grinned and popped the piece of pear into his mouth, chewing appreciatively.

Outside, a gust of wind rattled at the windowpane, and in the hall the clock chimed ten, the thin notes struggling to be heard above the gale.

"I pity any poor soul out on a night like this," remarked Lady Roseby, drawing her shawl more closely around her shoulders.

Roger Chapman dropped his napkin onto his plate and smiled ruefully. "I'm afraid I'm going to have to risk it," he said. "Noah will be wanting his stable, and that excellent meal has set me in good stead for the last part of our journey."

"Surely you're not going out in this weather?" Helena's mother protested. "Please stay the night. I can have a bed made up for you quite easily."

"And I have some particularly good brandy that I was hoping to share with you over a hand of cards," added Lord Roseby.

"You are most kind," said Mr. Chapman. "But the road to West Bay is sheltered for most of the way and it'll not take me much more than an hour to get home." He took out a silver watch from his waistcoat and narrowed his eyes. "However, there is no need for me to leave quite so soon. I'm sure Noah would appreciate another half hour in your warm stables, and I would be delighted to try some of that brandy, my lord." He settled back in his chair and smiled as he caught Helena's eye.

Helena stiffened. There was something about the way in which the Riding Officer had consulted his pocket watch that made her wonder if he were timing his departure precisely. Jamie had told her that high tide was at ten o'clock tonight, bringing with it the smugglers' cargo from France. In half an hour the men would be making their way up from the shore with the laden cart. Had the Riding Officer guessed that the smugglers would be taking advantage of the moonless night? Was he planning to catch them red-handed, just as he had promised?

Helena stared in dismay across the table at Mr. Chapman. He had twisted around in his chair to admire a print above the fireplace that her father had recently bought. Helena's mind raced as she tried to think what she could do. It was unlikely that she would be able to persuade their guest to stay after her mother had already tried to tempt him with the offer of a spare bed. And he might be suspicious if she seemed too keen to keep him at the manor house. Helena didn't imagine for one moment that Mr. Chapman had forgotten about their midnight meeting the last time he had been on the trail of the Roseby smugglers.

But a picture of the courthouse filled her mind, and the prisoners chained in the dock there to await the judge's sentence were not the Lyme Regis wreckers but men from Roseby, Jamie among them. Helena swallowed painfully. There was still a quarter of an hour before the Riding Officer was planning to leave. If she couldn't stop Mr. Chapman from going out to set his trap, she would have to go down to the beach herself and warn the smugglers.

HELENA LAID HER NAPKIN on the table beside her plate and stood up. "May I be excused, Mama? I have a headache." She knew that she was convincingly pale. She had felt the blood drain from her face once she realized what Mr. Chapman was going to do.

Lady Roseby looked concerned. "Of course, Helena. Would you like me to send Sarah to you with a tonic?"

"No, thank you, I'm sure I'm just tired," Helena replied. "Good night, Papa."

"Good night, Helena. Sleep well."

She nodded to the Riding Officer who was watching her closely, his eyes like blue fire. "Good night, Mr. Chapman," she said.

He gave a small bow. "I hope you feel better in the morning, Lady Helena."

Mansbridge opened the door of the dining room and Helena forced herself to walk out calmly and make her way up the stairs, moving slowly as if she really did have a bad headache. As soon as she was out of sight on the landing, she gathered up the skirt of her gown and ran along the passage to her bedroom. She wrenched off the heavy indoor gown and pulled on her riding habit, cursing under her breath as her shaking fingers struggled to do up the buttons of the jacket. Then she slipped back along the passage to the top of the stairs where she paused, gasping for breath. Luckily, the hall was empty this time, and she ran quietly down and unbolted the heavy back door without anyone seeing her.

Outside the rain had eased to a faint drizzle, blown sideways by the relentless wind. Clouds chased each other across the moon, allowing gleams of yellow light through. Helena paused at the corner of the stable yard and peered around, narrowing her eyes against the rain. A lantern was glowing inside the stable block, and silhouetted in one of the windows she saw a distinctive broad-brimmed hat. Watkins must be settling the horses for the night. He might even be saddling Noah, ready for Mr. Chapman to leave. The open-sided barn where visitors' horses were usually tethered was empty, so it looked as if the groom had taken the dun cob into the stable block where it was more sheltered from the wind.

Helena bit her lip to stop herself from cursing out loud in frustration. If Watkins was in the stable block, how was she going to take a horse to ride to Freshwater Bay? She had assumed that the stable block would be deserted and she would be able to collect Snowdrop just as she had when she had followed Jamie down to the beach the first time. She looked desperately around the yard, wondering if she could distract Watkins long enough for her to saddle Snowdrop; but surely he would notice the gray mare was missing when he went to fetch Noah for Mr. Chapman.

Then Helena's gaze fell on Oriel's stable door. The stallion was still kept separately from the other horses on the far side of the yard. She would be able to saddle him without Watkins seeing, as long as the groom stayed in the stable block. Helena felt her heart begin to race. There was no denying that Oriel would carry the warning to the smugglers more swiftly than any other horse, and with his midnight-colored coat he might even slip past the customs men without being seen. But no one at Roseby had ridden Oriel yet. Helena had always intended to ride him one day—but not at night, in a storm, far beyond the safety of the paddocks. Her stomach lurched as she remembered how the stallion had behaved when she and Jamie had first tried to lunge him.

But she had to warn the smugglers about Mr. Chapman. For their sake, and for Jamie's most of all, she would take the stallion.

She ran across the yard and into the welcoming shadows of the tack room. The fire in the stove cast a dim orange light, just enough to make out the saddles and bridles hanging neatly on the walls. The bridle at the end of the row was Oriel's, and Helena unhooked it and slipped it over her shoulder. Then she heaved a saddle from its rack—not a sidesaddle, but the one that Jamie had used on Piper earlier that day.

The yard was still deserted as Helena slipped out of the tack room, her steps uneven under the weight of the saddle, and crossed to Oriel's stable. The stallion greeted her with warm breath in her hair and stood quietly while she lifted the saddle onto his back and fastened the girth. Helena realized with annoyance that she had forgotten to bring anything to muffle his hooves, but then she decided that she'd rather leave him surefooted for the gallop ahead. They'd have to trust to the noise of the wind to hide the sound of hooves on cobbles as they left.

Helena thought for a moment. Mr. Chapman would almost certainly take the quickest route down to the bay, along the road through the village. She wasn't sure exactly what time it was now—it was too dark to see the coach house clock, and it only chimed on the hour—but she guessed it must be nearly half past ten. The Riding Officer would be leaving the manor house at any minute. The last thing Helena wanted was to meet him, which meant she'd have to take the longer way to the beach, up through the paddocks to the lookout on the Knoll then westward along the cliffs.

Pulling her shawl closer around her face, Helena took a deep breath and opened the stable door. Oriel followed her will-ingly, well used to these nocturnal outings. Keeping close to the wall, Helena led the stallion to the path that went through the garden and up to the paddocks. He skittered as they rounded the corner and were met by a blast of salty wind.

"Steady, lad," Helena murmured, struggling to keep her voice calm in spite of the fear that clutched at her stomach. Fear of being caught—and fear of the stallion that leapt and shied beside her. Then Helena remembered how Oriel had responded to her the night before, when she had shown him with the position of her body and the tone of her voice that she trusted him to listen to her and behave like any of the horses she had lunged before.

Gripping the reins in both hands, Helena took a deep breath. "Stop that nonsense," she told Oriel firmly, feeling her knees shake under the skirt of her riding habit.

The stallion stood still, his legs rigid, and looked down at her. Helena could see the whites of his eyes as she met his gaze, but he blew softly through his nostrils and didn't flinch when a gust of wind snatched at the weather vane on top of the coach house, making it spin madly.

"Walk on," Helena said, turning into the wind and tugging gently at the reins. Oriel tossed his head before falling into step beside her, his hooves leaving dark crescents in the wet grass.

When they came to the first paddock fence, Helena stood Oriel as close to it as she could, then climbed the railings until she could reach the pommel with both hands. Luckily there were no horses in the paddock to startle the stallion, and with an undignified scramble, Helena managed to haul herself into the saddle.

Oriel leapt sideways at once, hunching his back under Helena's weight. Gripping with both knees, Helena forced herself to sit deep in the saddle and gathered up the reins. *Treat him like any other horse,* she reminded herself, *and he'll behave like one.*

Oriel stopped, his ears flicking back and forth and his flanks heaving. Helena knew that she should make him walk quietly to get him used to her weight in the saddle and her commands before she asked him to go any faster. But there was no time for that. Roger Chapman would be leaving the manor at any moment. She tucked her skirt under her knees so that it wouldn't flap over Oriel's hindquarters and turned him to face away from the stable yard. Ahead of them, a wide grassy track led between the paddocks to the Knoll, where it met the cliff path that ran all the way from Weymouth to West Bay.

Bending forward from the waist and grasping a handful of thick black mane, Helena clapped her heels against Oriel's side. "Go on, boy!" she cried, her voice whipped away in the wind as the stallion plunged forward.

His hooves pounded against the soft turf, throwing up

clumps of mud that spattered Helena's clothes. She tried to shorten the reins, to take hold of Oriel's head and bring him back to a more balanced gallop, but he was spooked by the wind and the darkness, and pelted on with his nose stretched out and his mane flying against Helena's face in sharp stinging strands. Luckily the track was fenced in on either side which meant that the only direction Oriel could take was straight up the hill, toward the sea.

Helena crouched over his withers, just as she had seen Jamie do on Piper, and forced herself to trust the stallion to find his footing in the dark. She rested her hands halfway up his neck, the reins short enough that she could feel the bit in his mouth but without trying to slow his pace or steer him away from the path that led to the Knoll. She felt Oriel relax beneath her, the rhythm of his hooves settling into a steady gallop as he understood that Helena trusted him to choose his own pace. And in spite of the wind and the dark and the terribly urgent nature of their errand, Helena felt a bolt of pure joy.

The track swung around the eastern flank of the Knoll to skirt a small wood and opened out onto the cliffs beside the old coast guard's lookout. To the left, Chesil Bank stretched like an endless gravel path, the waves roaring and sucking angrily at the pebbles. Oriel skidded to a halt in alarm when the pale stone building loomed above them on the crest of the hill, and Helena was jolted onto his neck. She was gasping for breath and her legs ached from the effort of holding on, but she managed to push herself back into the saddle and kick Oriel forward.

The stallion shook his head, showering her with foam, and broke into an uneven trot. As they passed the coast guard's hut, Helena's skin prickled as if someone was watching her. Surely Roger Chapman couldn't have made it to the Knoll ahead of them? Her heart thudding painfully, she twisted around and caught a glimpse of a darker shadow in the tall glassless window that overlooked the bank.

The man wasn't wearing a hat and there was no sign of a dun cob, which meant it couldn't be Mr. Chapman. But Helena didn't want to waste precious seconds finding out the identity of the night sentinel. She scooped up the reins and urged Oriel into a canter, glancing back over her shoulder to make sure the shadow wasn't following her. She turned to see a tinderbox flare as the man lit a pipe, and in the brief flash of light she made out a narrow, long-nosed face that seemed vaguely familiar. One of the smugglers, perhaps? Helena was sure she would have recognized him if he had been a villager. But there was no time to wonder about the identity of the stranger now. She just hoped that whoever he was, he hadn't recognized her in return.

As the track sloped down into Freshwater Bay Oriel began to gallop faster, his breath coming in harsh ragged snorts.

Helena leaned back and gripped with both knees to keep her balance, while still allowing the stallion enough rein to pick his way down the steep incline. The bay opened out in front of her and she caught sight of the smugglers' galley, the shallow-bottomed boat that carried the cargo from the sailing ship to the shore. Empty now apart from the crew, it was rocking and bouncing over the waves, heading back to the ship that waited a few miles out to sea. Helena could just make out the oarsmen bent over their long paddles, scooping the moonlit sea like spoonfuls of pearls.

On the beach below her, half a dozen shadows crunched over the pebbles, weighed down by the barrels and oilskin bundles on their shoulders. A horse and cart stood at the end of the track that led up the gully to the main road. Helena guessed that the figure at the horse's head was Jamie, and she steered Oriel toward him. The soft grass of the track gave way to stones as they reached the shore, and Oriel's hooves suddenly clattered above the sound of the waves and the soft crunch of the smugglers' footsteps.

Jamie looked around, his body rigid with alarm. Then he recognized the stallion, and Helena saw his expression change from one of shock to anger.

"Nell! What do you want?"

Helena pulled Oriel to a standstill and struggled to catch her breath, her whole body shaking with exhaustion and fear.

"I had to come," she gasped.

"'Tis not a jaunt that you can join as you please," growled Jamie. "What were you thinking of, taking Oriel? You're more of a fool than I thought. An' with his hooves bare, so every Riding Officer in the county can hear you!"

"Just listen to me!" Helena retorted furiously. "I came to tell you that Roger Chapman is on his way."

Jamie narrowed his eyes. "How do you know?"

"He had dinner with my father this evening, but he said that he had to leave at half past ten. I left before him to warn you. Quick, you must all hide!"

Jamie turned toward the man who approached them at the head of the line, a glistening oilskin bundle balanced across his shoulders. It was Samuel Polstock.

Before Jamie could speak, the blacksmith frowned. "What are doing you here, Lady Helena? Jamie, I hope you didn't encourage her to come."

"No, Pa. Listen, Nell's brought word that there's a customs man on his way from Roseby. He'll be here any moment."

Samuel nodded, his face expressionless. Then he turned to the rest of the line and called out, "Right, lads. We're expecting company, so let's sow the crop an' get the beach clear."

While he was speaking, Jamie ran to the back of the cart and picked up a coil of rope, which he slung to the next smuggler along. A low murmur spread among the men, but Helena, watching from Oriel, was struck again by the absence of panic. Instead the men stayed calm, their movements deft and measured as they slung the loads from their shoulders and started to tie the long rope around each piece of cargo.

"What are they doing?" Helena whispered to Jamie as he came back to the cart.

"'Tis called sowing the crop," Jamie explained. "They'll tie the barrels an' oilskins together, then drag the whole lot out beyond the waves an' sink them in the bay. They weigh the rope down with stones, see? It won't hurt to leave it there for a day or so, an' it means the customs men won't lay their hands on it, even if they find us." He grinned, his teeth white in the shadows, and Helena realized that he was almost enjoying this battle of wits with the Riding Officers.

Oriel shifted restlessly on the stones, tossing his head and swinging his quarters around so that Jamie had to jump out of the way.

"You can head home now, Nell," he said. He looked up at her, his brown eyes serious. "Thank you. You did a brave thing, coming to tell us like that. An' taking the stallion too."

Helena smiled, shortening the reins and closing her legs against Oriel to hold him still. "He was brilliant, Jamie," she told him. "I know it was a risk, but I'd never have got here so fast on another horse."

Oriel snorted again, striking out restlessly with his front leg.

"Let's just hope Watkins doesn't notice he's missing an' raise a hue an' cry for a stolen horse!" remarked Jamie. "Now, go on, Nell, take 'im back afore anyone see he's gone."

"Are you sure you'll be all right?" Helena asked.

Jamie glanced over his shoulder to where the smugglers were already carrying their roped-together cargo back down to the sea. "Aye. We'll have this lot sown in no time, an' there's plenty of shadows 'round here to keep us out of the way of the customs men. Off you go, Nell, an' Godspeed." He reached up and patted Oriel's sweat-streaked neck, then ducked as the horse wheeled around, leaping away as soon as Helena clapped her heels against his sides.

They thundered back up the path, the stallion's powerful hindquarters thrusting them up the slope in a few long strides. Helena reined him to a halt on the brow of the cliff and looked down at the beach. It was deserted now, the stones bare of any trace of cargo or smugglers. On the far side, the cliff was covered in thick scrubby bushes, which Helena imagined to be made thicker with the shadows of hiding men. Even the horse and cart had vanished.

Suddenly Helena froze. A cream-colored shape was coming down the gully, picking its way along the stony track that led beside the river. Moonlight gleamed on a silver bit, and Helena strained her ears to hear the faint clop of hooves. The horse stopped at the foot of the track, and the shadowy figure of a rider loomed across the gray stones. He was wearing a broad-brimmed hat, and Helena knew that it was Roger Chapman.

His face flashed palely as he turned and looked straight at the horse on the cliff. Without waiting to see if the Riding Officer had recognized her, Helena turned Oriel's head and drove him into a gallop. Her fear of being discovered lent wings to the stallion's hooves, so that they seemed to fly along the cliff top faster than the wind-chased clouds scudding across the sky.

19

EVERY MUSCLE IN HELENA'S BODY protested when she woke the following morning. The air in her bedroom felt cold and damp, and she huddled under her eiderdown until Louise entered with hot water and a fresh undershift, warm and smelling of soap from the laundry room.

"Are you all right, my lady?" asked the maid, seeing Helena's pale face and black-circled eyes.

Helena pushed back the eiderdown and swung her aching legs to the floor. "I'm fine, thank you," she said. Her hair had still been damp when she went to bed, and now it hung in a thick tangle around her shoulders. She ran her fingers through the ends, wondering if she should ask Louise to wash it for her before breakfast.

There was a startled cry from the maid as she drew back the curtains and noticed the mud-soaked riding habit lying in a crumpled heap on the floor. She looked at Helena and frowned. Helena winced inwardly. She knew that Louise wouldn't dare to question her, but she hoped that the maid wouldn't mention it to any of the other servants. After all, Louise had told Sarah Canning, her mother's maid, about the bruise on her shoulder.

"Have I a clean riding habit for today?" Helena asked, as if it were nothing remarkable that her outfit had become so dirty overnight.

Louise nodded. "Yes, my lady. I'll just fetch it for you." With a brief glance at the clothes on the floor, she went over to the chest at the foot of the bed and lifted out a dark blue skirt and jacket.

Helena closed her eyes, feeling more tired than she had ever felt before. The exhilaration of the previous night's gallop had gone, and she felt only a dread that the smugglers had been found and that Roger Chapman had recognized her. She knew that she had to go to the stables and speak to Jamie as soon as she could.

Her mother and Will had already breakfasted and her father was not yet up when Helena arrived in the dining room. Eliza brought her tea and toast which Helena forced herself to eat, knowing that it would make her feel less weak and exhausted. As soon as she had swallowed the last mouthful, she wrapped a shawl around her shoulders and ran down to the stable yard. The rain clouds had been blown away overnight, but the wind had grown even stronger, spinning the weather vane on the coach house until the metal screeched in protest. The last of the autumn leaves whisked past Helena, dancing to music that only they could hear.

Helena made straight for Oriel's stable. To her relief, the stallion was pulling calmly at his hayrack. She had brushed off the worst of the mud and sweat last night and thrown a rug over him to keep out the chill, but he would need a good grooming today to restore the shine to his mahogany coat. Helena unbolted the door and slipped inside, anxious to feel for any heat or swelling in the horse's legs. She took off her glove and was just running one hand down his foreleg when Jamie appeared at the door.

Helena straightened up at once, stumbling a little as her skirt dragged in the thick straw. "Jamie! Is everything all right?"

"Shh," Jamie cautioned her, coming into the stable. "Not so loud. Yes, everything's fine. We saw the Riding Officer come down to the beach, but he didn't find anything we didn't want him to, an' we made our own way home as soon as he'd gone. We'll go back an' fetch up the crop in a couple of nights. You did the right thing, Nell, coming to warn us like that. We're all very grateful."

"I'm glad I got there in time," said Helena. She decided not to tell Jamie that she was afraid Roger Chapman had seen her on the cliff top.

"An' how is this fellow this morning?" asked Jamie, reaching up to ruffle Oriel's forelock.

"He's fine," Helena murmured. She closed her eyes for a moment, remembering the long-strided, effortless gallop that had carried her back along the cliffs. "You know, I think he's even faster than Piper."

Jamie frowned. "That's as may be, but you didn't know that when you took him. What if he'd thrown you an' left you on the cliffs with no one knowing where you were?"

"I couldn't take any of the other horses," Helena explained. She smiled as Oriel twisted his head around to blow in her hair. "Watkins was in the stable block when I came down to the yard."

"Lucky for us that Oriel's in this stable, then," said Jamie, catching Helena's eye and smiling. "So, shall we tell your father that he's safe to ride?"

"How can we without letting on when I rode him?" Helena pointed out. "We'll have to wait until Watkins lunges him, then he'll see for himself." She felt her heart sink with frustration as she realized that Oriel's future at Roseby was still uncertain.

The sound of a horse trotting into the stable yard interrupted them. Jamie looked over the door. His shoulders stiffened and when he turned back to Helena, his face was serious. "'Tis the Riding Officer," he said.

The stable floor seemed to sway alarmingly under Helena's feet. Had Roger Chapman recognized her on the cliff last night? She stared at Jamie, feeling the blood drain from her face. Then she heard her father's voice greeting the visitor as he ran down the steps to the yard.

"Mr. Chapman! Good morning to you, sir. What brings you here so early?"

There was a creak of leather as the Riding Officer swung himself down from the saddle. "Good morning to you, Lord Roseby. I came to apologize for leaving so abruptly last night. I had recalled a matter of business that I had to attend to."

"Business, you say?" echoed Lord Roseby, his tone light hearted. Her father was in a good mood this morning, Helena thought. "What business was it that needed your attention at such an antisocial hour?"

Chapman sounded serious as he replied. "Yesterday I received a report of some smuggling activity that was due to take place not far from here, my lord. I wanted to see if there was any truth in the report."

Helena caught her breath and looked at Jamie.

"Tempting prey indeed," remarked Lord Roseby calmly. "And did you manage to catch anyone?"

"Unfortunately not. The smugglers either moved faster than I anticipated, or they were warned of my pursuit."

The blood roared in Helena's ears and she reached out to clutch Jamie's arm.

"Then I wish you better luck next time," Lord Roseby said sympathetically. "But I must say, if you continue to round up lawbreakers with such efficiency as we have seen this assizes, I shall find myself spending more time in the courthouse than at my quarries or my home!"

The Riding Officer laughed politely. "'Tis nothing more than my duty, sir," he said.

Jamie unhooked Helena's fingers from his arm. "I'd best be going," he murmured.

Helena nodded and stood in the shadows beside the door as Jamie let himself quietly out of the stable and headed for the paddocks, pausing at the corner of the yard to pick up a bucket and fork before vanishing out of sight.

In the center of the yard, Lord Roseby was inviting Mr. Chapman to stay for a tour of the stables.

"I'd be delighted to, my lord," replied the Riding Officer. "I must admit that I'm very curious about your excellent prospects for the Bridport race."

"Prospects?" echoed Lord Roseby. "No, I just have the one horse entered—the chestnut gelding we were discussing last night."

"Really?" said Roger Chapman, his voice politely doubtful. "What about the dark stallion?"

"Do you mean Oriel?" Helena's father seemed puzzled. "He won't be competing in the race. As you know, we've not had him here for long and he's proved more than a handful so far. He's certainly not shown a temperament that's fit to be ridden.

But he looks nicely bred, so we're hoping he'll settle in time. Why don't you come and see him for yourself?"

Helena heard footsteps crossing the cobbles toward her and she busied herself with adjusting Oriel's rug, knowing there was no way to slip out of the stable without being noticed.

"Helena!" Her father sounded surprised to find her there, and Helena remembered that he had made her promise to keep away from the stallion. She just hoped that Mr. Chapman's presence would discourage her father from questioning her disobedience.

"Good morning, Papa," she said, turning around with one hand on Oriel's warm, comforting shoulder.

"He's a fine-looking horse indeed," said Roger Chapman, looking over the door and nodding. "And with a turn of speed like that, I should think there's not a horse in the county that could better him."

Helena felt her throat tighten in alarm.

"You must be mistaken, Mr. Chapman," said Lord Roseby, frowning. "This horse hasn't been out of the stable since he arrived, except to the paddocks. But I agree that he seems docile enough today, so perhaps we'll have a chance to see what his paces are like before he's with us much longer. Who knows what secrets that handsome animal is hiding from us?"

Mr. Chapman stared at Helena, his ice-blue gaze seeming to look straight into her thoughts. "As you say, my lord, I must have made a mistake. I could have sworn I saw this horse galloping on the cliffs very recently."

To Helena's relief, Mansbridge appeared at that moment, his gray hair blown into tufts by the wind and his nose red with cold.

"My lord, Lady Roseby wonders if you and the gentleman would like to take tea with her this morning?"

"That sounds like an excellent idea," agreed Helena's father. "I was going to take Sultan out, but I can delay for an hour or so. Will you join us, Mr. Chapman?"

"Thank you, sir, but I have an appointment in Abbotsbury at noon. With your permission, though, I should like to speak to you again about the stallion." His eyes met Helena's for a moment, then he looked back at her father. "In my experience, one can never be too careful about horses you know little about. It might even be better to sell the stallion now before too many secrets are uncovered. And if you agree, then I'd be very interested in buying him myself."

20

HELENA'S HEART SEEMED TO stop beating as she waited for her father to answer. She pulled a wisp of hay from Oriel's mane and crumpled it in her fingers, feeling it prickle against her skin.

Lord Roseby smiled. "I can see you've an eye for a good-looking horse, Mr. Chapman. I haven't decided yet whether Oriel will be staying at Roseby, but I'll bear your offer in mind if I do want to sell him."

The Riding Officer nodded. "Please do that, Lord Roseby. Perhaps Lady Helena could help you make up your mind? She seems to know the stallion as well as anyone."

A shadow flashed across Lord Roseby's face, and Helena winced, knowing that she would have to explain later why she was in Oriel's stable when her father had warned her to leave the stallion to the grooms. "My daughter has always been a keen horsewoman," he said. Then he turned and beckoned to Watkins to bring Mr. Chapman's cob.

The Riding Officer swung himself into the saddle and

looked down at Helena and her father. "Good day to you both," he said. "Lord Roseby, I look forward to hearing your decision about the stallion." He closed his heels against Noah's sides and the dun cob cantered away, his hooves crunching over the gravel.

Lord Roseby looked somberly at Helena over the stable door. "Nell, I don't believe I've given you permission to have anything to do with Oriel yet. You do understand that I had only your safety in mind, don't you?"

"Yes, Papa," Helena said quietly, glancing down at the piece of hay that she was twisting between her fingers. "But you can see how quiet he is now. Watkins hasn't had any trouble with him since he's been going out in the paddocks."

"Yes, Watkins told me that the stallion seems to be settling down at last. But that's no excuse for you to disobey me."

"No, Papa."

Her father sighed, and when Helena looked up she saw that his hazel eyes were warm with amusement. "I can see I'm not going to be able to keep you out of here, am I?" he said. "Very well, you may groom Oriel if you wish, but you're not to handle him outside the stable until Watkins has tried lunging him."

"Thank you, Papa. I promise to be careful."

"I hope you will. Now, I must go and join your mother before our morning tea is stewed. See you later, Nell." He walked away across the yard, calling to Salome and Batista who came running out of the barn where they had been nosing for rats.

Feeling suddenly choked with emotion, Helena buried her face in Oriel's mane, pressing the silky strands against her cheeks with both hands. Her father couldn't sell Oriel now! But Helena was very worried about what Mr. Chapman had meant by his reference to uncovering secrets. Had he been talking about Oriel's past—or had he been threatening to tell her father that he had seen her twice at night when smugglers were about?

The horse jumped away from her as Jamie appeared in the doorway. "What's wrong, Nell?" he exclaimed, seeing her flushed face.

"It's all right," Helena said quickly. "Mr. Chapman didn't say anything about last night. Not directly, anyway."

"What did he say, then?"

"He saw me riding Oriel on the cliffs," Helena confessed.

"What? Last night, you mean?"

Helena nodded unhappily. "It was when I was leaving. He didn't see you, though, I'm sure of it."

"Well, if he said nothing to your pa about it, then he probably isn't certain that he saw you," Jamie pointed out.

"But there's more than that," Helena told him, her heart sinking lower with each word. "Mr. Chapman wants to buy Oriel. It's no surprise. After all, he's seen how fast he goes, and

Oriel's dark brown coat gets lost in the shadows better than the dun cob's ever could." She stopped, running her hand down Oriel's glossy shoulder.

"What's that got to do with us, though?" asked Jamie. "I mean, I know we don't want your pa to sell Oriel, but Chapman can't think that he'd stop the smugglers just by buying a horse."

Helena shook her head, frustrated. "You don't understand. I'm sure Mr. Chapman was trying to get me to convince my father to sell Oriel in return for not asking more questions about last night."

Jamie was silent for a few moments. Then he shrugged. "I think you're worrying too much, Nell. We got away with it last night an' that's all that matters. Mr. Chapman knows where to find us if he thinks he knows anything about what happens in the bay. An' he knows that your pa is capable of making up his own mind about Oriel, whatever you say." He let himself out of the stable and walked across the yard to the stable block.

Helena leaned on the door and watched him go, trying hard to feel encouraged by her friend's words. But she couldn't help fearing that the Riding Officer knew she had more to tell and was prepared to use the secret knowledge they shared to get what he wanted—either the arrest of the Roseby smugglers or the stallion.

AT DINNER THAT AFTERNOON, Helena couldn't stop yawning, and her mother grew quite concerned. "Are you not sleeping well at the moment, Helena?" she asked. "You've been looking pale for days now. Perhaps a tonic would help? I could ask Mrs. Gordon to prepare you one before you go to bed."

"Honestly, Mama, I'm fine," Helena said quickly. Mrs. Gordon's tonics were strange black potions, as thick as molasses but with none of the sweetness; they tasted like water that vegetables had been boiled in. Helena couldn't believe that anything so unpleasant could possibly do her any good. She shivered as the wind slapped against the window and made the curtains bulge. "I'm sure I'll sleep well tonight, even if this gale keeps up."

Lord Roseby glanced up from his roast beef. "We've not had a storm like this all year," he remarked. "I pity any sailor out tonight, that's for sure."

"What did Mr. Chapman want this morning?" asked Lady Roseby, slicing a boiled potato into neat quarters.

"He wanted to apologize for leaving so suddenly last night. Apparently he heard that smugglers were landing a cargo near here." Lord Roseby took a sip from his wineglass. "And that wasn't all. Just before he left, he suggested that he might make me an offer for Oriel. He claimed he'd seen the horse up on the cliffs and liked the look of his paces. You wouldn't know anything more about that, would you, Nell?" He looked questioningly at her from the end of the table.

Helena shook her head. "No, Papa," she replied, trying to keep her voice level.

"How very strange," said Lady Roseby. "Mr. Chapman must have seen a horse that looked similar. And I'm surprised he'd want to buy a horse that even we know so little about."

"Well, he made a good point about that," Lord Roseby admitted. "He said that it might be worth accepting an offer for him now, before we find out he's even more difficult than we thought. After all, we don't even know if he's been ridden before, so we're taking a gamble if we keep him at Roseby."

Helena bit her lip in an effort to stay silent. She couldn't bear to hear Oriel being described as difficult and unpredictable when she knew that he was the swiftest, most perfect horse she had ever ridden! But there was more reason to keep Oriel's talents a secret now. The Riding Officer would be even keener to buy him if he knew just how fast he was, how perfect for chasing smugglers in the dead of night.

Inspired, Helena said suddenly, "Papa, it would be just as much as a gamble for Mr. Chapman if he were to buy a horse he knew nothing about."

"Well, he's a good horseman, and he seems willing to take that risk." Her father smiled as he helped himself to more fried celery.

"But think how dreadful you'd feel—we'd all feel—if something bad happened to him because of Oriel." Helena crossed her fingers under the table and hoped that Oriel would forgive her for exaggerating his reputation. "You couldn't possibly sell a dangerous horse to a respectable gentleman like Mr. Chapman, could you?"

Lord Roseby set down his knife and fork and narrowed his eyes at Helena. For a moment she was afraid that her father had seen through what she was trying to do, but then he nodded. "You're right, Nell. It would be unfair not to wait until we know more about the stallion before we consider selling him to anyone. I certainly couldn't forgive myself if a horse that I had sold caused any injury, especially when we already know that Oriel can be difficult to handle." He glanced at Lady Roseby. "Your mother and I have agreed that you can continue to groom Oriel in the stable. But as you have just said yourself, there's a long way to go before we can trust Oriel completely, and you must leave it to Watkins to decide when the horse is ready to be lunged."

Helena nodded, breathing out in relief, and behind her the wind sighed at the window as if in agreement. For now, Oriel was safe at Roseby Manor—ironically, thanks to his bad reputation. And by the time everyone found out just how wrong they were about him, Helena was sure that her father would be as determined to keep the stallion as she was.

21

THE GALE BLEW ITSELF out during the night, but not with-out leaving evidence of its strength. When Helena looked out of her bedroom window the next morning she saw that one of the beech trees at the end of the garden had lost a branch. The torn limb lay splintered on the grass in a scattering of sodden leaves, its twigs whipping angrily at the air like outstretched hands.

Helena dressed and hurried downstairs but the dining room was empty, a plate of half-eaten toast and a cold cup of tea at her father's place suggesting that he had been called away urgently. As Helena turned to go out again, she almost bumped into Eliza Clark. The young kitchen maid's eyes were wide with shock and she seemed out of breath, as if she had been running.

"Is everything all right?" Helena asked.

"No, my lady!" Eliza burst out, the silver teapot sliding alarm-ingly across the tray that she was carrying. "There's been a ship-wreck on the bank! All the men from the village have gone down to the shore a couple of hours since, an' your father too."

"A shipwreck!" Helena felt a pool of dread form in the pit of her stomach. "Does my mother know?"

"Yes, Helena, I know," said a voice behind her. Lady Roseby came into the dining room and rested one hand on Helena's arm. "Your father came to tell me before he left. He's taken Hawk and Mansbridge down to see if there's anything they can do." She closed her eyes for a moment, her face pale with concern. "Now, Nell, have some breakfast. There'll be no church service this morning since Mr. Forbes has gone to the bank as well. As soon as you have eaten, we must get ready to look after any survivors. I've told your father that he can bring them straight here."

Helena nodded. She could remember this happening once before, several years ago. She had only been six or seven years old, but she could still remember wave-drenched, bruised men being carried on pallets into the main hall and laid in front of the massive fireplace.

"Here's some fresh tea, my lady." Eliza's voice broke into her thoughts, and Helena smiled her thanks as she sat down and held out her cup.

Lady Roseby sat opposite her and began to spread butter onto a piece of toast.

"Where's Will?" Helena asked, wrapping her hands around the teacup to warm them.

"I've told Charity to keep him in the nursery," replied Lady Roseby. "It's best if he stays out of the way while we're busy with the survivors of the shipwreck." Her expression darkened and she added, "That is, if God spares them."

Helena bowed her head and uttered a silent prayer that the villagers from Roseby had reached the shore in time to help the sailors. Just then, she heard the back door opening and her father's voice, low and weary.

Lady Roseby hurried out of the dining room. "What news, William?"

Helena followed her mother into the hall, her heart plummeting when she saw her father's strained, gray face. Water blackened his hair and clothes, and a ragged-edged tear stretched down one leg of his breeches. The footmen stood behind him, Mansbridge looking frailer than his sixty-odd years as he struggled to remove his sodden jacket.

"'Tis bad news, Jocelyn," Lord Roseby said quietly. "There were no survivors. By the looks of it, 'twas a cargo ship so at least there were no passengers. But I reckon there would have been at least twenty crew, all lost."

Lady Roseby drew in her breath sharply, then reached out and touched her husband's arm. "God rest their souls," she murmured. She turned to Eliza, who was twisting her apron with anxious hands. "Eliza, please go and tell Mrs. Gordon to make tea for the men. And, Helena, you can help me fetch some linen. It is the least we can do, to wrap the poor sailors decently before they're brought up from the shore." She glanced at her husband, who nodded.

"Thank you, my dear," he said. He broke off as there was a knock at the door.

Hawk, who was standing nearest to the door, opened it. Roger Chapman stood on the top step, a greatcoat over his uniform. "I am sorry to disturb you, my lord," he began. "I wondered if I could speak with you in private?"

For one brief moment, Helena feared that he had come back to talk to her father about buying Oriel, but then she saw that the Riding Officer's face was grim and lined, and his eyes were darkly shadowed as if he hadn't slept. He had come about something much more serious than the purchase of a horse.

"Of course, Mr. Chapman" said Lord Roseby. "Mansbridge, please bring some tea to my study."

"Yes, my lord." The footman shuffled off, his head bowed under the weight of what he had seen that morning.

Helena watched him, feeling her stomach churn with horror at the cruelty of wind and sea.

Lady Roseby smiled gently as if she could read her daughter's thoughts. "We must try to be brave, Nell. Come, let's go and find those sheets. We'll all feel better if we have something to do."

BY THE TIME THE clock in the hall chimed eleven, a pile of crisp white sheets stood ready on the floor of the laundry room. Helena smoothed her hand over the topmost sheet and straightened up, rubbing the small of her back which ached from stooping over the linen chests. A movement in the doorway startled her and she looked around.

"Sorry, Nell, I didn't mean to make you jump." It was Jamie, his hair plastered to his scalp from rain and sea spray, and his drenched shirt clinging to the outline of his body. His eyes didn't meet Helena's but stayed fixed on the floor.

"Have you been down to the beach?" she asked.

He nodded.

Helena waited for him to go on, and when he didn't, she said awkwardly, "Here are the sheets. Do you want to take them now?"

"No," Jamie said gruffly. "I—I'm not needed down there anymore. Your father sent me to ask if you'd like to go for a ride this afternoon."

"That sounds like a very good idea." Lady Roseby came into the room, a calico apron over her gown and her fair hair tucked into a neat white cap. "Go on, Nell. Hawk can take the sheets to the beach. Some fresh air would do you good, and I should imagine we'll be eating dinner late today."

Helena looked at Jamie. "Can you give me a few minutes to get changed?"

"Of course. I'll go an' get the horses ready." His voice was flat and expressionless and Helena felt a pang of sympathy that made her want to reach out to him. She couldn't imagine what horrors he had seen that morning, but a quiet ride, away from Roseby and all its sadness, would probably do him as much good as it would her.

THE WIND HAD SOFTENED to a stiff, salt-laden breeze by the time Helena ran down the steps to the stable yard. There was no one about, and she guessed that most of the men were still down at the shore, carrying on their grim task of removing the bodies.

Jamie emerged from the stable block wearing a dry shirt and leading Snowdrop. Helena went over and pressed her cheek against the mare's smooth white neck, breathing in the familiar warm smell. She felt drained after the morning's tragedy and was looking forward to getting away from the manor and the fearful pictures that haunted her mind.

"Ready, Nell?" Jamie asked. She nodded, and Jamie lifted her into the saddle then went back into the stable block and brought out Sultan, Lord Roseby's sturdy liver chestnut hunter.

"Piper's out in the paddock," he explained to Helena, "an' your father thought this one could do with some exercise."

"Good idea," Helena agreed. Jamie's face was still pale, but she didn't want to force him to talk about what he had seen on the beach if he didn't want to.

They followed the path that led east along the River Bredy toward Abbotsbury. It was one of Helena's favorite rides, sheltered by trees with the murmuring of freshwater instead of the relentless crash of waves. The two horses seemed content to walk quietly, their heads nodding with the rhythm of their hoofbeats.

Jamie and Helena rode in silence until the trees stopped and the track curved sharply right to join the road that ran parallel with Chesil Bank from West Bay to Weymouth. Usually they would cross straight over the road and follow a narrow path to the beach to canter back through the reed beds that lay along the edge of the stones. But today Jamie halted and looked back at Helena.

"Do you want to go back the way we've come, Nell?" he asked.

Helena knew he was giving her a chance to stay away from the bank, but the ride so far had soothed her spirits, and the watery sunlight offered more warmth out here than under the shade of the trees. "I don't mind going down to the beach," she said. "They'll have finished by now, won't they?" However calm she was feeling now, she had no wish to see the motionless linen-wrapped shapes being carried away.

Jamie nodded. "Aye, I should think so. Come on, then." He nudged Sultan with his heels so that the gelding trotted over the road and onto the soft grassy path. The land sloped gently down to the sea at this point, the cliffs to the west giving way to low, rolling hills from here to Weymouth.

Snowdrop jogged and snatched at the bridle when her hooves touched the turf.

Helena smiled. "Go on, then, girl." She leaned forward and let the gray mare canter behind Sultan across the meadow and down to the reed bed.

Jamie reined Sultan to a stop on the broad track that ran behind the reeds. "Look, Nell," he said, pointing. "The path's flooded. We'll have to go along the beach." The reed bed had overflowed so that the track was hidden beneath a long stretch of shiny silver floodwater.

"Very well." Helena turned Snowdrop onto the narrow path that led through the reeds to the beach. The mare picked her way carefully over the stones, her head lowered and her nostrils flared. "Come on, Snowdrop, you've done this before," Helena urged her.

"Let her take her time," Jamie called from behind. "The stones will be slippery from the rain an' we're not in any hurry."

Helena twisted around in the saddle to look at him. Sultan was walking more easily than the mare, his enormous hooves treading easily over the fist-sized pebbles.

Suddenly Snowdrop's head shot up and the stones rattled loudly under her hooves as she jumped backward.

Helena grabbed the pommel to keep her balance. "Steady, girl," she soothed, running one hand down Snowdrop's mane. "What's the matter with you?"

She peered over the mare's shoulder, trying to see what had spooked her. A few yards ahead, several charred branches lay in an untidy heap, and the stones around were blackened and sticky with wet ash. Helena frowned. It looked like the remains of a recent fire, but who would have been lighting bonfire in last night's storm?

She glanced up as Jamie rode the big chestnut horse alongside her. His face was set in a grim mask as he looked down at the half-burned branches, and Helena suddenly feared what he was about to tell her.

His troubled brown eyes met hers. "Do you know what this is, Nell?"

Helena shook her head, although a dark suspicion was forming in the back of her mind.

"It's a wreckers' bonfire," Jamie told her, his voice dull with pain. "Last night's shipwreck was no accident. This fire was lit to send the ship onto the reefs."

22

"DID YOU KNOW ALREADY?" said Helena.

Jamie nodded and gazed past her to the slate-gray sea. "It was obvious when we went to the beach this morning."

"How?" Helena asked.

Jamie turned back to her, his eyes bleak with horror. "Nell, there were never meant to be any survivors from the wreck. It wasn't just the sea that killed those men. Some of them had been beaten to death. That's what wreckers do, you see, so they can lay claim to everything that's washed up from the ship." His voice was strangely matter-of-fact, as if the only way he could describe what he had seen was to distance himself from the terrible emotions it stirred up.

Helena felt a dizzying wave of horror sweep over her and she twisted her fingers into Snowdrop's mane, as much to keep her in the saddle as for comfort. "Had the wreckers gone by the time you got there?"

"Yes, an' all the ship's cargo with them. We don't know what the ship was carrying, but that makes no difference. Wreckers would kill for driftwood."

"But why should a bonfire here send the ship onto the reefs?" Helena looked around, confused. "Surely the sailors would see the fire on Beacon Hill and know exactly where the reefs were?"

"They'll have put the beacon out first," Jamie told her. "All the ships know that the reefs lie directly below the beacon, so it's safe to sail to the west of it. But if that fire is moved one mile east, like this bonfire here, the ships sail straight into the reefs."

A picture flashed into Helena's mind of a ship overwhelmed by towering black waves that hurled sails and timber onto the reef again and again until only a few splinters of wood were left. She imagined a handful of sailors fighting the waves to reach the shore, thanking God as they felt stones crunch beneath their feet, only to be attacked in cold blood by the men who had lit the false beacon. What sort of men could wreck ships deliberately and murder innocent men for the sake of a cartload of sea-battered flotsam?

She remembered Mr. Chapman's dark warnings about news of a wrecking gang heading toward Chesil. "Do you think it's the gang from Poole?" she asked.

"Perhaps," said Jamie. "If they'd heard that the gang from Lyme have been caught, they might have thought there was room on this coast for them." He shortened his reins and closed his legs on Sultan's flanks. "Come on, let's get back. We don't want to be out after dark, an' Mr. Chapman will want to know that we've found where the fire was lit."

"Mr. Chapman?" Helena echoed.

Jamie nodded and a glimmer of bleak humor flashed in his eyes. "Aye, 'tis him who will be investigating the wreck."

"That must be why he came to see my father this morning," Helena said. "Well, I hope he finds these men soon, before any more ships are lost."

She nudged Snowdrop forward, and the mare walked on, skirting the remains of the fire with one ear twisted toward it and her nostrils flared. The two horses crunched over the stones until Beacon Hill loomed on the right, where the land sloped steeply up to begin the long line of cliffs to West Bay. Helena looked up at the beacon, the basket of charred kindling a mere speck on the horizon. Who would have thought that one small flame could mean the difference between life and death for a whole shipload of men?

Suddenly Snowdrop lost her footing and stumbled onto her knees. Helena's right leg was jolted off the pommel and she half fell, half slithered off, landing heavily on the stones.

"Are you all right, Nell?" Jamie reined in Sultan and jumped off, ducking under the horse's head to help Helena to her feet.

"I'm fine." She gasped, brushing down her skirt and

straightening her hat. "I wasn't concentrating and I let Snowdrop trip."

Jamie bent down and ran his hand down Snowdrop's forelegs. "She seems all right," he said. Then he stopped, his attention caught by something that lay among the stones. "Hang on, what's this?"

He picked up the object and held it out to Helena. It looked like some sort of laborer's tool.

"Do you think that's what Snowdrop tripped on?" she asked.

"Perhaps," said Jamie. "It's an odd thing to find on the beach, that's for sure." His voice trailed away, and Helena saw the color drain from his face.

She looked more closely at the object. It was a mason's dummy, the short-handled mallet with a round metal head. Helena's heart began to pound so loudly that she could hardly hear her own thoughts. She had seen this particular mallet once before, with the distinctive nail scar running from the crown to the handle. But the soft shine had been dulled by salt-water, and the scar was half hidden under a dark stain that could only be blood.

"That's your uncle's mallet," Helena whispered. "Jamie, he must be one of the wreckers!"

"We can't know that for sure." Jamie tucked the mallet inside his coat and stepped forward to lift Helena into the saddle.

She wrenched away from him and stared in disbelief. "You

know that's Mathias's mallet! And he said himself that his tools went everywhere with him. Why else would it be here?"

Jamie frowned. "Be careful what you're saying, Nell. It's a big thing to accuse a man of murder."

"Does that mean you're not going to take the mallet to Mr. Chapman?" Helena felt as if she was looking at a stranger as she searched Jamie's cold, expressionless face.

"It's not that simple, is it?" Jamie lifted Helena onto Snowdrop before she had time to object, then pulled himself up into Sultan's saddle and kicked the gelding forward.

"I think it is that simple," Helena said quietly as she urged the mare to keep up with Sultan's long strides.

Jamie twisted around to look at her, his expression hard to read in the twilight. The afternoon light was fading now and the white-tipped waves glowed in the dusk. "Mathias Jarrow knows all about the Roseby smugglers, Nell. How could he not, living with us? He knows that my father is the lander, he knows where we keep the cargo, he knows whose horses we use. If I give his name to the customs men, he could bring us all down with him."

Helena shook her head, trying to clear the shock and confusion from her mind. "I still think you should take the mallet to Mr. Chapman. After all, Jarrow won't know it was you who found it."

Jamie reined Sultan to a halt and glared at Helena, more

angry than she had ever seen him. "Is that what you think, Nell? That Jarrow will go quietly when he's arrested an' not offer to trade the smugglers for his wretched neck? Don't try an' tell me what to do. It's nothing to do with you, so just keep out of it."

Too stunned to reply, Helena gazed at Jamie for a moment. Then she kicked Snowdrop into a canter, forcing the mare to stumble over the stones until they reached the track that led away from the beach. Angry tears blurred Helena's eyes, and she drove Snowdrop on faster until they were galloping along the hedge-lined path, branches whipping at Helena's clothes and the mare's breath coming in ragged snorts.

Helena let Snowdrop slow to a trot as they entered the village, suddenly ashamed that she should have taken her frustration out on the gentle horse. Inside, she was still seething. How could Jamie say that the wreckers and the smugglers were nothing to do with her? She knew that they would be risking the smugglers' secret if they reported his uncle to the customs men. But if Mathias Jarrow had really murdered those sailors, he couldn't be allowed to get away with it.

As she entered the yard, Watkins was leading a well-built bay horse into the open-sided barn, and a man in the distinctive navy uniform of a Riding Officer was crossing the yard toward the house. It was Tom Clark, the brother of Robert the thatcher, and his face looked grim and set.

Watkins tied the bay horse beside Mr. Chapman's dun cob and came over to take Snowdrop's bridle. He followed Helena's gaze to the steps, where Tom Clark was just disappearing around the corner. "He's come with an urgent message for Mr. Chapman," he told Helena.

"Is it about the wreckers?"

"I don't know, Lady Helena. He didn't say. Now, let's get this mare inside an' fed. 'Tis long past her dinnertime, an' yours, I dare say."

"Yes, of course," said Helena, allowing the groom to lift her down.

"Jamie not with you?" asked Watkins, looking down the drive.

Helena blushed. "No, he's a little way behind."

The groom shrugged. "Well, he'll take care of Sultan when he gets back. In you go now, my lady, afore you catch a chill." He led Snowdrop away across the cobbles, the gray mare's head hanging low after her hard gallop.

Helena headed for the steps, feeling worn out and cold right through to the bone. She stopped as two figures ran down toward her, the man in front pulling on his greatcoat.

"Good afternoon, Lady Helena," said Roger Chapman, threading his arm through his sleeve in time to lift his hat to her.

"Good afternoon, Mr. Chapman." Helena couldn't resist adding, "Have your men caught the wrecking gang yet?"

The Riding Officer stopped. "Not yet, my lady, but it is only a matter of time. Tom tells me that the remains of a false fire has been spotted eastward along the bank, but we have found no trace of the wreckers themselves yet. Is there something you wish to tell me? Perhaps something you've seen out riding?"

Helena froze. This was her chance to tell Mr. Chapman about the mallet, the bloodstained weapon that would surely lead him straight to one of the wreckers. But then she thought of Jamie, and his fears for the whole village if Jarrow was arrested, and she knew that she couldn't tell Chapman about the mallet, not yet. It was up to Jamie to make that decision.

She shook her head and looked the Riding Officer squarely in the eye. "No, I have nothing to tell," she said.

23

"WILL YOU BE RIDING today, my lady?"

Helena spun around, scraping her elbow painfully on Oriel's stable door. Jamie stood behind her in the middle of the stable yard, holding a head-collar and grooming brush. He looked pale and tired, with dark rings under his eyes.

"Er, no . . . thank you, Jamie," Helena said, rubbing her arm. "I promised I'd help my mother today. I just came down to see Oriel." She felt uncomfortable as she remembered how their ride had ended the day before; from the flat, hard tone of Jamie's voice, he hadn't forgotten their quarrel either. "Is everything all right?" she asked hesitantly, thinking that he seemed even more troubled than yesterday.

Jamie's face was an unreadable mask. "Oh, aye, I'm sure everything's all right, now you've done your duty."

"What do you mean?" Helena stepped forward and laid one hand on his arm, but he pulled away.

"I should have known you wouldn't understand," he said. He shrugged, and this suggestion of indifference hurt Helena far more than the ice that dripped from his words.

"I don't know what you're talking about," she whispered. The wind tugged a strand of hair free from her hat so that it whipped against her cheek, but she didn't make any attempt to tuck it back again.

Jamie glared at her, his brown eyes defying her to argue with him. "I know you told Chapman about the mallet," he said. "The customs men have been at our house all night asking questions about Jarrow an' searching through everything. They even woke up the twins. What are the girls supposed to know, for heaven's sake? But it were too late. Jarrow never came home yesterday. Looks like he knows he's a hunted man. We'll just have to hope he doesn't go to the customs men first an' turn King's evidence."

Helena's mind reeled. She recalled Tom Clark's errand yesterday that had summoned Mr. Chapman from the manor. He must have found out something else, apart from the mallet, that would lead them to Jamie's uncle. Helena looked at Jamie, her eyes pleading. "I promise, I didn't tell Mr. Chapman anything," she said, but his expression remained hard and disbelieving.

A rush of anger flared in Helena that her best friend should be so quick to distrust her. "Look, believe me or not, I don't care. The Riding Officers have been pursuing these wreckers for weeks. Why shouldn't they discover things for themselves? You know full well that Jarrow was involved, and it's only a matter of time before he's caught. And you should know by now that I wouldn't do anything to put the smugglers in danger."

She pushed past Jamie and marched across the stable yard, but she wasn't quick enough that she didn't hear Jamie's parting words, murmured quietly after her.

"Just because you know about what we do, Nell, doesn't make you one of us."

HELENA FOUND HER MOTHER in the back hall talking to Will's nursemaid. Lady Roseby was wearing the long calico apron again and her face looked tired. She turned when she saw Helena and smiled. "There you are, Helena. Please could you look after Will today? Mary has sent a message to say that she won't be coming in, so I've asked Charity to help Mrs. Clark with the washing."

Helena nodded, feeling her heart sink as she realized that Jamie's mother, Mary, had probably been kept at home by the customs men who were looking for her brother. She blinked fiercely to force away the tears that pricked behind her eyes.

"Are you feeling all right, my dear?" asked Lady Roseby.

Helena wondered if her mother knew the reason Mary Polstock had stayed home today. "Yes, Mama. It's just the wind making my eyes water. Of course I'll look after Will."

"Stand and deliver!" shouted a small voice. "Your money or your life!"

She turned to see her brother charging down the passageway toward her, his boots drumming against the stone flags as he galloped his wooden hobbyhorse at breakneck speed. He skidded to a halt at the foot of the staircase, his cheeks flushed and his blue eyes glowing with excitement.

"Look at my horse, Nell! I've called her Bess after Dick Turpin's horse!" he declared, stroking the hobbyhorse's plump hessian cheek.

"Do you think Bess would like to come to the parlor and listen to a story about a man called Robinson Crusoe?" Helena asked, thinking that she could read the chapters her governess had asked her to.

"Does he have a horse, too?"

Helena smiled. "No, but he has some goats. They're wild at the moment, but he's going to tame them."

"That sounds like a good story," said Will. He wheeled his hobbyhorse around. "Race you to the parlor, Nell!"

THE MORNING PASSED SWIFTLY, with Helena curled on the sofa, the book balanced on her knees, and Will sitting on the floor beside her, round eyed as he listened to the story. The fire leapt unevenly in the grate as the wind whistled down the chimney and sent fingers of smoke reaching into the room. Helena found herself wishing she could join Mr. Crusoe on his desert island, to escape not just the relentless cold drafts but also whatever was going on in the village at the moment. Pictures slid into her mind of the Polstocks' cottage being searched by grim-faced customs men, of Mary trying to comfort her little girls who didn't understand what their uncle had done wrong.

"Keep reading, Nell!"

Will's voice roused Helena from her troubled thoughts, and she found her place on the page and started reading again. There was nothing she could do to help Jamie's family now.

Helena and her brother ate dinner with Lady Roseby alone, as their father wasn't due back until later. When they had finished, Will slipped out of the dining room and returned with his hobbyhorse. "I don't want to listen to stories anymore," he announced. "Can we go for a walk? Please, Nell. Bess wants to go outside too," he added, brandishing the wooden hobbyhorse at her.

Helena shook her head. "The grass might be wet and I don't think Bess would appreciate getting muddy hooves," she explained, glancing down at Bess's polished wooden stem. Then, seeing her brother's face fall, she said, "But that doesn't mean you and I can't go out. We could pretend to be riding horses just like Bess. You can be Dick Turpin and I could be the sergeant chasing you!"

Will's face broke into a smile. "That sounds fun. Shall we go now?"

Lady Roseby pushed back her chair and laid one hand on his shoulder. "Some fresh air sounds like a very good idea. Perhaps you'd like to go and see if Mrs. Gordon has some apples for you to take? I'm sure if you don't eat them, Bess will!" When the little boy had gone, Helena's mother said, "A walk should make him sleep well tonight! But don't be out too long; you don't want to get caught if it starts raining."

"Yes, Mama," said Helena. She went upstairs to fetch a shawl and repin her hair. As she stared at her reflection in the looking glass, she wondered if Mr. Chapman had found Jarrow yet. Would Jamie's uncle really try to save his neck by betraying the Roseby smugglers?

Helena shook her head impatiently. News of any arrests would reach the manor soon enough. Taking a shawl from her linen chest, she ran downstairs and collected Will from the kitchen, his pockets bulging with apples.

They crossed the gardens toward Home Farm, past the fallen branch that would be cleared for firewood before long. Harry Savage was in the farmyard, leading a honey-colored cow into the barn. He lifted his cap politely as they passed. "Good day to you, Lady Helena, Master Will."

Will let go of Helena's hand and raced over to the barn, scrambling halfway up the gate to peer inside. "Are you putting all your cows indoors, Harry?" he asked.

The farmer smiled. "That's right, Master Will. There's

another storm coming an' they don't like being outside in bad weather." He paused and looked at Helena, his forehead creasing with concern. "You're not going far, are you, my lady? That's a nasty wind blowing an' it'll bring rain afore long, I'm sure."

"We won't be long," Helena assured him. "I just thought we'd go as far as St. Luke's Chapel." She turned to look west along the cliffs where thick black clouds were swelling on the horizon. "We certainly don't want to get a soaking from those," she agreed. "Come on, Will, let's get going." She held out her hand, and her brother jumped down from the gate and trotted back to her.

Helena led Will up the stony track that led out of the farm-yard and across the fields toward St. Luke's Wood, a copse of ancient gnarled oak trees that stood on the sheltered inland slopes below Beacon Hill. There had once been a monastery here, and Helena loved to shut her eyes and imagine the robed monks shuffling along the flint path to and from the village. All that remained of the religious house was the chapel and that was in a far from perfect state, with crumbling walls and half its roof missing so that the nave was roofed by the sky. No one worshipped there now, but there was a stillness about the ruins that reminded Helena of all the years of prayer and study that had gone on within the pale stone walls.

The track that led up to the summit of Beacon Hill ran

alongside the copse. As they neared the wood, Helena heard hoofbeats coming toward them. She stopped and looked up the hill, holding her hair out of her eyes with one hand.

A black-and-white pony appeared around the corner, plodding steadily with its head down and its quarters hunched against the wind. Its rider wore a greatcoat with the collar turned up to his chin and a broad-brimmed hat pulled low over his ears. It was Zachary Heddle, the parish constable from Far Cheney.

He raised one hand in greeting when he saw Helena and her brother. "Good day to you, Lady Helena." He reined his pony to a halt and looked down at her, frowning. "'Tis no weather for you to be out," he told her. "I've just been up to light the beacon. Just in time, too. While I was up there I saw a ship coming past Portland toward West Bay. Let's hope they make the harbor afore the storm sets in."

Helena looked up the track and saw the orange flame flickering in its wire cage on top of the hill. "Look, Will," she said, bending down and pointing. "There's the beacon to tell the ships where the reefs are." She straightened up and smiled at the elderly parish constable. "It's all right, Mr. Heddle, we won't be out long."

"Very good, my lady." He touched the brim of his hat and clapped his heels against the sides of his pony. "Let's be getting home, Patch." The pony jerked up its head, then ambled off down the track.

Will tugged at Helena's hand. "Come on, Nell, I want to see the chapel."

"All right, but just for a moment, then we must go home. We don't want to get caught in the rain." She allowed herself to be led across the track and into the wood. The path ran past a huge oak tree, the biggest Helena had ever seen, that sat like a guardian at the entrance to the copse. Above their heads, the branches clashed like brittle swords, and the light around them faded so that it felt like night had come in the middle of the afternoon.

Helena stopped, the hair on her neck prickling in alarm. She was certain she had heard voices above the din of the windblown branches. Men shouting, more than one, their words muffled by the wind. She peered ahead. Was that a lantern glowing among the trees? It seemed to be coming from the ruined chapel.

Suddenly there was a crashing sound beside them like a deer taking flight. Helena turned and saw a man running away, his dark coat flapping like raven's wings and his leggings flashing creamy white in the half-light. He glanced back over his shoulder, and at that moment a bolt of lightning lit up the trees, freezing everything in a harsh white glare.

Helena felt the ground sway beneath her feet. She had seen that narrow, long-nosed profile before, watching the waves from the Knoll on the night she had gone to warn the smugglers.

"Why's that man running away from us?" asked Will, puzzled.

"I don't know," Helena answered, forcing herself to stay calm. "Come on, let's go home. It's not safe to be in the woods when there's lightning." She grasped Will's hand and led him quickly back the way they had come. Her heart was beating so hard, her legs felt unsteady, so that she slipped on the muddy path and nearly fell.

"Careful, Nell!" exclaimed Will. "You nearly pulled me over then."

"Sorry," Helena gasped. "I'm all right now. Keep going." But she was far from feeling all right. There had been enough light to recognize the long-nosed man this time, running through the woods. It was Mathias Jarrow, Jamie's uncle, whose blood-stained mallet they had found on the beach. The voices and the half-glimpsed lantern could mean only one thing. The wreckers were hiding in the ruined chapel.

HALF RUNNING, GASPING FOR breath, Helena dragged Will back across the fields, through the farmyard, and into the safety of the garden.

Will stopped just inside the gate and bent over, hugging his ribs. "I've got a stitch," he complained. "Why did we have to run all the way back? Was it something to do with that man?"

"No, not at all," Helena soothed him hastily. "I thought we might get caught in the storm, that's all." She didn't want Will to say anything to her mother about what they had seen in the wood, not until she'd had a chance to tell Jamie. Whatever he thought of her, Helena was not going to go straight to the Riding Officers. She knew that he deserved to know first where his uncle was hiding.

She took Will to the kitchen and left him with Mrs. Gordon, who was making a syllabub for dinner and was only too happy to let the little boy scrape out the bowl. Then she ran down to the stable yard, wrapping her shawl more closely around her shoulders as the wind threatened to snatch it away.

Drops of rain spat against her face like pebbles, and the beech trees behind the stable block sighed and bowed as if the weight of the gale were making their knees buckle.

The yard was empty, but lanterns glowed in the windows of the stable block. Helena found Jamie leading Snowdrop into her stall. He squeezed past the mare, patting her on the rump, and stopped in surprise when he saw Helena. "What are you doing here?" he said, frowning. "I don't have time to talk— there's all the horses to bring in from the paddock."

"Jamie, I've got something really important to tell you."

"Well, you can make yourself useful an' help me get Monument an' Fleet in first."

He threw a head-collar toward her, and Helena stumbled backward as she caught it. "Where's Watkins?" she asked.

"Gone to Abbotsbury with Isaiah to collect a load of feed. Come on." Jamie led the way across the yard, walking so briskly that Helena had to break into a run to keep up with him. The heavy leather head-collar dragged against her skirt, and the wind tore her hair from under her hat and ruffled it into her eyes so that she could hardly see. "Jamie, wait!" she puffed. "You must listen to me. I think your uncle is hiding in the old chapel in St. Luke's Wood."

Jamie stopped dead and turned to her. "What? How do you know?"

"Will and I went for a walk there just now. I heard voices

and saw a lantern, then a man ran past us, and I'm sure it was Jarrow," Helena explained breathlessly, one hand pressed against her aching side.

Jamie frowned. "Who else have you told?"

"No one!"

"Not your friend Mr. Chapman?" His eyes narrowed suspiciously.

"For goodness' sake, Jamie! Of course not! And I didn't tell him about the mallet, either. But you can't let the wreckers get away, not after what they did."

A flash of lightning lit up Jamie's face for a moment, deathly pale under his brown hair. "We won't let the wreckers get away, Nell," he promised. "As soon as we've finished here, I'll go an' tell my dad what you saw in the wood. He'll know what to do. You have to trust me, Nell," he added seriously.

Helena nodded, the strength of the wind as they reached the open paddocks making it impossible to speak. She slipped through the gate and went over to Monument. The gray horse stood with his head high, the whites of his eyes showing in alarm.

"Easy, lad," Helena soothed, stretching up to slip the head-collar behind his ears. Behind her, Jamie was struggling to catch Fleet, who had been spooked by the storm and jumped away every time he tried to put the head-collar on.

As she struggled with the buckle, Helena's gaze fell on the

flattened bulk of Beacon Hill, a dark brown silhouette against the slate-gray sky. Something was wrong, but at first she couldn't think what. She narrowed her eyes, trying to work out what was making her uneasy. Then she realized. The flame in the beacon had gone out.

Helena wheeled around to Jamie, who had finally managed to catch Fleet. "Jamie, look!" she cried above the noise of the wind. "The beacon!" She pointed past Monument's nose, making the gelding spring backward.

Jamie stared at the horizon. "They've put it out, Nell! They must be planning another wreck tonight!" He turned toward the gate, dragging Fleet behind him. "Come on, we have to find my father."

Helena pulled at Monument's leading rein, forcing the horse to jog beside her. "Jamie, wait!" she shouted. "That might take too long. We need to relight the beacon."

On the path ahead, Fleet jolted to a standstill and Jamie looked over his shoulder. "What do you mean?"

Helena led Monument alongside. "There's a ship out there right now. The wreckers might have lit the false beacon further along the beach, but if we relight the beacon, the sailors will know which way to go."

"How are we going to do that?"

Helena looked at him, determination making her suddenly clear headed. "I could do it. I could take Oriel."

Jamie shook his head and clicked Fleet forward again. "It's too dangerous," he said. "The wreckers might catch you."

"No, they won't," Helena insisted. "Oriel's too fast for them."

"Well, if someone's goin' to ride up to Beacon Hill in this storm, it should be me," he argued.

"Stop wasting time! Let me take Oriel, I've ridden him before. And you know better than me where to find your father—and what to tell him."

Jamie glanced down at the ground, and Helena suddenly feared that he was about to say they couldn't do anything because of what Jarrow knew about the Roseby smugglers. "We can't let them wreck another ship," she added, while behind her Monument threw his head up against a gust of wind, jerking the lead rope taut in Helena's hands.

Jamie looked at Helena. "I know," he replied. "Come on, let's take these two inside an' get Oriel ready."

They led Monument and Fleet across the yard at a trot, their hooves clattering on the cobbles. When each horse was tied in its stall, Helena ran to the tack room to fetch Oriel's saddle and bridle. She was just lifting down the bridle when Jamie appeared in the doorway carrying a heap of pale cloth.

"Here, it'll be easier if you wear these," he said, thrusting the bundle toward her.

Helena realized it was a pair of breeches. "Thanks," she said briefly. At any other time she would have been thrilled at the thought of riding properly astride, free from the heavy skirts that chafed her knees.

"Put them on in here while I tack up the stallion," Jamie ordered her. "Watkins is up at the house so we should have time to get you gone before he comes back." He reached behind her and picked up a small metal box from a ledge above the stove. "Here's the tinderbox. You know how to use it?"

Helena nodded. She tucked the tinderbox securely inside her jacket, where it felt cold and sharp edged against her ribs. At least she would notice if it fell out, she thought. Jamie took the bridle from her and picked up a man's saddle, then went out of the tack room, closing the door behind him. In the soft orange light cast by the stove, Helena quickly undid her skirt and let it fall to the floor. She pulled on Jamie's breeches, feeling a moment's curiosity in the smooth material that gripped her legs and felt so much lighter than a heavy, constricting skirt. The breeches were far too long and gaped at the waist, but Helena rolled up the ankles and turned the waistband over until she was confident they wouldn't slip down. Then she ran out of the tack room, feeling the tinderbox bang against her side.

Jamie had already saddled Oriel, and he led the stallion out, his face serious. "The wind'll be worst on the cliffs," he told her, "so take the track through Home Farm an' go across the fields

to the inland side of the hill. The same way we took Piper an'
Snowdrop, remember? Once the beacon is lit, come straight
back, you hear?"

"Yes, I will," said Helena. She paused. "Jamie, will your father
fetch the Riding Officers? Even . . . even if it means that Jarrow
is arrested?"

His brown eyes met hers steadily. "My father will do whatever he thinks right, Nell. He won't let the wreckers go unpunished."

Helena nodded. "I know," she said. She held Jamie's gaze for
a moment, then reached up and grasped the saddle with both
hands. She bent her left leg just as she had seen her father
do, and Jamie gripped her knee and hoisted her easily into the
saddle. The leather felt hard and cold under the thin breeches,
but Helena knew she was a hundred times more secure in the
saddle than when she wore her thick skirt. Oriel shifted
underneath her, and she revelled in being able to feel every
movement of his spine and shoulders. She gathered up the
reins and looked down at Jamie.

"Ready?" he asked, squinting up at her through the rain that
was falling harder now.

"Ready," she replied.

"Then go, an' Godspeed," said Jamie.

He stepped back, and Helena dug her heels hard into
Oriel's flanks. The stallion leapt forward, snatching at the bit,

galloping flat out in just a few strides. This time, Helena was ready for the strength in his long strides and she crouched low in the saddle, gripping hard with both knees. She let Oriel follow the path through the garden until just before they reached the paddocks, then pulled hard on the left rein to send him along the edge of the garden to Home Farm.

Through the farmyard they raced, Oriel's hooves clattering over the stones and suddenly going silent again as they reached the turf track across the fields. The wind and the rain seemed to fade away, and Helena was acutely aware of the constant dialogue between her hands and Oriel's mouth, her heels and his flanks, as he listened for the tiniest of commands. It was almost as if the stallion were an extension of her own body as he swerved to avoid a hole, then gathered his quarters beneath him to climb the hill.

When St. Luke's Wood loomed ahead of them, a surging mass of windblown trees, Helena leaned to the right. Oriel turned with her, his hooves striking unevenly against the stony track until he found his stride again. Now the hill fort lay just a few hundred yards ahead.

"Come on, boy," Helena whispered into the thick black mane that foamed around her face. "We're nearly there!"

And then there were shouts from the shadows in front of them, and a gunshot cracked through the air. It was the wreckers.

Oriel shied, almost losing his footing on the stones. Helena looked up, terror thickening her blood to ice, even as she instinctively shortened the reins and clapped her heels against Oriel's sides to keep him going. She could just make out several figures running down the track toward her. They must be on their way back from lighting the false fire, she realized. If she kept going this way, she would run right into them and risk either her or Oriel being shot.

Dead ahead of her was the hedge that she and Piper had swerved from. It was over five feet high and nearly as wide, bristling with thorny branches that flicked like whips in the gale. To jump the hedge in broad daylight would take nerves of flint; to jump it in twilight like this would be madness. But it was the quickest route to the summit, and the wreckers would not be able to follow that way.

Oriel's ears flickered and his head went up, but he kept on galloping. Helena measured the steadily decreasing distance between the horse and the hedge. Oriel's strides were a shade longer than Piper's, and he would need to sit back on his hocks to clear the height of the hedge. But she didn't want to interfere with the stallion's pace too much in case he became unbalanced. She sat deep in the saddle, closing her legs against his sides. The shouts to her left grew louder, and another gunshot went off, crashing above her head with a din that left her ears ringing.

Three strides, two strides, and the hedge reared up in front of them, even taller than Helena remembered. But Piper had shied away because she had doubted him. The chestnut gelding had sensed her uncertainty and become uncertain himself, just as her father had warned her. If Helena made it clear that she trusted Oriel to jump the hedge, then he would. Taking a deep breath, Helena gripped the reins even tighter and clapped her heels against his sides.

Oriel didn't falter for a second. His powerful hindquarters bunched underneath him, and he soared into the air. Helena thrust her hands forward to keep his head free and bent forward over his withers, feeling the wind rush against her face and branches clutch at her legs as Oriel cleared the hedge by inches.

Then they were on the other side, landing with a jolt that almost toppled Helena out of the saddle. She pushed herself back, her hands on his neck and mane, and kicked the stallion up the slope. "Come on, Oriel!" she cried, the wind snatching her words away.

The horse stretched out his neck and galloped on, scrambling up the steep hill with tireless thrusting legs. The shouts on the other side of the hedge were lost to the storm, and there were no more gunshots.

The ground flattened out in front of them and Helena realized they had reached the summit. Oriel leapt down the ramparts and fell into a trot, his breath coming in loud snorts. Helena urged him back to a canter, reaching inside her jacket with her left hand for the tinderbox. The beacon loomed out of the darkness like a bleak, leafless tree overlooking the long stretch of Chesil Bank.

Helena reined Oriel to a halt beside the wooden post and looked down at the shore. There was no moon, but she could just make out the heaving black waves crashing in a rush of white froth along the bank. It was high tide and the reef was invisible, but Helena knew that it was waiting just under the surface, below Beacon Hill. She turned her head to the east, peering along the bank toward Weymouth and Portland. Her heart seemed to stop beating for a moment. There was a bright orange flame flickering against the dark gray stones, sending out a signal as clear as day. The wreckers had lit their false beacon.

Helena felt a surge of rage. She would not let them wreck another ship! Oriel had brought her this far; all she had to do was relight the beacon.

And then, further out, she saw a glimmer of white sail, rising and falling on the angry sea. It was a ship, and it was heading straight toward her.

25

HELENA HELD THE REINS in one hand and stretched up with the other, praying that the wreckers had doused the beacon with soil, not water. To her relief, she could feel a layer of earth covering the kindling.

"Steady, Oriel," she murmured as she brushed the worst of the soil off the kindling. The sticks were still mercifully dry and she rattled them together to shake off the remaining soil, making it rain onto her head in a gritty shower.

Then she reached into her jacket for the tinderbox. Her fingers were stiff with cold, and she nearly dropped it as she fumbled with the lid. Oriel sidestepped restlessly underneath her, and she spent precious seconds calming him and bringing him back to the beacon. With the reins looped over one wrist so that she could use both hands, Helena opened the lid of the tinderbox. At once the scrap of linen was caught by the wind and threatened to blow away. Helena quickly anchored it with her thumb, making the linen flutter madly like a trapped moth.

With her other hand, she struck the flint against the steel. The first spark failed in an instant and the second lasted not much longer, leaving a faint white glow on the inside of Helena's eyes. Cursing, she struck again, knowing that all this time the ship was sailing trustingly toward the reef, guided by the false fire.

The linen flared at last and Helena held the tinderbox up to the beacon. As she stretched up, her thumb slipped. To her horror, the burning scrap of cloth was snatched away by the wind and hurled over the edge of the hill, glowing briefly like a firefly before disappearing altogether. For one dreadful moment, Helena thought she was going to be sick. Then a burst of lightning turned the churning sea to silver, so that the masts of the ship looked like jet black fingers thrust up from the waves.

Helena clenched her jaw in fury. That ship would not be lost! Closing her legs against Oriel's sides to keep him still, she wrenched open her riding jacket and pulled her shirt out of the waistband of the breeches. She grasped the cloth in both hands and ripped a strip off the hem. It wasn't the usual sort of tinderbox kindling, but at least it was dry. With her hand closed protectively over the precious scrap of material, she kicked with her right leg to send Oriel's hindquarters around until they were facing inland. Now the rain spat against Helena's back, so that she could shield the cloth in the tinderbox while she struck the flint again.

Her hands were shaking so much that she missed the steel completely with her first attempt, catching her wrist instead so that a jolt of pain shot up to her elbow. Helena ignored the beads of blood that welled up from the graze and tried again. This time a spark leapt off the metal and singed the cloth. Helena curved her left hand around the tinderbox, not daring to breathe as she willed the material to catch light. The singe mark spread, scoring a thin brown line up the cloth until suddenly the fire took hold and started to devour the material with a tiny orange tongue.

Wedging one corner of the cloth under her thumb, Helena reached up to the beacon again. She thrust the flame between the bars of the cage, scraping her grazed wrist painfully against the metal. "Please, God, let it catch light," she prayed.

Suddenly there was a flash of bright yellow, and a flame shot up through the kindling. Helena jumped and dropped the tinderbox, so that it fell out of sight among the shadows on the ground. Hastily scooping up the reins to stop Oriel from leaping away, Helena looked up at the beacon. The fire was steadily taking hold, licking the branches with a hungry yellow tongue. Brighter and brighter it flared, until Helena could no longer keep Oriel close to the flame, and she let him canter a short distance away.

Then she reined him in and looked past the beacon, out to

sea. The wind whistled around her bare skin where her jacket hung open and her ripped shirt was still untucked, but Helena didn't care. She had relit the beacon. Surely now the ship would be saved?

A flash of lightning lit up the coast for a brief heartbeat and Helena saw the ship again, even closer to the shore now, and dangerously close to the reef. Was it just her imagination, or had she seen dark silhouettes frantically pulling at the sails? She peered through the darkness, desperately trying to tell if the sailors had seen the beacon and were turning their ship around. All the time, the waves lifted the vessel and let it drop again like a child's toy.

Another glare of lightning, and this time Helena saw the mainsail sagging against the mast, while on the other side of the ship the wind snatched at a billowing topsail as it was hoisted by tiny figures on the deck. They had seen the beacon and were trying to change their course.

"Please, God, give them strength," Helena whispered. There was nothing more she could do now. If the sailors could just steer their ship for another quarter mile, they would reach the harbor at West Bay. The wreckers would not have their cargo tonight.

Suddenly worn out, Helena kicked Oriel into a trot toward a gap in the ramparts at the far end of the hill fort. This was the longer way home, along the track that led around the flank of the hill. She would have to trust that the wreckers had gone because she couldn't jump the hedge downhill. Oriel stumbled as his hooves struck stones, and Helena let the tired horse walk, keeping the reins short so that he didn't get unbalanced. She wondered if Jamie had found his father by now. She remembered the seriousness in his expression as he had promised her that the wreckers would not go unpunished. Did that mean Samuel Polstock would take the law into his own hands and hunt down the wreckers himself? He would have the support of every man in Roseby if he wanted, Helena knew.

A sudden burst of gunfire from the woods below made Oriel stop and throw up his head in alarm. Flashes of yellow appeared among the trees where muskets were reloaded and fired again, and angry shouts were raised above the noise of the wind. Helena felt her stomach turn over. Had the villagers attacked the wreckers' hideout?

Oriel reared with the next volley of gunfire, and Helena threw herself forward over his neck until he landed back on his forelegs, his whole body quivering with fear.

"Easy, lad, easy," she soothed, closing her legs against him and making him walk on. The stallion's flanks felt hot and soaked with sweat, and the reins were slippery with foam. She kept him close to the side of the hill, watching the track ahead as it ran past the woods. It was the quickest way home, but Helena had no intention of getting herself or Oriel shot.

Suddenly several figures crashed out of the trees onto the track. Helena froze, Oriel stopping the second he felt her muscles tense. Some of them were men from the village—she recognized Samuel Polstock's broad-shouldered silhouette and the tall, fair-headed figure of Harry Savage. But there were other men among them, neither wreckers nor smugglers. They wore scarlet coats and distinctive flat-topped caps, and short swords hung from their broad white belts. These men were dragoons, soldiers stationed along the coast to help the Riding Officers.

Helena's mind whirled. Had Jamie's father fetched the customs men so they could attack the wreckers' hideout together? And if the wreckers had been caught, how long would it be before Mathias Jarrow betrayed the Roseby smugglers?

Suddenly there was a clatter of hoofbeats, and a stocky pale-colored horse cantered up the track toward Helena.

"Who goes there?" shouted the rider, reining his horse to a standstill.

Helena had recognized the short-legged cob before she heard the familiar voice. Now she kicked Oriel forward until she knew the Riding Officer would be able to see her.

"Lady Helena!" Roger Chapman sounded as if he could

hardly believe his eyes. "What are you doing here?"

Helena's throat suddenly tightened, making it hard to speak. "I—I saw that the beacon had gone out," she stammered. "I went to relight it."

"What?" The Riding Officer peered past Helena to the top of the hill where the fire sent its steady orange signal into the night. He swore disbelievingly under his breath and turned back to her, his face a pale disk in the darkness. "You put yourself in great danger by doing that, Lady Helena. Did you know the wreckers were hiding in the woods?"

Helena nodded.

"As did the rest of Roseby, it seems." Roger Chapman nodded his head toward the men that had gathered at the edge of the wood. "When I arrived with the dragoons, we found some of the villagers had already surrounded the ruined chapel. But we were glad of their help. This was a desperate gang of men."

Helena twisted a lock of Oriel's mane between her fingers. She had to know what was going to happen now. Was Jamie's uncle going to reveal the smugglers' secret? "Were all the wreckers caught?" she forced herself to ask.

"Caught or shot." There was a note of blank finality in the Riding Officer's voice.

"Shot?"

Roger Chapman looked grave. "Three of them were killed

when they tried to escape. One of them was a man called Mathias Jarrow. It's his trail we've been following from Weymouth. We had word from a Riding Officer there yesterday that he was involved with the wrecking gang and might have come to stay with his sister in Roseby. This afternoon we found a map with the ruined chapel marked on it among his belongings."

Helena shut her eyes for a moment. God forgive that she should ever feel relieved by the news of a man's death, but at least this meant that Jarrow could never betray the Roseby smugglers to save his own neck.

When she opened her eyes again, Roger Chapman was looking at her with an unreadable expression on his face. "Come, Lady Helena, it's time you went home." He turned his dun cob and started to walk down the hill.

Oriel fell into step beside them, Helena too exhausted to do much more than keep upright in the saddle. Further along the track, the men from Roseby were making their way home, their heads bowed against the rain. Among the men who remained at the edge of the woods, Helena could see that the wreckers had been roped together. Scarlet-coated dragoons surrounded them, their muskets held ready in case any of the prisoners was foolish enough to try to escape.

She caught a glimpse of the face of one of them, a man her

father's age whose hair was long and beard ragged as if he had been living outdoors for a while. He wore no jacket, in spite of the cold wind, and his shirt and breeches were stained with mud and splatters of something darker and more sinister. He must have sensed Helena looking at him for he turned to meet her gaze, his eyes flint pale in the shadows. Helena flinched but didn't look away. Instead, she remembered the horror she had felt when she had watched the ship struggle in the waves beneath the unlit beacon, and her mind burned with the thought of where this man would end up, in the dock with shackles on his hands and feet.

Roger Chapman reined Noah to a halt beside the track that led across the fields to the manor house. "Will you be all right from here, Lady Helena?"

"Yes, thank you," she replied.

He followed Helena's gaze and added, "The law will take care of them now, you can be sure of that."

"Thank goodness they were caught before they could wreck any more ships," said Helena.

"You did well tonight, Lady Helena, to relight the beacon." Mr. Chapman studied her in silence for a moment, and Helena winced as she felt his gaze take in her mud-spattered breeches and torn shirt. "You are a most unusual young lady," he commented. "You seem willing to take great risks for the sake of other people."

Helena gripped the reins tighter. Was Mr. Chapman talking about the sailors on the ship below the unlit beacon—or the smugglers she had warned on the night he saw her on the cliff top?

"I am as relieved as you are that the wreckers have been caught," said Mr. Chapman quietly. "But my work does not end here. I still have a duty to catch the smugglers that operate along this coast. You do understand that, don't you?"

Helena forced herself to meet his eyes. "Yes, Mr. Chapman, I understand," she said honestly. She hadn't imagined for one moment that catching the wreckers would make the Riding Officer any less determined to find the smugglers.

Suddenly Roger Chapman shot her an unexpected smile. "I am glad to see that the stallion is safe to be ridden," he remarked. "Perhaps Lord Roseby will keep him after all."

Helena nodded, wondering what her father would say when he found out she had been riding Oriel.

They were interrupted by a shout from behind as the sandy-haired Riding Officer, Evan Price, rode up on his gray horse. "We're ready to take the prisoners away," he announced.

"I'll be with you presently," said Roger Chapman. He glanced back at Helena. "Good-bye, my lady." He raised his hat, then wheeled his cob around and trotted down the track toward the waiting dragoons.

Helena gathered up the reins and turned Oriel across the fields toward the manor house. The stallion seemed to know where he was going and Helena sat limply in the saddle as he picked his way over the turf, his head lowered against the rain. Her hair had come loose from the pins long before she had reached the beacon, and now it clung uncomfortably to her shoulders and sent icy drips down the back of her neck. The ill-fitting breeches were rubbing the inside of her knees, and every muscle in her legs ached.

A faint glow and the sound of anxious voices came from the stable yard behind the manor house. As Helena and Oriel rounded the corner, the voices fell silent. Blinking against the sudden glare of bright lanterns, Helena saw her mother rush forward, a man's greatcoat thrown over her gown.

"Oh, Helena, thank goodness you're safe!"

Helena let the reins fall onto Oriel's neck, suddenly so tired that she could hardly stay in the saddle. Her father noticed her unsteadiness and stepped forward to half lift, half catch her as she slid to the ground.

"Nell, Nell," he said, hugging her close. "What on earth were you thinking of?"

Helena twisted her head to look up at him, the wool of his jacket warm and comforting against her cheek. "I had to relight the beacon," she explained, "to save the ship from the wreckers. You do understand, don't you?"

"I think I do," Lord Roseby said quietly. Then he straightened up and watched Jamie come forward to take hold of

Oriel's bridle and lead him into his stable. "It looks like you two have got the measure of that horse," Helena's father commented. "I take it that today wasn't the first time you rode him?"

"No, Papa," Helena admitted. "Please don't blame Jamie. It was all my idea. Oriel is wonderful, not dangerous at all, and he gallops faster than you could imagine!"

Lord Roseby raised his eyebrows. "He seems to have looked after you well enough tonight, young lady. But I'm not impressed that you disobeyed me again."

Helena met his gaze steadily. "I'm sorry, Papa. But I wouldn't have done it if I hadn't been so sure that you were wrong about Oriel. He's a good horse—you just need to trust him."

Her father smiled and reached out to brush a lock of wet hair away from Helena's cheek. "I think you've managed to prove that, Nell."

Jamie reappeared from Oriel's stable, his face flushed in the light from the lanterns. "Are you all right, my lady?" he asked, coming over to Helena.

"I'm fine," she promised. "And so is Oriel. Jamie, we jumped the hedge on Beacon Hill! You know, the one I didn't jump on Piper." She glanced guiltily at her father, but he didn't seem to have noticed. "They caught the wreckers," Helena went on quietly.

Jamie nodded, his face deathly pale. "Aye, I heard the shots. The dragoons came racing through here not long after my pa left, so I guessed there'd be enough men to surround the chapel." His eyes searched hers for an answer to the question he could not ask.

Helena took a deep breath. "Mr. Chapman told me that some of the wreckers were shot, trying to escape. Y—your uncle was among them."

Jamie's expression gave away none of the relief Helena knew he must be feeling. "That's the end of that, then," he said softly.

"Yes, that's the end of that," she echoed.

Lady Roseby stepped forward, shrouded inside her husband's greatcoat like a slender, pale-feathered bird. "Come inside now, Nell," she ordered. "Jamie will see to Oriel. I know what you did was brave, but I want you to promise you'll never do something as dangerous as this again." Helena nodded, and her mother's face relaxed in an unexpected smile. "And next time you take the stallion out, you might have to ride him sidesaddle. Think what your aunt Emma would say if she could see you now!"

Helena glanced down at her soaked, mud-spattered breeches and grinned.

"Yes, in you go," agreed her father. He looked at Oriel's stable door, his eyes narrowed thoughtfully. The stallion was invisible in the shadows at the back of the stable, but a faint crunching sound told Helena that he was already tucking into his hay.

Lord Roseby turned back to Helena. "You know, if Oriel's as fast as you say he is, perhaps I should think about putting him into the race. He's certainly fit enough if he can gallop all the way to Beacon Hill like that."

Helena stared at her father in delight. Oriel was going to be entered in the Bridport horse race! What better way to prove once and for all that he belonged at Roseby? Then she frowned. "But what about Piper?"

Lord Roseby smiled. "Oh, I still intend to ride Piper. I couldn't let all that training go to waste, could I?"

"So who will ride Oriel?"

Her father looked serious for a moment. "'Tis a pity that too many eyebrows would be raised if a young lady were to ride in the race," he said. "I'm very proud of you, Nell. It took courage and skill to ride the stallion like you did today, and I know few men who could have done the same."

Helena felt herself blush.

Then, to her surprise, her father turned to the stable lad who was standing beside them, Oriel's bridle hooked over one shoulder and the saddle in his arms. "Jamie, would you be willing to ride the stallion? After all, you've done a grand job with training Piper."

Jamie's face lit up. "Certainly, my lord," he declared. "'Twould be an honor, an' I'll do my best by Oriel."

"I know you will," said Lord Roseby, nodding.

Helena stepped forward and flung her arms around her father. "Thank you, Papa! You won't regret this, I promise."

CHAPTER

26

THE AUTUMN GALES HAD well and truly blown themselves
out by the time the day of the horse race dawned, leaving still,
cold air and soft turf that held the imprint of the horses' hooves
without sucking at their legs and slowing them down. Helena
was in Oriel's stable at first light, polishing the stallion's coat
until it gleamed like a mahogany mirror.

She paused as Jamie appeared in the doorway, his breath
forming a silver cloud and his cheeks red with cold. His eyes
shone with excitement and he looked tense, but it wasn't the
same tension that had gripped his shoulders and shortened his
temper when the wreckers had threatened their village. In the
end, there had been no need to show Jarrow's bloodstained
mallet to the Riding Officers, and Helena had watched Jamie
throw it into the sea from the cliffs above Freshwater Bay after
one of Oriel's training gallops. The stable lad hadn't wanted his
mother to see it—she had enough sad memories of her brother.

"He'll have no coat left if you brush him much more," Jamie
teased, leaning against the doorpost with his arms folded.

Helena grinned at him. "Nonsense! I just want to make sure you're riding the best-looking horse today."

"Oh, there's no doubt of that," Jamie agreed. "But you'll have to leave him now. It's time for his breakfast, an' we want him to finish eating a good few hours before the race."

Helena tucked the brush into the grooming box and ran her hand over Oriel's shoulder, enjoying the satin feel of his coat and the smooth muscles underneath. Then she picked up the blanket that was draped over the stable door and buckled it onto the stallion to keep him warm. "Don't go getting dirty again," she warned him, letting herself out of the stable.

She went into the house, picking her way through the piles of greenery that lay in the back hall. The Bridport horse race was traditionally the day that the house was decorated for the Christmas season, and tendrils of ivy and holly branches were waiting to be woven through the balusters and draped along the mantelpieces.

A holly twig snagged Helena's skirt, and she bent down to unhook it.

"Are you all right, Lady Helena?" said Jamie's mother, Mary, who had come out of the kitchen with a pile of clean linen in her arms.

"Yes, thank you, Mary. Or I will be, once this holly agrees to let me go! Have my parents breakfasted yet?"

"They've just finished," Mary told her. "An' you should

hurry if you want any yourself, my lady. It'll be time to leave very soon."

Helena unhooked the last holly barb from her skirt and straightened up. "I'm too nervous to eat anything," she confessed.

Mary tucked the linen under her arm and patted Helena's hand. "Don't you worry, Nell, my sweet," she said. "From what my Jamie's been telling me, that stallion is the finest animal this side of Bristol, an' further too."

Helena smiled gratefully at the housekeeper. "You're right," she said. She broke off as the clock behind her started to chime. "Nine o'clock! I must get changed, Harding will be ready to take us soon." Impulsively, she stretched up and planted a kiss on Mary's soft cheek, then turned and ran up the stairs.

Louise was waiting in Helena's bedroom with a basin of hot water to help her wash and dress. Sinking her cold hands gratefully into the water, Helena sat still while her maid unpinned her hair and brushed it into shining brown waves before curling it into ringlets that framed her face and exposed her neck. Then Louise helped her into the outdoor gown that Susan Clark had made. The dress rested on her cream-colored petticoat like a waterfall of green silk, rustling faintly when Helena turned to see her reflection in the mirror. She had to admit that Louise had been right to suggest this color—it made her eyes look as green as a cat's, and the generous folds of the skirt shone like silver when they caught the light.

"Will you be wearing your amber necklace, my lady?" Louise asked.

Helena smiled. "Yes, I think it will go well with this gown, don't you?"

Louise nodded and stretched up to fasten the string of heavy amber beads around Helena's neck, while Helena slipped a matching ring onto the third finger of her right hand. The jewelry had been a present from her parents for her last birthday, and it gleamed softly against her skin.

Taking a deep breath, Helena smoothed down the folds of her gown and turned to face Louise. The maid's eyes sparkled appreciatively. "You look like a picture, my lady," she breathed.

"Thank you, Louise," said Helena, feeling more than usually satisfied with her appearance. "Now, help me with my hat, then I will be ready."

With her bonnet pinned firmly in place, Helena gathered up her skirt in her hands and ran down the stairs to the back hall, where her parents and Will were waiting for her. They were all dressed in their finest outdoor clothes, but with shawls and mufflers to keep out the cold December wind. Helena's father smiled when he saw her, helped her into her shawl, then held open the back door to let his family make their way down to the yard.

The Rosebys were traveling to the race in their carriage.

Jamie and Watkins would ride Oriel and Piper ahead of them, and Lord Roseby would mount at the start.

By the time Helena reached the stable yard, Jamie had saddled Oriel and led him out. To Helena's delight, the stallion let out a gentle whinny when she rounded the corner. She ran over and pressed her cheek against his neck, warm and silky and with a sheen like jet in the sunlight. "See you at the start, Oriel," she whispered, then stepped back and let Jamie swing himself up into the saddle.

"We'll see you there," he told her, his brown eyes dancing under the brim of his hat.

"Let's get going, lad," Watkins called from the other side of the yard, where he had just mounted Piper. The chestnut gelding tossed his head, flicking his amber mane in a thousand skeins of silk.

"It looks like Piper's agreeing with you." Will laughed, standing beside the carriage with his hand firmly in his mother's.

The two riders lifted their hats to the watching family and turned their horses down the drive, eight hooves crunching rhythmically over the frosty gravel.

"Come on then," urged Lord Roseby, opening the door of the carriage. "We don't want to be late."

Lady Roseby took his hand and allowed him to help her into the carriage. "Come, Will," she said, patting the seat beside her.

Helena's little brother scrambled into the carriage, then

Lord Roseby helped Helena up the steps and climbed in behind her.

Harding flicked his whip over the perfectly matched bay rumps in front of him, and with a creak of leather harness and wooden wheels, the carriage rolled across the cobbles. Helena settled back on the padded seat, tucking her hands under the rug. Normally they would use the closed carriage on such a cold day, but the open carriage made it easier to look around and greet other people who were traveling to the race.

The road got busier as they approached the field outside Bridport where the race would start. Harding slowed Apollo and Jupiter to a walk and joined the queue of carriages and carts waiting to enter the field. On the other side of the hedge, Helena could see a row of stalls being set up, selling hot pies and spiced fruit, with a coconut shy and apple bobbing for the children. Will wriggled out from under the rug and stood up to get a better look, making the carriage rock.

"Sit down, Will, or you'll have us all in the ditch," warned his father.

As soon as they were through the gateway, Harding stopped the carriage and let them all get down. Clutching her father's arm, Helena held her skirt out of the mud with her other hand and gazed around in delight. There were people everywhere, warmly wrapped in hats and mufflers so that only their eyes and wind-reddened cheeks showed. And weaving between the people, cloudy breath steaming from their nostrils, were horses of every shape and size, from barrel-chested farm cobs with bristling tails and hogged manes to long-legged Thoroughbreds whose veins stood out beneath their fine skin.

Lord Roseby lifted his hat to someone, and Helena turned to see Faith Powell, her pretty face flushed with the cold and wisps of blond hair escaping from her bonnet. "Good day, Lord Roseby, Helena. Have you seen my husband yet?"

"Is Mr. Powell competing?" Helena asked.

Faith nodded. "I'm rather worried about how Whistler will fare against all these Thoroughbreds," she confessed.

"Here he comes," said Lord Roseby, pointing toward the gate.

Jonathan Powell trotted his skewbald hunter across the field toward them, the horse's enormous hooves throwing up clods of mud. "Good day, Lord Roseby!" he called out. "A fine day for the race, wouldn't you say?" He reined Whistler to a standstill beside them, and Helena reached up to pat the horse's warm brown and white neck.

Suddenly a hunting horn sounded, and Whistler's head shot up, his ears pricked. The crowds fell quiet and turned expectantly in the direction the sound had come from. A loud voice rang out over their heads. "Ladies and gentleman, the Bridport horse race is ready to begin! Will all horses and riders please make their way to the start?"

Helena looked around for Oriel and Piper. She saw a familiar chestnut horse picking its way delicately through the muddy field toward them, and she tugged at her father's sleeve. "There's Watkins, Papa," she said.

Nodding good-bye to the Powells, Lord Roseby straightened his top hat and walked over to the horses. Watkins jumped down from the saddle. "All ready for you, my lord," he said.

"Thank you, Watkins." Lord Roseby bent his left leg so that the groom could hoist him into the saddle and watched while the groom adjusted the stirrup leathers for his long legs.

Helena went over to Oriel, her heart suddenly pounding with nerves on his behalf. But the mahogany horse looked untroubled by the tide of people that flowed around him, only sidestepping when a small brown and white terrier darted past, yapping. Jamie scooped up the reins and ran one hand down the silky black mane. "Easy, lad," he murmured.

"How does he feel?" Helena asked.

Jamie smiled. "Oriel feels great, but I'm not so sure about me," he joked.

"Nonsense," Helena argued. "You'll both be fine." She noticed Jamie looking intently at her and frowned. "What's the matter?"

Jamie shook his head. "I was just noticing your new gown, that's all," he said quietly. "You look beautiful."

"Beautiful?" Helena echoed. A warm flush spread up from her neck. "Well, thank you." Unconsciously, she lifted one hand to touch the amber beads that rested on her collarbone.

Jamie's brown eyes were unusually serious. "You look a proper lady of the manor, Nell," he told her.

Helena laughed, feeling the tension that had crackled between them vanish like spent lightning. "A lady of the manor? That's as well, I suppose. I shouldn't wish to look like a smuggler!"

She broke off and frowned. Instead of joining in her laughter, Jamie was staring past her with his eyes wide in alarm.

Helena spun around. Roger Chapman was standing behind her.

"MR. CHAPMAN!" HELENA EXCLAIMED.

The Riding Officer bowed politely. "Good day to you, Lady Helena. Your mother has kindly invited me to watch the race with you."

"Oh, yes, of course," Helena stammered, wondering if the Riding Officer had overheard what she had just said. She hadn't forgotten his promise on the night the wreckers had been caught to keep looking for the Roseby smugglers.

"All horses to the start!" the steward called again before Helena could say anything.

"I have to go, Nell," said Jamie.

Helena darted forward and straightened the dark green cloth under Oriel's saddle. "Godspeed," she murmured.

"Good luck, Master Polstock," Roger Chapman called up to him, raising his hat. "And to you, Lord Roseby," he added.

"Thank you, Mr. Chapman," Lord Roseby replied. "Ready, Jamie?"

"Aye, sir," said Jamie firmly. The two horses trotted toward the far side of the field, their dark-coated riders rising in time to their hoofbeats.

"Shall we go and watch the start?" suggested Mr. Chapman, offering his arm to Helena.

She turned to him, butterflies suddenly dancing so violently in her stomach that she could hardly speak. "Thank you," she murmured, taking his arm.

The Riding Officer looked down at her for a moment. "May I compliment you on your gown, Lady Helena?" he asked. "A most becoming color, in my opinion. Your seamstress did well to find such fine fabric."

Helena stared at him in alarm, trying to detect any hidden meaning behind his words. Could he possibly suspect that she was dressed in smuggled silk? "Thank you, sir," she said, thinking fast. "My aunt, Lady Windlesham, is kind enough to bring us fabric whenever she visits London. She seems to think that we live among barbarian hordes who wear nothing but calico and wool!" she added.

Mr. Chapman smiled politely at Helena's joke, and she breathed a sigh of relief when he didn't pursue the topic of her gown but turned to offer his other arm to Faith Powell, who was watching her husband ride away. "Mrs. Powell?" He led the two of them deftly through the crowds to the rope that marked the edge of the course, where Lady Roseby was standing with Will.

"There you are, Nell!" Will shouted as they approached. "I thought you were going to miss everything. Look, there's Papa and Jamie." He pointed to the far end of the line of horses.

"Ready?" bellowed the steward, standing on a crate and raising a white flag. "Go!"

The flag dropped and the horses surged forward, hooves drumming against the turf as they leapt away from the start line.

"Go on, Oriel! Go on, Piper!" Helena shouted, her voice swallowed up by the deafening cheers from the rest of the crowd.

The line of horses grew more ragged as they approached the hedge at the end of the field, the less confident horses and riders falling behind to take a lead from the others. A few dug in their toes at the last minute and refused to jump, sending their riders sailing into the bristling bank of thorns. The rest of the horses swarmed over in a blur of heads and hooves and disappeared out of sight into the next field.

Helena searched quickly among the loose horses that were now cantering back toward the start, checking for dark brown, bright chestnut, or skewbald, but it looked as if Jamie, her father, and Mr. Powell had made it safely over.

Lady Roseby turned to Helena, her blue eyes sparkling. "An excellent start!" she declared. "Now, shall we go and find Harding before the lane gets completely blocked?"

Helena nodded. Already, the spectators had turned away from the rope and were surging toward the waiting carriages or, for those on foot, the gate that led out of the field. It wasn't practical to watch the horses all the way along the course, so the competitors would follow the route marked out across the fields and hedges while their supporters went along the lanes to the finish. Harding had already brought the carriage to the gate, and quickly stepped forward to help Helena and her mother up the steps. Roger Chapman swung Will in after them and was about to climb in too when Lady Roseby leaned over the side, calling, "Faith! Come with us, please!"

Faith Powell had been about to join the queue waiting for the cart provided by the organizers of the race, but she turned with a grateful smile and ran over to the Rosebys' carriage. "Thank you, my lady," she gasped.

Harding sent the carriage bowling forward, steering them past slower carts until they were almost at the head of the procession making for the finish.

"Hold tight!" he warned as Apollo and Jupiter turned through a gate into a broad grassy field. He snapped the whip over the horses' heads and they cantered across the damp turf, lurching to a halt just yards from the finish.

Helena scrambled out of the carriage and ran as fast as she could to the finish.

Mr. Chapman appeared beside her. "Can you see them yet?"

Helena shook her head. "Not yet."

Just then a pair of small boys with wind-reddened cheeks bundled past, and Helena stumbled forward. Roger Chapman reached out and grasped her arm to stop her falling into the rope that marked the edge of the racecourse.

"Are you all right, Lady Helena?"

Helena disentangled herself from his grasp as politely as she could and smoothed down the folds of her skirt. "Yes, thank you," she replied. She looked over her shoulder, willing the horses to appear over the hedge at the end of the field, but there was no sign of them. Floundering for something to say to her companion, she asked, "Will you be coming to the New Year Ball, Mr. Chapman?" Lord and Lady Roseby hosted a party every year on New Year's Eve—the greenery that would be decorating the house by the time Helena returned today would be carefully watered to ensure that it stayed fresh and glossy until then—and it always seemed to Helena that her parents invited everyone they had met during the last twelvemonth.

The Riding Officer shook his head. "I'm afraid not, my lady. I have been asked to take up a position in Portsmouth before Christmas."

"You mean, you're leaving?" Helena exclaimed in surprise.

"Yes. News of the wreckers' arrest has spread, it would seem, and my presence been requested especially by the customs supervisor."

"C—congratulations," Helena stammered. "Do you know who will replace you at West Bay?"

Roger Chapman raised his eyebrows a tiny fraction. "I have heard that Mr. Jessop is returning from Warwickshire. Apparently, he liked it so much here that he asked to be transferred back."

Helena smiled. "It will be nice to see him again," she said, glancing away so that the Riding Officer could not read her expression. In her mind, she let out a most unladylike whoop of glee. The smugglers would be delighted with this piece of news! Elderly Mr. Jessop posed far less of a threat to their operation than Mr. Chapman.

When she looked up again she saw that Mr. Chapman's eyes were serious. "Be careful, Lady Helena," he said quietly. "Whatever you may believe, smugglers are lawless men, and the incident with the beacon has left me concerned by your apparent willingness to put yourself in danger."

"I—" She broke off when she heard the sound of drumming hooves, and spun around to see the hats of the leading riders bobbing above the hedge at the end of the field. Helena narrowed her eyes, straining to make out their faces, but they were too spattered with mud to be recognizable at this distance.

The first horses jumped the hedge, landing so close together that a bright bay with a hogged mane stumbled badly and sent his rider flying into the mud. The others swerved to avoid him and galloped for the finish, their riders driving them forward with hands and heels working like pistons.

Helena held her breath. At the front of the close-packed group, two distinctive heads nodded together, necks stretched out and nostrils flared. Shining bronze and mahogany brown galloped side by side, but which one was ahead, it was impossible to tell.

NEARER AND NEARER THEY galloped. Helena opened her mouth to cheer them on, but no sound came out. Then they swept past, the rest of the horses close on their heels, and the crowd roared deafeningly in Helena's ears. The steward leapt up and down on his crate, madly waving a scarlet flag and shouting out the name of the winner, but his voice was lost in the din.

Helena turned to Roger Chapman in confusion. "Did you see who won?"

The Riding Officer smiled at her, the seriousness of their interrupted conversation apparently forgotten. "It was the stallion, Helena," he told her. "Oriel won!"

He took her elbow and guided her through the crowd, which got thicker as they neared the end of the course. With a final squeeze, Helena found herself pressed against a warm mahogany shoulder, streaked with mud and sweat and flecked with white foam. She looked up into Jamie's ecstatic face, split with a huge grin, his teeth white against the mud that plastered his cheeks.

"He did it, Nell!" he whispered. "We won!"

Helena reached up and ran her fingers through Oriel's mane as the stallion turned his head to blow into her hair. "You beautiful, beautiful horse," she murmured.

"Well done, Jamie!" called Lord Roseby over the heads of the crowd. "A brilliant ride."

"Hurrah for Oriel!" shouted Will, thrusting his way between two farmers and reaching up to pat the stallion's foamy chest.

"And hurrah for Piper too," added Lady Roseby, squeezing through behind him. "He came in second, after all." She looked up at her husband and smiled. "Well done, William."

"Perhaps I should have tried harder to persuade your father to sell me the horse when I had the chance," murmured Roger Chapman in Helena's ear.

She wheeled around, shocked.

"Don't worry, Lady Helena." He laughed. "I've got my eye on the horse that came third, actually." He pointed to a gray Thoroughbred that was tossing its head and scattering foam over the people standing nearby. "He's called Devlin's Pride. I've heard his owner is looking to sell him after today."

Helena smiled. "He looks a fine horse," she remarked, her heart thudding with relief. Was there any news that could make this day more perfect? Mr. Chapman was leaving West Bay and Mr. Jessop was returning, so the Roseby smugglers would be safe for a while longer, and the Riding Officer had openly declared that he no longer had any interest in buying the stallion. And best of all, Oriel had won the Bridport horse race! Suddenly Helena felt a pang of concern for her governess, who had been watching the race with equally anxious eyes. "Where's Mrs. Powell?" she asked.

"She's over there with her husband," said Mr. Chapman, pointing toward the finish where the fair-haired young woman was patting the neck of an exhausted-looking skewbald. "It looks like Whistler got around safely after all."

Just then, a gray-whiskered man wearing a brown tweed jacket pushed his way through to Oriel's shoulder and peered up at Jamie. "Your name, lad?" he demanded.

"James Polstock, sir," replied Jamie.

The man made a note on a piece of paper. "And the horse?"

"Oriel, owned by Lord Roseby," Helena couldn't resist putting in, feeling her cheeks flush with pride.

The man glanced at her. "Thank you, miss," he said. "So, that's Lord Roseby's horses first an' second. A good day for him, I'd say." He looked down at the list. "Devlin's Pride third, Starling fourth, an' Alex of Araby fifth," he read aloud. "Right, that's the lot." He turned and shouldered his way out of sight.

Lord Roseby appeared beside Helena on foot, the dark blue wool of his jacket hardly recognizable under a liberal coating of mud. "Come, Nell," he said. "Let's give Jamie and Watkins a chance to take these brave horses home, shall we?"

"Of course, Papa." Helena pressed her hand against Oriel's shoulder once more, feeling his skin warm through her glove. Then, with a final delighted grin at Jamie, she followed her father and Mr. Chapman through the crowd to the waiting carriage.

IT WAS NEARLY DARK by the time the jubilant group returned to Roseby Manor, and candlelight glowed welcomingly from every downstairs window. News of Oriel's victory spread through the household like wildfire, and before long Helena heard her father giving Watkins permission to celebrate the win with a party in the barn for the stable lads. The Rosebys themselves would celebrate more quietly with a late dinner, including Will, who was allowed to stay up past his bedtime as a special treat.

After helping her mother to decide on the menu and unwrapping the heavy silver cutlery from its protective silken cloths, Helena excused herself, saying that she wanted to wash and repin her hair before dinner. She knew that Oriel would have been settled in his stable by now, but there was no way she could sit down to eat without saying good night to him. And besides, she wanted to find Jamie and tell him that Roger Chapman was leaving.

Pausing only to take a shawl from the chest beside the back

door, she ran down the steps to the stable yard. The cobbles gleamed like jet in the faint light that came from the windows of the stable block. Watkins would extinguish the lanterns later on, after his final check of the horses. At the far end of the yard, the open-sided barn was alive with the sound of voices and old Abel Woodford's fiddle, scraping out a lively jig. A blur of figures whirled in the center of the barn, feet flying and shrieks of laughter as dancing partners were spun out of the circle and back in again.

Helena watched for a moment, wary of disturbing the celebration, then crossed the yard to Oriel's stable. The stallion was pulling hay from the rack, but he turned as she approached and put his head over the door, his velvety nostrils quivering in a silent welcome. Helena reached up and rested her hands on either side of his face, marveling again at his exquisitely sculpted head.

"Nell! What are you doing out here?" It was Jamie, carrying a wooden cask.

"I wanted some air before dinner," Helena explained. "And to congratulate the winning horse, of course!"

"Not the winning rider, then?" Jamie pretended to be disappointed.

Helena laughed. "All right, both of you." She glanced over her shoulder at the barn. "It looks like the party is going well."

"Aye, it is indeed," Jamie agreed. "So well that I've had to fetch another keg from the Black Feathers!" He nodded at the cask in his arms.

"Actually, I have something to tell you," said Helena. "Can that wait a minute?"

"Of course." Jamie set down the cask and straightened up, looking puzzled. "What is it?"

"Don't worry, it's good news. Mr. Chapman has been transferred to Portsmouth! Mr. Jessop is coming back to replace him."

A broad grin spread across Jamie's face. "That's good news indeed," he agreed. "'Twill make our business easier, that's for sure. How did you find out?"

"He told me himself, just now," Helena explained. "I . . . I think he tried to warn me, as well. He said something about not putting myself in danger from lawless men." A thought suddenly struck her, and she gazed at Jamie in alarm. "Do you think he will tell Jessop that I'm involved with the smugglers?"

Jamie shook his head. "I doubt it. An' Jessop's hardly likely to believe him, if he did. Anyway, you won't be helping us out in the future, will you?"

"Why not?" Helena exclaimed. "We have Oriel now! He's faster than any Riding Officer's horse, you know he is."

"Whoa, Nell!" Jamie laughed, putting one hand on her arm. "You can't join our company, an' well you know it."

Helena opened her mouth, about to argue, when she heard

voices coming from the tack room. Jamie stiffened and drew her into the shadows beside the wall of Oriel's stable.

A figure emerged from the door of the tack room, a tall slender-framed man wearing white breeches and silver shoe buckles that gleamed in the light from the stable block. A thickness of shadows in the doorway behind him suggested there was someone with him.

Helena bit her lip to stop herself from gasping out loud. What was her father doing out here, and who was that with him?

Then the second figure emerged, broad-shouldered and nearly as tall as Lord Roseby. "I won't keep you from your supper any longer, my lord."

Helena felt every muscle in her body tense. The speaker was Jamie's father, Samuel Polstock. At once her mind leapt to the worst possible reason for their unlikely meeting, when both should have been celebrating the success in the race. Had her father found out that Samuel was a smuggler? Helena felt her stomach lurch at the thought. Surely her father would not order the arrest of his own friends and neighbors?

As a hundred fears surged through her mind, Helena realized that Jamie was grinning at her in the shadows. "Does my father know—" she began in a whisper, then stopped as Jamie put a finger to his lips and nodded to the figures by the tack room.

Looking around, Helena saw that her father was handing Samuel a soft leather purse, the heavy chink of metal against metal revealing that it held money, and no small sum, either.

"That should cover the next shipment," her father murmured, so quietly that Helena could only just hear.

Samuel tucked the purse into his pocket. "Aye, my lord," he said. "We're expecting the next boat in four days. You'll be wanting your usual amount of tea an' silk, I presume?"

Lord Roseby nodded. "Yes, please. Good luck with the landing, Samuel." Nodding a farewell, he walked briskly across the yard and ran up the steps, disappearing out of sight around the corner.

Samuel Polstock straightened his jacket and strode back to the barn, passing barely a yard from where Helena and Jamie stood in the shadows.

As soon as the blacksmith's footsteps had faded away and merged with the music from the barn, Helena stepped away from the wall and turned to face Jamie. "Are you going to tell me what's going on?" she demanded. Fear and confusion made her angry, together with the fact that Jamie was leaning against the wall and grinning at her as if he was enjoying a private joke.

Taking pity on her, he straightened up and walked over to her. "Nell, Lord Roseby knows that my father runs the smuggling operation in Roseby." As Helena started to protest in alarm, Jamie held up one hand to hush her and carried on. "He's always known. You see, your father's what we call the venturer. He provides the money that my father sends to France to buy our cargo. Without him, Nell, there would be no smuggling in Roseby at all."

Helena stared at Jamie in utter disbelief. How could this be true? Her own father was a smuggler?

Jamie went on. "It's Lord Roseby who made my father promise never to carry arms. He wants no risk of anyone getting injured, not us nor the customs men. He knows we smuggle only what we need, an' it keeps us from having to buy from smuggling gangs further along the coast, who do carry arms."

Helena found her voice at last, and a thousand questions flooded into her mind. "Do all the smugglers know who the venturer is?"

"No, Lord Roseby is determined that he's kept secret. My pa only told me when I had to collect the money for him one month."

"And does my father know about me?" Helena asked uncertainly.

"About you helping us out?" Jamie grinned. "No. Pa didn't see there was any reason for him to know."

Suddenly Helena's mind cleared. All that time she had spent worrying about whether her parents knew about the smuggling that went on in the village, when her father was responsible for financing the whole operation! Behind her, Oriel snorted in the warm darkness of his stable, and she turned to look at him, smiling when she caught sight of a faint mahogany gleam in the shadows.

"Surely that makes it all right for me to help you?" she asked, turning back to Jamie.

He shook his head, his eyes suddenly serious. "No, Nell. 'Tis for the villagers to land the cargo, not your pa, an' not you. That's how it works, see? Look at you—you're a lady now." He gestured to Helena's dress, and she blushed. "An' a fine one at that," Jamie went on. "You've got to study dancing an' French, to get ready for getting married an' having a big house o' your own. But me? I'm a stable lad an' a smuggler. That's the way things are."

Helena wanted to protest, but inside she knew Jamie was right. Her life had always been following a different path from his, and there was no escaping that. She smiled at him. "But we'll always be friends, won't we?" she asked.

Jamie smiled back at her. "Always," he promised.

From the barn, Abel's fiddle struck up again, the high-pitched notes leaping and falling through the frosty air.

Jamie gave an exaggerated, sweeping bow and held out his hands to Helena. "May I have the pleasure of this dance, my lady?"

Helena curtseyed, her skirt sweeping the cobbles with a soft rustle. "The pleasure will be mine, kind sir," she replied.

She stepped toward him and took hold of his hands and let him sweep her lightly around the yard, their only audience the mahogany stallion that watched over his stable door.

A terrible shipwreck, a mysterious horse, and the adventure of a lifetime . . .

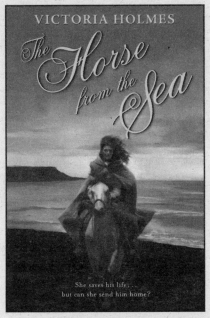

VICTORIA HOLMES

The Horse from the Sea

She saves his life . . .
but can she send him home?

Hc 0-06-052028-0
Pb 0-06-052030-2

Nora Donovan bravely saves a shipwrecked stallion and a Spanish soldier, nursing them both back to health in secret. But can she take them across the mountains and onto a ship that will take them safely home?

AVON BOOKS
An Imprint of HarperCollinsPublishers

WWW.HARPERCHILDRENS.COM